D0336568

Troubled Waters

Also by Rosie Harris

Turn of the Tide

Troubled Waters

ROSIE HARRIS

WILLIAM HEINEMANN : LONDON

First Published in the United Kingdom in 2002 by
William Heinemann

1 3 5 7 9 10 8 6 4 2

William Heinemann
The Random House Group Limited
20 Vauxhall Bridge Road, London, SW1V 2SA

Random House Australia (Pty) Limited
20 Alfred Street, Milsons Point, Sydney, New South Wales 2061,
Australia

Random House New Zealand Limited
18 Poland Road, Glenfield
Auckland 10, New Zealand

Random House (Pty) Limited
Endulini, 5a Jubilee Road, Parktown, 2193, South Africa

The Random House Group Limited Reg. No. 954009

www.randomhouse.co.uk

A CIP catalogue record for this book is available from the British Library

Paper used by Random House are natural, recyclable products made from wood grown in sustainable forests. The manufacturing processes conform to the environmental regulations of the country of origin

Printed & bound in the United Kingdom by
Creative Print & Design, Wales (Ebbw Vale)

ISBN 0 434 00826 5

To Vivienne Rowlands
And also to my many friends in Wales, and all those
who have ever enjoyed a holiday there.

My grateful thanks to Lynne Drew, Joanna Craig, Anna Dalton-Knott, Mary Chamberlain and Caroline Sheldon for all their help and support.

Chapter One

Screaming, Sara Jenkins ran out into the rain-sodden night clutching Myfanwy, her baby sister, to her chest. She was sure the flames were licking at her heels and that at any moment they'd be stinging like the strap her Dada used on her bare bum when he was in one of his sanctimonious moods and determined to drive out the Devil that made her so wicked.

The hem of her nightie was flapping against her ankles, her bare feet slipping on the greasy pavement. Behind her a flame was curling through the bedroom window like a bright orange flag, waving victoriously against the blackness of the night, branding itself on her memory.

The child in her arms whimpered in protest against the damp night air and she pulled the shawl it was wrapped in higher to protect the baby's face and to smother its noise.

It was then that she thought of her mother and realised that she was still upstairs in bed and probably trapped by the acrid smoke that seemed to fill the entire house.

A crowd was gathering, alerted by the pungent smell of the smoke that was billowing out into the night.

Yelling, 'Mam, our Mam, where are you?' Sara

turned back towards the house. As hands grabbed at her she fought them off. Thrusting the baby at one of the women she ran towards the smoke-filled building, repeatedly calling out to her mother.

One of the men grabbed at her arm. 'It's no good, *cariad*, you can't go back in there! Think yourself damn lucky you got yourself and the baba out when you did.'

She turned on him angrily. A slip of a girl, still boy slim, her dark eyes saucer wide with fear in her elfin face. 'Leave go of my arm, Alun Pritchard, my Mam's still in there!' she gasped.

'It's too late to do anything now, my lovely. The whole of the upstairs seems to be full of blinding smoke. All of you sleeping, were you?'

She shivered violently. 'Dada's still at the pit.'

He patted her shoulder. 'Someone's gone to fetch him.' He pushed Sara towards his wife, the plump motherly woman who had taken the baby from her. 'There's nothing more you can do here, so go along with Martha and she'll brew you some tea. You'll feel better after that, girl, you see if you don't.'

'But Mam's still in there,' Sara protested as Martha, holding the baby in one arm, placed a hand protectively along Sara's thin shoulders. 'She's asleep in bed, worn out, see.'

'Come along with me,' Martha urged. 'The fire brigade boyos will fetch her out so there's no need for you to worry. Look, they've got their ladders up to the window already so it will only be a matter of a few minutes. Come on now, and my Alun will bring her along to our house the moment they've brought her down.'

Sara took a lingering glance back at her home, still wondering whether she should ignore all their warnings and try and find her mother herself. Downstairs looked almost normal, but grey smoke still billowed from the gaping holes where the bedroom windows had been before the firemen had broken the glass with their axes to try and gain entry.

Sara had been sitting in the wooden rocker in the living-room, trying to pacify Myfanwy so that her mother could snatch an hour or so of sleep, when she'd first smelt the smoke.

For one moment she'd thought it was coming into the house from outside and had something to do with the pit. She'd wondered if there'd been some sort of explosion. Her thoughts flew to her father who was working the night shift. Then she'd noticed the wisp of grey smoke curling under the door and she knew it was nothing to do with the pit, but was right here in her home.

With Myfanwy still in her arms, she'd gone to investigate. The moment she'd opened the door a blinding cloud of smoke had billowed into the room, making her cough and choke. When she'd found it impossible to get upstairs she'd run out into the street screaming for help.

Alun Pritchard from the house next door was first on the doorstep, followed by some of the other men who lived nearby. They'd wasted no time. They'd sent for the fire brigade, and one of the younger ones had made off at a run for the pit to fetch Ifor Jenkins.

It was only when Sara began whimpering about

her Mam still being in the house that any of them knew that Gwen Jenkins was inside.

The firemen did their best. They put up ladders and tried to get in through the bedroom windows, but the smoke was so thick and so acrid that it choked them. There was no hope of rescuing Gwen.

No one could understand how Sara and the baby had managed to escape until Ifor Jenkins arrived home. Then, bit by bit, between her hysterical sobs, she explained how she'd been downstairs with the baby, but her Mam had been upstairs in bed.

'Trying to get some sleep she was,' Sara sobbed. 'Tired out, see, because the baby was being so mardy. I thought if I took Myfanwy downstairs, where Mam couldn't hear her crying, it would give Mam a chance to sleep. She was getting into bed when I left her. There was a candle burning on the chest by the bed, but she said she'd snuff it out before she went to sleep. I don't know what happened after that. Perhaps she forgot about it, or it fell on the bed and set fire to the covers. It was a feather bed, that's why the smoke was so terrible and smelt so awful.'

'Go on!'

'The next thing I knew was that there was smoke coming into the room downstairs. Choking me. I dashed out of the house with Myfanwy. For the moment I forgot our Mam was still up there,' she whispered pathetically as she looked up at the dark figure of her father, shrouded in coal dust, his eyes white pools in the black grime of his thin face.

Ifor Jenkins regarded his fourteen-year-old

daughter solemnly. His dark eyes glittered fanatically. 'It's the will of the Lord,' he pronounced in a tone that had no compassion or feeling of any sort. 'His wrath is terrible to behold.'

'She was only trying to get some sleep, Dada. She was worn out, see, with Myfanwy crying so much.'

Ifor Jenkins regarded his daughter sternly. 'Lying there in bed reading one of those stupid love magazines?'

Sara shook her head. 'I don't know about that, Dada. Only that she was trying to get some sleep. Myfanwy was crying and keeping her awake so I tried to help by bringing her downstairs so that Mam could have some quiet.'

'The Devil's trash, that's what those magazines are,' Ifor intoned as though he was not listening to a word Sara said. 'Don't you dare let me catch you reading one, mind!' he thundered.

Sara bit down on her lower lip to stop herself saying anything. She knew he hated her Mam reading *Love Letter*, the magazine Martha Pritchard, their next-door neighbour, passed on to her after she'd finished with it.

Soppy sentimental rubbish it might be, but it took her Mam out of herself and into a world where a woman didn't spend all her waking hours cleaning and scrimping and trying to make ends meet. It was a world where the men didn't come home from work grimy from head to toe with coal dust and expect to find a tin bath of hot water waiting in front of the fire, and their wife standing by to scrub the ingrained filth from their back.

In the stories in *Love Letter* the women were

treated kindly, not bawled at when things went wrong. They wore pretty dresses and lived in lovely homes where there were always fresh flowers, and soft music in the background, and they served up delicious meals to their families and friends.

Sara and her mother both knew that Ifor disapproved of them reading such things. He called them fairy stories for stupid women who didn't know when they were well off.

Often Gwen would hide the magazine down the back of her chair when she heard Ifor's footsteps in the road outside and pray that he wouldn't spot it. Whenever he did he took a sadistic pleasure in making her toss it straight into the fire. Then he made a point of docking twopence from her housekeeping money to teach her a lesson she wouldn't forget. He always made a great ceremony of putting the twopence into the collection box for Fallen Women when he went to the Tabernacle Chapel.

Sara knew how this humiliated her mother, but there was nothing either of them could say or do. Once or twice, Sara had tried to stand up for her mother, and on one occasion she had said the magazine was hers, but it had done no good. In addition to punishing her mother in the usual way, her father had taken off his strap and tanned her bare backside even though she was thirteen at the time. The indignity had hurt worse than the lashing, though that had drawn blood and the weals had still been there three weeks later.

His harshness was something Sara found difficult to understand. On Sundays, and when he wasn't working down the pit, he was such a pillar of respectability. In his best navy blue three-piece suit, white shirt with its stiffly starched collar that shone like a piece of polished bone, his dark tie neatly knotted around his scrawny neck, polished black shoes and dark trilby, he was almost a dandy.

When he was going to work, his clothes were shabby and shiny. He wore a collarless flannel shirt and a wool muffler tied round his neck. Sometimes he tied his trouser legs with a piece of cloth or a strap just below the knee.

When she'd been very small, Sara had thought it was two different men who lived in their house, and she'd been frightened of both of them.

Now, listening to her father pontificating about it being the Lord's will that her mother had been taken from them and consumed by fire, and that it was a warning to other women who idled their time away reading trash which was such an abomination in the eyes of the Lord, Sara felt so angry that she couldn't even cry.

Her mother had been in poor health ever since Sara could remember; a small stout woman with a shapeless figure from constant childbearing. In winter she suffered from bronchitis and from early December until the end of March she had a poultice of goose grease smeared on brown paper fastened to her chest to make her breathing easier. She still had breathing difficulties in the summer months, only then it was caused by pollen as well as the coal dust that was in the air.

Every year there was the regular pregnancy that ended either in a miscarriage or a stillborn baby, and that, too, her father blamed on her mother's fecklessness.

When she had managed to carry Myfanwy to full term and the baby had been born alive, Sara had been almost as relieved as her mother. Perhaps now the onslaught of accusations would cease and there would be peace in their home.

Myfanwy had been such a tiny, scrawny baby that Sara had feared she wouldn't live, but she had survived those early weeks. It had taken its toll on her mother, though. Gwen Jenkins had been exhausted most of the time, and Sara found that instead of going to school, she had to stay at home and look after the house, nurse her mother and care for her baby sister.

Ifor didn't encourage visitors, so apart from their next-door neighbour Martha Pritchard, few knew the real Ifor Jenkins, the sadistic martinet who ruled his wife and elder daughter with a heavy hand, and dictated how they must live their lives.

Martha and her husband Alun had some inkling of what went on behind their neighbours' closed door. Through the thin walls they often heard Ifor's voice raised in anger, heard the thud of his fists, or the cry from Sara when his strap flayed her.

Next day, Gwen Jenkins would be in bed with a bad headache. Sara's chastisement, however, was always carried out in such a way that it was invisible to the casual eye. A girl rising fourteen was hardly likely to lift her skirt and show the cuts and weals on her bare bottom.

The pale fingers of dawn were already making their

way across the sky before the firemen had finished dampening down the Jenkinses' house and removing any pieces of smouldering timber and furniture. It was essential for the fire to be completely out so there was no risk to the houses either side in the terrace.

The devastation to the upper floor was mostly smoke damage but apart from the mess caused by the water the rooms downstairs were not badly damaged at all.

Even so, it would be several days before the place had dried out sufficiently for Ifor and his daughters to live there. Neighbours offered them beds and invited them to share their food, but Ifor would have none of it. He insisted that he must stay at home, it was the will of the Lord. 'Sara can clean the place up and we can sleep downstairs,' he stated.

Martha Pritchard refused to listen to him. She said if he was determined to stay in that damp, smoke-stained house then he could please himself, but she took charge of Myfanwy and in spite of what Ifor Jenkins said she claimed that Sara needed the chance to get some proper rest as well.

Exhausted, Sara curled up in Martha's truckle bed and fell into a deep dreamless sleep the moment her head touched the pillow.

Martha nursed Myfanwy to sleep in her arms, then made up a bed for the baby in the empty clothes basket and carried it upstairs where she placed it alongside the double bed where she and her husband, Alun, slept.

Chapter Two

Looking back, Sara was sure that if it hadn't been for the kindness shown to her by Martha and Alun Pritchard she would never have survived the days leading up to her mother's funeral.

Right from the first moment Martha had taken charge of Myfanwy and organised and counselled Sara. It was not in harsh stentorian tones such as her Dada used, nor in weak, breath-catching gasps like her mother, but in a firm, friendly voice. And even though she responded automatically, Sara felt the warmth that emanated from the older woman and drew strength from it.

When they awoke to a grey dawn the morning after the fire, and the enormity of what had happened struck Sara like a sudden blow, she broke down and wept piteously. Martha gathered her into her arms, and sat nursing her and crooning words of comfort as if she was a small child until they were forced to attend to Myfanwy's piteous cries of hunger.

'We've no way of feeding her so she'll die as well now,' Sara sobbed as she rocked the mewling child in her arms and watched helplessly as Myfanwy's little hands scrabbled ineffectually at her dress.

'Nonsense! Where's her bottle?' retorted Martha.

'Mam gave her the breast always, see.'

'Surely she had a bottle in the house, though, to give her a drop of water now and then?'

'Never! Only ever let her sip off a spoon.'

'*Duw anwyl*, that's a problem,' Martha said, looking worried. Then her plump face brightened. 'I've got an idea. I'm not sure if it will work, mind, but it could be the answer!'

'What's that then?' Sara looked at her expectantly, her worries about Myfanwy temporarily taking her mind off her mother.

'Janie Harries has a young baby. Bit older than your Myfanwy, but she still has him on the titty even though she's started weaning him. Now, if she is willing then she could feed your Myfanwy and that would solve all our problems.'

'Do you think she would?'

'Only one way to find out! Give the baba to me and we'll pop along and ask.'

Wrapping the baby warmly in a big carrying blanket, Martha then wound one end of it around her own body so that the child was cocooned against her. 'Come on, you come with me and then if Janie agrees you'll be able to take your little sister along to her whenever she needs a feed.'

'Do you think we should ask Dada first?' Sara questioned. Her brown eyes were cautious.

'What for? He can't feed her, now can he? Women's business this, *cariad*. Come on before the poor little dab starves to death.'

The moment the words were out of her mouth Martha wished she could bite her tongue off, but Sara didn't seem to notice.

When they reached Janie's house Sara listened

mutely as Martha cajoled the other woman into agreeing to suckle Myfanwy.

While the baby was being fed, Martha took Sara back to her place so that they could have something to eat themselves.

'Come on, girl, get some food down you,' she insisted when Sara said she wasn't hungry. 'Need all your strength in the coming days, you know. You'll have to look after the baba as well as your Dada!'

Because of the damage done to the bedroom by the smoke and water that had been used to put out the fire, it had been agreed the night before that Gwen Jenkins's body should be placed in its coffin right away in the morning. It was then to be taken straight to the Tabernacle Chapel where it would remain until the day of the funeral.

Sara watched in grief-stricken silence as her father and Alun Pritchard manhandled her mother's body, wrapped in a white sheet, down the steep narrow staircase. They laid Gwen Jenkins's body on the living-room table while they waited for the hearse to arrive with the coffin.

As if in a dream, Sara, dry eyed, her elfin face drained of colour, stood motionless by the side of the table as if guarding the body. Martha watched anxiously. When Sara stretched out a hand to draw back the sheet covering Gwen's face and head she gently but firmly restrained her from doing so.

Alun had been one of the first to go into the smouldering bedroom and Martha knew how horrified he had been by the sight of Gwen's charred face and singed hair. She was fearful of the distressing effect it would have on Sara.

Martha felt that Sara would be consumed by guilt if she saw her mother like that and it was not the sort of memory a young girl should have to carry through life.

Sara shook Martha's arm away. 'I only want to kiss her goodbye.'

'Later, *cariad*. When your Mam's been washed and made a bit tidy, like.'

Sara looked bewildered. 'I can do that, I'll wash her face.'

To Martha's relief, at that moment there was a commotion in the road outside as the hearse arrived.

'Sara, can you find me a clean nappy?' Martha said hurriedly. 'Little Myfanwy needs changing, soaked right through, so she is.'

By the time they had attended to Myfanwy, the undertaker had brought in the coffin and Gwen's body had been put into it and carried out to the waiting hearse.

For a moment, when they came back into the room, Sara seemed to be oblivious to the fact. Then she saw the empty table and tears rolled silently down her cheeks. Once more, Martha gathered the young girl to her ample bosom.

When Sara had recovered sufficiently, Martha suggested that now that her mother's body had been taken away, they should try and salvage what clothes and belongings they could from the smoke-blackened bedroom.

Most of Ifor's best clothes were intact in the

boxed-in floor-to-ceiling cupboard that stood in one corner of the main bedroom. Sara's own clothes, and most of those Gwen Jenkins had ready for the baby, were in the smaller back bedroom where Sara slept and were also undamaged although they smelt strongly of smoke.

The next few days were unreal to Sara. Her father was too busy buying himself a new double bed and organising the funeral to have any time for her or Myfanwy. As a prominent member of the Tabernacle Chapel he wanted to be seen to do the right thing by his wife and this was far more important than talking to Sara or considering her feelings.

Although normally he heartily disliked Martha Pritchard, he was forced to turn to her for assistance. As well as helping with Myfanwy he needed her to arrange food for those mourners who might return to Taff Court when the service and internment were over.

'Ham sandwiches, tea and lemonade,' he decreed.

'What, no drink at all, Ifor Jenkins?' Martha asked in surprise.

'Of course not! They will drink tea or lemonade,' he told her curtly. 'Alcohol is a tool of the Devil and a sin in the eyes of the Lord.'

'And what about something more for them to eat? Bit of variety, like.'

'Ham sandwiches will do nicely.'

She shook her head despairingly. 'At least put out a few bakestones and some *bara brith*,' she pressed.

'It's a funeral, not a party,' he snapped.

Martha sighed noisily, but didn't bother to argue with him. They'd already had one verbal tussle and she didn't want another. The first one had been to persuade Ifor to buy Sara something suitable to wear to the funeral.

'What is wrong with her school clothes?' Ifor defended. 'A black crêpe band round the arm and they will do perfectly well.'

'The poor girl deserves something better than that. She needs something special. It's her mother's funeral, remember!'

It had been a long drawn-out argument, but Martha had won in the end. She'd managed to get enough money out of him to buy Sara a new black skirt, a white blouse and a black beret.

'And we'll put a black crêpe armband on your school mackintosh, Sara,' she promised when they returned home.

On the day of the funeral, as a mark of respect, every window in Taff Court was shrouded either by blinds or tightly drawn curtains. Those neighbours not going to the service demonstrated their sympathy by standing on their doorsteps as the funeral party assembled. Mourners stretched all the way from Taff Court, through the streets of Pontypridd, to the doors of the Tabernacle Chapel in Bridge Street.

As Martha watched them set off her heart ached. Ifor looked spruce and confident in his navy blue suit, a black crêpe armband and black tie denoting that he was in mourning. Sara thin, almost scrawny in her new black skirt, white blouse and school mac.

What did the future hold for Sara and baby Myfanwy, Martha wondered sadly?

In chapel, Sara was in a trance for most of the

service. Her eyes were glazed and fixed on the shining wooden coffin. When her mother's favourite hymns were sung, though, the tears welled up in Sara's eyes and rolled unchecked down her ashen cheeks.

Suddenly she was a little girl again, cuddled up to the plump warm body of her mother. And her mother was singing to her. She was singing the hymns they both loved, the ones about children, about all things bright and beautiful, about love and happiness and the joy that lay ahead.

It was as if the familiar words melted the ice that had frozen her senses since the moment she had realised her mother was dead. It was so cruel that she should die now, when she had finally achieved the dream she had set her heart on, a baby that was going to live.

As the last strains of the organ died away, Sara dabbed her eyes and made a solemn promise. She'd saved her baby sister from the fire so Myfanwy was now her responsibility. She'd look after the tiny innocent little scrap and protect her from harm. She'd care for her and see she grew up into the girl her mother would have been proud of had she lived.

She looked round the crowded chapel and felt trapped. She wanted to leave, to hurry back home where she was needed. Panic filled her. She should be looking after Myfanwy, not sitting here surrounded by all these people, most of them complete strangers.

Her heart hardened, she felt completely detached from what was going on around her. Her eyes rested on the polished wooden coffin but she felt no emotion. She knew her mother's body was in that shiny box, but her tears had dried now. The time for crying was over, she was no longer a child. Dada would have to stop taking his belt to her; from now on he must treat her like a grown-up and stop bullying her.

Her eyes were shining as she left the church, not with tears, but with the determination that she would do the very best she could for Myfanwy.

All the way back to Taff Court her brain was buzzing with plans for the future. She imagined Myfanwy as a happy little toddler, then growing up into a cheerful schoolgirl, and finally becoming an adult.

She would protect Myfanwy from her Dada's temper and never let him use his strap on her. She would tell Myfanwy endless stories about their Mam and how sweet and kind she'd been and make sure that the memory of her was always kept alive in her sister's mind.

Chapter Three

In the weeks that followed, the people in Taff Court were very divided about the way the Jenkins family were dealing with the aftermath of the fire at their home.

Some of the chapelgoers admired the way Ifor Jenkins bore the loss of his wife, Gwen, with such dignity. Most of the others either thought him a hypocrite, or a sanctimonious fool. They would turn away to hide their embarrassment as he voiced aloud, over and over again, that it was the will of the Lord that his wife had died in the fire.

Many, like Martha Pritchard, thought the real person to be admired was Sara. Although barely fourteen, Sara had not only put on a brave face, but she was also rallying to the situation she found herself in as a woman twice her age would have done.

Sara had not only taken over the full responsibility of caring for her baby sister, Myfanwy, but she was also putting her heart and soul into running their home.

Every morning there was a row of Myfanwy's nappies blowing on the clothes-line stretched across the Court, along with Ifor's shirt and vest and her own cotton dress and apron.

Every morning Sara was out first thing, her

sleeves rolled up to the elbows of her scrawny arms, sweeping away any litter from the front of the small terraced house. Twice a week, with a bucket of water and a pumice stone, she would set to vigorously scrubbing the front doorstep and the stone window-sill until they were a luminous shade of grey.

The pit owners, who were the landlords of all the houses in Taff Court, had arranged for new windows to be put in upstairs, and for any other structural damage to be repaired. They refused to do anything at all about redecorating the bedrooms, though, and Ifor turned a deaf ear when Sara started pleading with him that he should do it.

'Look, *cariad,*' Martha Pritchard offered, 'if you can persuade your Dada to buy some paint then I'll get my Alun to slap it on for you. Dab hand with the old paintbrush is my Alun and a nice clean worker into the bargain. He'll have the place looking like new in next to no time.'

At first Ifor showed no interest in the idea at all. Then when he realised that he wouldn't have to lift a finger and that all he had to do was supply the paint, he gave in.

'I'll buy a tin of paint, but tell your Alun that he is to do my bedroom first. If there is any left over then he can use it up on the back room,' he told Martha.

'There's selfish you are, Ifor Jenkins,' Martha exploded. 'Unless, of course, you are planning on letting Sara and Myfanwy share the bigger room and you're going to move into the small back room. That would make sense, really,' she went on thoughtfully, 'since there are two of them and there's only one of you now.'

Ifor drew himself up to his full five feet eight inches and glowered down at the plump matronly woman who was confronting him. 'Talking out of turn, aren't you, Martha Pritchard?' he scowled. 'My sleeping arrangements and what use I make of the rooms in my home are my affair, not yours!'

'Keep your hair on, it was only a suggestion! It must be a bit cramped in that back bedroom, though, for Sara's bed and the baby's crib.'

'And it would be even more cramped in there if I moved my double bed in, that's if it would even fit in that room in the first place.'

'That's true enough,' she agreed. 'Perhaps the answer is to let Sara have the big double bed. If you do that, then when winter comes she can cuddle up in it with the baba when it's squalling so that it doesn't disturb you. There will be plenty of sleepless nights over the next twelve months while little Myfanwy is cutting her teeth, or have you forgotten about all that?'

'Sara will cope.'

'Oh, I'm sure she will. A gem of a girl you've got there, Ifor Jenkins.'

'She's only doing her duty, so don't go turning her head with too much foolish praise.' He frowned censoriously. 'You have quite a way with silly words, haven't you, Martha Pritchard. No doubt you've picked them up from all those trashy love stories you fill your head with all the time. I haven't forgotten that you were the one who encouraged my Gwen to read those sort of books, and that ended up in her being burnt alive and almost made me homeless. I hope you remember that from time to time.'

'I don't know what sort of accusations you are trying to make, Ifor Jenkins, but you need to watch your tongue,' Martha retorted furiously. Her plump face flushed angrily. 'Those stories brought a great deal of comfort to her, see. They took your poor Gwen's mind off her drab, miserable existence, let me tell you.'

'If she needed comfort she should have turned to the Good Lord. He's always there, listening out for our prayers. And, what is more, woman, you don't have to pay twopence a time either,' he snapped, his eyes narrowing and his mouth tightening.

It took Alun Pritchard an entire weekend to paint the front bedroom. He did that one first as Ifor had instructed, hoping all the time that there would be enough white paint left for the smaller room.

'It's going to be tight, Martha,' he said worriedly. 'I've skimped as much as I can on the big room, but I'm not sure that I've enough paint left to make a decent job of Sara's bedroom. Do you think Ifor Jenkins would buy some more paint if I asked him?'

'You'd be wasting your time doing that!' Martha told him. 'You know what an old skinflint he is unless it is something for himself.'

'Yes. He's more than likely to tell me not to bother at all with the back bedroom.'

Martha's plump face suddenly split into a wide smile. 'I tell you what, boyo, why don't we get a small pot of red paint and mix it in with the white you have left to make it go further. Then you can use that to paint Sara's room. Doing it pink will brighten it up no end, and I'm sure she'd be delighted.'

Alun nodded in agreement. 'Sounds a great idea to me. Don't say a word to her about it then. Let it be a surprise. I'm on day shift next week so I'll do it one evening when Ifor's on night shift.'

'That makes sense,' Martha chuckled. 'If Ifor sees what you're up to he's bound to have something to say about it.'

'He'll probably tell me that pink is an evil colour,' Alun joked.

'If he gets to know what's going on he'll certainly do his best to spoil things for poor little Sara,' Martha agreed morosely. 'Mean spirited as they come, that man is!'

'You will also remember to tell Sara that the paint smell is bad for the baby and that she will have to sleep in her father's room for the night,' Alun reminded his wife. 'It'll all be dry by next morning and then when she walks in there she'll get the surprise of her life.'

Martha entered enthusiastically into planning the surprise for Sara. As well as buying the tin of red paint she also bought a length of pretty flowered border to go up as a frieze. When Alun was ready to start work she invited Sara to bring Myfanwy to her place for a few hours.

'Come on, girl, your Dada's gone to work so come along in with me and give my man a chance to get on with things unhindered. We can have a cup of tea and a nice chat, and Alun will work all the faster with no one there talking to him. Anyway, it's better for the baby to be out of the smell. Alun will make sure the bedroom door is shut tight when he finishes, so you leave it that way until morning.'

Sara was more than happy to comply. She'd known Martha for as long as she could remember and enjoyed her company. Martha always knew what was going on, and always had so much to tell them. Yet she was so kind-hearted that she had a good word to say about everyone.

Martha might be middle-aged, but she was so cheerful and full of chatter that Sara had always thought of her as being younger than her own mother, even though she was a few years older.

Martha's home was spotless, well furnished and welcoming. She loved cooking and was very generous with her cakes and pies. Most of Sara's own cooking skills were the result of what Martha had taught her and what she had picked up from watching Martha at work in her kitchen.

Alun Pritchard was a man of few words, but equally kind-hearted. Like his wife, he enjoyed his food and both he and Martha were overweight but contented.

When she'd been small, often when her father and Alun Pritchard were both at work, her mother used to take her in to visit Martha Pritchard.

While her mother and Martha sat and drank tea, gossiped and sampled Martha's latest batch of cakes or scones, Sara would play with toys that Martha kept in a cupboard under the stairs for whenever children came to the house. There was a box of bricks, toy cars, dolls, boxes of puzzles and picture-books and she brought these out for Sara to play with on the floor in front of the fire.

Every so often Martha went on a visit to Cardiff where she said there were streets and streets full of shops, some of them joined up to one another by arcades which had glass roofs. Sara listened entranced as Martha told them about these and the wonderful posh departmental stores like Howell's and David Morgan's, where they sold everything from pots and pans and china to furniture and wonderful clothes.

She was so eager to see them for herself that she begged her mother to take her to Cardiff as a special treat when she left school at fourteen.

Her mother had agreed and had been squirrelling a few coppers away each week in readiness, and Sara had been counting the months, then the weeks, until it would happen.

They'd kept their plan secret from her father knowing he would disapprove, possibly even forbid them to go. Sara suspected that they would go while he was at work and without telling him.

That was before Myfanwy had been born; before her mother had been so ill; before the fire.

After the fire Sara was haunted by guilt in case it was God's way of punishing her for her wickedness in not only wanting to visit Cardiff but also keeping it all so secret from her Dada.

When she confided in Martha about this, Martha had hugged her close and told her not to be so silly.

'Why would God punish you for wanting a harmless treat like that?' she asked in astonishment. 'You put such thoughts right out of your head this minute,' she said firmly. 'Your Mam had told me all about your plans, and even when she was laid up after Myfanwy was born, she was still looking forward to going. I'd said I'd have the baba for the day, or I'd come along with you and show you round, like. Oh yes, your treat was still on the cards, *cariad*, and don't you ever forget that.'

Sara spent the early part of the evening with Martha. When Alun came home to say he had finished work on the room, they both wanted her to stay at their place overnight.

'No, I couldn't do that,' Sara protested. 'I must be at home when Dada gets back from work to have his bath and breakfast waiting for him.'

'Fair dos, then, but you mustn't go in the bedroom until the paint has dried because of the smell of it getting on the baba's chest. You understand now? Sleep in your Dada's room tonight, mind.'

'I might stay downstairs in the chair.'

'Nonsense! There's silly to have a good comfortable bed empty upstairs and you perched on a chair downstairs. Get into your Dada's new bed and have a good night's sleep, girl. Promise me now?'

Chapter Four

Sara was still fast asleep in the new bed her father had bought to replace the one that had been reduced to a mass of ashes when he came home next morning. Myfanwy, too, was asleep in her crib that Sara had moved into his bedroom for the night.

When he entered the house Ifor Jenkins was incensed to find that Sara was not up preparing his breakfast, and that his tin bath of hot water was not ready for him to step into the moment he entered the house.

Removing the leather belt from his trousers, and kicking off his heavy boots, he padded upstairs. He'd teach her a lesson she'd not forget in a hurry, he thought angrily.

He found the door of Sara's room tight shut, and he felt a moment of alarm when he opened it and found she was not in there, and neither was the baby. Where the hell was she, he wondered, as the smell of fresh paint filled his lungs. The change to the drab little room shocked him, but he was so bemused by the girls' absence that he spared no thought for the frivolous new decoration.

Then he saw that the door to his bedroom was also closed and he opened it as quietly as he could. A cold flash of anger surged through him as he saw her spread-eagled in the centre of his bed. She was sound asleep, the covers thrown back to her waist.

Ifor stood at the foot of the bed, clenching and unclenching his fists. He had intended to chastise her for her negligence, but now, as his gaze fastened on her firm young breasts starkly visible through the shabby cotton nightdress, he felt his body trembling with an intoxicating excitement.

It was the Lord's will, something out of his hands and beyond his control, he told himself afterwards. It was the only way he could justify what happened next.

His reasoning deserted him at the sight of her pubescent body and he began shedding his clothes like a snake sloughing its dead skin. Still grimed with coal dust and rank with sweat, he found himself slipping into bed alongside his young daughter.

The heat from her body stirred his senses and made it impossible for him to resist the desire rising inside him. Physical responses that he normally held in control were suddenly rampant. His mouth was on hers, stifling her screams as he pushed away the rest of the bedclothes. With trembling hands he roughly parted her stick-like legs and plunged into her.

The shock of what was happening, and the sudden tearing pain, frightened Sara so much she could scarcely breathe. She wanted to cry out, but her father's mouth was clamped so tightly over her own that she couldn't. She tried to struggle, to fight him off, but every vestige of strength had seeped from her limbs. She felt physically sick, hysterical with fear, and filled with an overpowering horror at what was happening to her body.

She wept inwardly, knowing she was powerless. How could he do this to her? Her own Dada to violate her in such a manner. It was the worst evil imaginable, and he was a man who believed fervently in the Lord.

When her father finally rolled off her, satiated and exhausted, Sara wriggled her thin body away from him and inched her way towards the side of the bed. By the time her bare feet touched the linoleum he was already snoring. Mortified, she scrubbed at herself with her nightdress, then clutching her clothes, and carrying the crib with Myfanwy still asleep in it, Sara crept downstairs.

Her mind still swam with ugly visions and she was shivering violently. When the poker rattled against the bars as she stirred the dying embers of the fire, she held her breath in case it should rouse her father.

She stayed huddled there, frozen with fright, until the kettle that was balanced on a trivet at the side of the fire began singing as it came to the boil.

Her hands were shaking so much that she found pouring the water from it on to the leaves she'd scooped into the big brown teapot almost impossible. The water splattered against the rim, sending needle-sharp dabs of pain on to her bare legs and feet. Her sharp intakes of breath and tiny yelps of pain roused Myfanwy.

The baby's crying momentarily restored everything to normality for Sara. Picking her up she cradled the small urine-soaked baby in her arms, taking comfort from the feel of the tiny vulnerable body pressed against her own.

How could her Dada have treated her like that, how could he have done what he had, she asked herself over and over again as tears streamed down her cheeks.

Her mother had told her the facts of life and she had seen and heard enough from other women and girls living in Taff Court to know all about what went on between men and women. Because of her mother's dire warnings, she had never had anything at all to do with boys. And she'd certainly never even kissed one!

'Keep yourself for the man you are going to marry,' her mother had told her gently. 'He will love you all the more for your innocence.'

In her day-dreams she had sometimes visualised the man she would marry when she was older. He'd be fair haired, tall, with blue eyes and fresh golden skin. And when he smiled he would have beautiful white teeth. He wouldn't be a miner. He'd be a teacher, perhaps, or someone with an important job in Cardiff or Newport. He'd take her away from the mining community of Pontypridd to a world where people worked only by day and enjoyed themselves in the evenings and at weekends.

They'd have a home bright with flowers and music, like the women in the love stories her mother had read so avidly, and they'd have golden-haired blue-eyed children who would play on the green lawn that surrounded the beautiful house they lived in.

She knew it was a dream, just as her mother knew

the stories she read were sheer fantasy. It made her happy to think about it, especially when Myfanwy was crying or being sick.

Sara poured herself a cup of tea and suddenly felt so old and used that she wished she were dead. Her Dada had taken away so much more than her innocence; he'd taken away every vestige of hope that she'd had for her future happiness.

Draining her cup, Sara started to unwrap the sodden little bundle in her arms. No matter how abused and sore her own body felt, Myfanwy still needed attention. She fetched a bowl and flannel and gently sponged the child's scrawny little body, dried and dressed her.

Automatically, she heated up some milk, poured it on to a slice of bread and mashed it up with a sprinkling of sugar into a bowl of pobs that the young baby could manage.

Barely four months old and being weaned already, she thought sadly. Janie Harries had promised to suckle Myfanwy a couple of times a day. Her own baby was eight months and partially weaned but her milk was still plentiful.

'You feed her pobs in the morning when she's so hungry she won't be able to resist,' Janie advised, 'and bring her to me around midday and again around tea time. Between us we'll keep the poor little mite going.'

Her father had been scornful of the idea. 'Letting that woman feed her is filling the child with evil,' he'd ranted. 'We all know about Janie Harries and the time she spends at the pictures. Twice, sometimes three times every week she is at the cinema.

Rank wickedness! Why her husband stands for it I will never know.'

'She doesn't go there any more, Dada,' Sara told him, 'not since the baby arrived. She only did it for a couple of months before Gareth was born to help pass the time.'

'There were plenty of other things she could have done to pass the time. If she'd spent it praying to the Good Lord, or helping other people, it would have been better for her and for the child she was carrying.'

'Well, she's trying to help now by offering to feed Myfanwy,' Sara pointed out. 'If it wasn't for her kindness I don't know how I would manage because Martha says too much cow's milk isn't good for such a young baby. Even the small bit I have to give her between feeds at Janie's gives her colic. That's why she cries so much.'

'She cries because you don't look after her properly,' he snapped. 'How many times have I come home from work and found her lying there in her crib bawling her eyes out?'

'I have to put her down while I get your bath ready and prepare a meal for you, Dada,' Sara explained wearily.

'Don't you dare contradict me!' he told her harshly.

She'd half expected a thrashing. Only the knowledge that she had to take Myfanwy down for a feed, and that Janie Harries would be quick to spot if her eyes were red or puffy from crying, had stayed his hand. He knew Janie was something of a gossip and would relish a bit of scandal.

Sara sighed as she spooned the milky mess into the baby's resisting mouth. She shuddered, wondering what Janie Harries would have to say if she knew what had happened this morning? If that got out then her name would be blackened not only in Taff Court but also in the whole of Pontypridd. She wished there was someone she could confide in, someone who would tell her that none of it was really her fault and that she wasn't responsible for the terrible sin that had been committed.

Martha might understand. Or would she? Sara wondered what the outcome might be if she confided in Martha. Would she tell her she was wicked to have let it happen?

It had been Martha who had suggested she should sleep in her Dada's bed while her room was being painted, in case the smell might upset Myfanwy, Sara reminded herself.

'Sleep there just for the one night, *cariad,*' Martha had said. 'Your Dada doesn't have to know if you don't want to tell him. You'll be up getting his bath ready before he gets in from the pit in the morning. It's only for one night. The paint will all be dry by morning, see! Your room will be all fresh and nice for you, my lovely.'

She'd dropped off to sleep, blissfully comfortable in the huge bed, wondering what her own room would be like when she next saw it and now it was almost mid-morning and she hadn't even taken a peek at it!

Settling Myfanwy back in her crib she crept upstairs again. The sound of her father's snores as she tiptoed past his bedroom door brought her nerves to screaming pitch. Then she opened the door to her room and for a moment she stood there unable to believe her eyes.

The drab brown walls had been transformed into a soft glowing pink and right the way around there was a three-inch frieze of red and pink roses on a green background. Martha had even made new curtains in a crisp, rose-splattered cretonne to hang at the window.

It was so beautiful that for a brief moment it gave Sara new hopes for the future. One day, she vowed, she'd have the whole house decorated so that it was as pretty and glowing as her room was at the moment.

Then the thought of what she had endured at the hands of her father eroded her pleasure. If she could turn back the clock, to the time when her room was drab and ugly, she would have gladly done so. Quietly she closed the door and went downstairs.

Her heart heavy, she steeled herself to go next door to thank Martha and Alun for all their hard work.

'There's pleased I am that you like it, *cariad*!' Martha smiled.

'It's absolutely wonderful!' Sara told her. Her dark eyes filled with tears. 'Mam would have thought it beautiful, too.'

She longed to confide in Martha about what had happened that morning but innate caution kept her silent. She shivered at the thought of what would follow if her Dada suspected she'd told Martha, or anyone else for that matter. Once he got her on her own he'd feel justified in taking his belt off and tanning the hide off her.

And if anyone heard about that they would say it was her fault for saying such a disgraceful thing about her father. Most people, especially the members of the Tabernacle Chapel, considered him to be a pillar of respectability. It would be her word against his and she knew who would be believed.

No, Sara decided, no one outside their home must ever hear about it. He would blame her, make her out to be wanton and say she had tempted him. If that happened they might take Myfanwy away and put her in a home, and Myfanwy was her responsibility. She owed it to her mother's memory to look after her little sister and do the best she could for her. She had made that promise at her mother's funeral and she was determined to keep it.

She'd never be able to forget what had happened that morning between herself and her father, so she would tell herself that it was all an evil dream.

She'd make sure nothing like that ever happened again. If she told no one, not even Martha, then although it would remain a dark secret shadow in their lives, it would be something known only to the two of them.

Chapter Five

'Christ, mun! What are you playing at? You can't do this to me! Those days are behind us.'

There was a look of shock on Ifor Jenkins's face as Tecwyn Taylor, the foreman of number three shift, turned him away at the coalface.

'Sorry I am, Ifor, but there it is. Not easy to pick such a small team, I can tell you. Sleepless night I've had over it and no mistake.'

'Sleepless!' Ifor's voice rose. 'I'll have more than a sleepless night if you turn me away, Tecwyn Taylor. I've a young daughter as well as a baby not yet fully weaned to provide for, how can I do that with no work? How? How? I ask you!'

Tecwyn Taylor turned his back on the ranting miner. 'You're always bloody telling us how the Good Lord looks after each and every one of us so I suggest you ask Him to do just that and look after you and your problems,' he muttered over his shoulder as he walked away.

Ifor's jaw dropped. 'What the hell does he mean by that?' he gasped, looking round at the group of miners who, like himself, had been stood off because there was not enough demand for coal to merit a full shift.

'You heard he what he said, Ifor Jenkins, you ask the Lord to help you.'

'Why should you fare any different from the rest of us? We've all got families to support.'

'That's right, boyo. We're all in the same boat.'

'Push off home, Ifor Jenkins, and give that girl of yours a hand with the babby, she looks worn out.'

'Bright young thing your Sara used to be, but she's like a little ghost these days.'

'Poor little dab, looks as though she's got the cares of the world on her back.'

'Looks haunted to me. Not hiding some terrible sin, is she, Ifor?'

A dull flush spread over Ifor's sallow cheeks as he turned his back on the crowd of men and began to walk towards the pit gates.

'Fancy a hand of cards before you go?' someone called, and as the crowd's laughter wafted after him in waves, Ifor spun round.

'Card playing is evil, the Devil's distraction, and makes sinners of every one of you. The Lord will demand retribution so heed my warning and mend your ways, all of you, or your punishment will be dire.'

'*Darw*! Ifor the prophet has spoken!'

'Fair dos, he knows what he's talking about!'

'You mean when it comes to sinning?'

There were loud guffaws and their tone dropped so that Ifor was unable to hear what was being said, but he sensed it was far from flattering. He strained his ears, trying to make out even the odd word. He heard Sara's name, over and over again, and his blood chilled.

What did they know, what evil rumours were being spread, he wondered? Sara wouldn't have breathed a word to anyone about what was going on, he was sure of that. She was mortally terrified by his threats.

He stopped in mid-stride, cold dread clawing his conscience. The possibility that someone like Martha Pritchard, who was always poking her fat nose into his affairs, might suspect something and start a whispering campaign, set his heart hammering.

He knew that what he was doing was the ultimate venial sin, but he justified it to himself on the grounds that it was the Lord's will. The Lord had taken Gwen from him and a man needed physical solace. The Lord had given him Sara and at her age she was ripe and ready. And since he offered up every act to the Lord, like Abraham when he was preparing to sacrifice his son, it justified what he was doing, he told himself.

The same with taking Sara out of school. He made that quite clear to Gwladys Jones, the schoolteacher, when she came snooping round to see why Sara seemed to be permanently absent.

'She's turned fourteen so she's old enough to be finished with school and to make herself useful,' he stated firmly, his dark eyes levelling with Gwladys Jones's slate-grey ones.

'I know that, but Sara is such a bright girl it seems a pity that she can't stay on for another year,' Gwladys Jones persisted. 'If she worked hard, who knows, it might be possible to enrol her as a pupil teacher.' Her solemn face broke into a cold smile. 'I'm sure an intelligent man like you would welcome an opportunity like that for your daughter, Mr Jenkins.'

She'd turned on her prim school-marm charm so he responded in the same vein. With a deep sigh he'd told her that he agreed with what she said.

'There's nothing I would like more than for my eldest daughter to continue with her education, Miss Jones, but since her Mam has died I need Sara here to care for the baby and run the home.'

Gwladys Jones nodded thoughtfully. 'I do understand. I know the problems you must be experiencing, Mr Jenkins. For many years I have had to face a very similar predicament,' she confided. 'Both my elderly parents were bedridden, and I was faced with the dilemma of continuing with my work or staying home to look after them.'

'And so how did you solve your situation?' he asked politely.

'By paying a housekeeper to look after them while I was at work, and then shouldering the burden myself in the evenings and at the weekends. I managed for four years like that so I know it can be done.' She sighed plaintively. 'Both of them died within weeks of each other only a few months ago.'

'The Lord giveth and the Lord taketh away,' Ifor Jenkins intoned solemnly.

'And since the Lord has given your daughter Sara the talent to learn, it's unfortunate that it's not possible to foster it,' Gwladys Jones said quickly.

Ifor's dark eyes narrowed. Being glib of tongue himself, he was quick to recognise the gift in others.

'I'll think carefully about what you've said regarding Sara's future,' he promised smoothly.

'Good! I am very pleased to hear you say that.' She stretched out a slim, firm hand. When he took it she covered his hand with her other one. 'Perhaps we should discuss it again after chapel next Sunday?' she said, an earnest look on her long, sombre face.

The matter had completely gone from his mind when he left the Tabernacle Chapel the following Sunday and found Gwladys Jones waiting for him. There was open admiration in her eyes when she saw him dressed up in his Sunday-best suit.

He raised his trilby in greeting and tried to remember what commitment he had made when they'd previously discussed Sara's schooling. As they walked side by side down the road towards Miss Jones's house they talked about the service, the preacher, the weather and countless other topics, but neither of them once mentioned Sara or her future.

Ifor found that Gwladys Jones's educated voice and her sensible questions and answers were a balm to his soul, and when she invited him in for a cup of tea he felt it would be churlish to refuse.

The house was old, rather shabby, and smelt musty. From the way it was furnished it had obviously been her parents' home. He listened with renewed interest as she told him once again how she'd nursed them through long illnesses until they'd both died a few months earlier.

'So now I'm on my own,' she said wistfully. 'I won't be staying here for very much longer, there are too many memories. I feel the time has come for a fresh start.'

'You mean you intend to move away from Pontypridd?'

She considered his question for a long moment before answering, her head tipped slightly to one side. 'Possibly. There is nothing to keep me here. Having nursed my elderly parents for such a long time has meant that my social life has been very curtailed and so I have very few friends these days.'

'The Tabernacle Chapel, and the school where you teach, surely those must mean something to you?'

Gwladys Jones sighed. 'The voice of the Lord will stay with me wherever I am. As for the school, there are plenty of teaching jobs in other towns and villages.'

'Don't be too hasty,' Ifor warned. 'This depression that's been caused by the General Strike can affect us all so it's better to be amongst friends at such a time. A considerable number of men have been laid off at the pit again this week, and even those of us who have been kept on have had our hours cut, and are on a short working week.'

'Is your job safe?'

'Praise be to the Lord, yes! A week ago I was not so sure. Sent home along with a great many others, as you well know, since you were at my house when I arrived home when I should have been working. I prayed to the Good Lord and he answered my prayers. Next day I was reinstated,' he added piously.

Gwladys frowned. 'You are working a shorter shift, though?'

'That's true. And that means making economies all round.'

'And is Sara thrifty?'

Ifor sighed. 'Not as clever at spinning out the housekeeping money as her mother was. She doesn't have the time to cook proper meals, and she certainly doesn't clean the house as thoroughly either. She claims the baba takes up most of her day, but since the child is less than a year old, and spends most of its time asleep, I cannot see how that can be so.'

'Now, now,' Gwladys tapped his arm gently, 'you mustn't be too harsh on the girl. She's only fourteen, remember, and I'm sure she's doing her very best. Without an older woman to turn to for advice or guidance she is bound to make mistakes.'

'Sara turns to Martha Pritchard, our next-door neighbour, especially when it comes to looking after the baby, but I'm not at all sure that she is the right person to instruct her,' Ifor confided.

'It's not always the best thing to be too reliant on one's neighbours,' Gwladys murmured as she refilled Ifor's cup. 'They end up knowing far too much of your business.'

Ifor looked at her admiringly. Gwladys Jones was a remarkably sensible woman, he decided. He was glad he had taken the trouble to get to know her better. Sara could benefit from listening to her wise counsel.

As if reading his mind, Gwladys went on, 'If you think I can help Sara in any way then you have only to ask me.'

'Thank you. I might well take you up on that. I feel that the Good Lord planned for our paths to cross,' he added earnestly, 'and it would be foolish to ignore His help.'

She coloured slightly; her long solemn face brightened so that for a moment he thought what a fine-looking woman she was.

He studied her covertly. Although not exceptionally tall she had a presence that made her appear imposing. Her manner was so confident and she had such an air of authority that few other women he knew seemed to possess, that he was greatly impressed.

He thought of his late wife. Gwen had been a slightly built, elfin-faced girl when they'd married, but years of childbearing and ill health had turned her once-slim figure into a shapeless mass, and her face into a grey mottled smudge.

This woman was wearing a plain grey dress that fitted so neatly that you were left in no doubt as to the trimness and firmness of her mature body. At chapel she had been wearing a full-length black coat which he assumed was in deference to the fact that she was still in mourning for her parents. Her brown hair was smoothly waved and taken to the back of her head in a neat roll. Even though her face was long and sombre she had a firm nose and jaw, and her skin looked smooth and unlined.

Most of the time she kept her narrow lips pressed tight together as if holding her words in check. He could easily visualise her standing in front of a class, confidently commanding their attention and respect. There was a sharp intelligence in her slate-grey eyes that indicated she would stand for no nonsense.

He was glad Sara was not still at school. This woman was so shrewd that she might well suspect that all was not as it should be with the girl. If she interrogated Sara then there was always the possibility that she might spin some garbled story about what was happening at home.

Momentarily, he even doubted if it was wise for him to be associating so closely with Gwladys Jones; she was so astute, so clever at extracting information.

The truth was, Ifor Jenkins admitted to himself, she fascinated him and he found her mentally stimulating. It had never been any good discussing political or religious topics with Gwen. She had listened, nodding every so often like an automaton, but nothing of what he said ever penetrated her mind. She'd long ago given up accompanying him to the Tabernacle Chapel, although, he had to admit, she had made sure that Sara went regularly and to Sunday school.

The trashy magazines Martha Pritchard passed on to her had fouled Gwen's mind, he thought angrily. It had been her one vice, her link with the Devil, that he had never been able completely to stamp out.

Ifor was quite sure that Gwladys Jones didn't stoop to such reading. She wouldn't have time. From the discussions they'd had, it was obvious that she kept right up to date with what was happening in the world around her. She even shared his political opinions, and thought that it had been both foolish and criminal of the mine owners, back in May, to claim that they must either reduce the men's wages or close the pits down.

They both agreed they never wanted to witness

anything like that happening again. It was as if the whole world had come to a standstill. Within twenty-four hours there'd been no trains, trams or buses, and no newspapers.

Mines, steel works and ports had all lain idle. And even though the General Strike had been called off less than two weeks later it had been a long time before everything was back working at full scale. When the miners returned to work they had been forced into accepting the mine owners' conditions.

He'd never been able to make Gwen understand any of these issues. In the lean years before the General Strike eventually happened, she had whined at him as though it had been his fault because they were short of money for food immediately before Myfanwy was born. She had taken to her bed most of the time, leaving Sara to manage things in the home.

Gwladys Jones would have coped, he felt sure of that. She was one of those inwardly strong, resourceful women.

Simply being in her company inspired him. And the way she listened to his reasoning, and agreed with his theories, made him realise that she was someone who appreciated his viewpoint. Fervently, but silently, he thanked the Good Lord for bringing them together.

Chapter Six

Sara Jenkins sat back on her heels and surveyed the expanse of linoleum she'd been polishing for the last half an hour.

'There you are, Gwladys Jones, you'll be able to see your face in that,' she muttered as she straightened up.

She spread some sheets of old newspaper over the newly polished floor so that there would be no footmarks if anyone walked on it. Whatever happened it must remain pristine until five o'clock when Dada was bringing Miss Jones home for high tea before they both went off to Sunday worship at the Tabernacle Chapel in Bridge Street.

Sara checked the time on the enamel alarm clock perched on the mantelshelf and breathed a sigh of relief. It was only half past three so she had plenty of time to change Myfanwy's nappy and dress, and then have a wash herself and put on her own clean dress before the great event.

Gwladys Jones had been her teacher at school for the last two years she had been there, and Sara remembered her as being terribly strict. She never smiled, rarely praised anyone, and kept a ruler in her hand all the time she was teaching. It was heaven help anyone she caught fiddling with their pencil or making a noise of any kind when they should be listening to what she was saying. Without a word of warning she would bring the ruler down across their knuckles with a resounding crack.

She was strict about time, too. One minute late and you stayed in the classroom for the entire break time. She never kept you in after school, but that was only because she always had to hurry home to look after her sick parents.

Sara bustled around, straightening the room after polishing the floor, spreading a crisp white, freshly ironed tablecloth on the wooden table, and putting out the best china in readiness. She hoped she wouldn't say or do anything to spoil the occasion for her Dada.

He had been very precise about what he wanted her to serve for their meal. She had boiled the gammon joint herself and then left it to cool in its own water before rolling it in breadcrumbs. She had cut off a mere morsel to taste and then wondered if Miss Jones would find it too salty. Hopefully, the jar of home-made sweet chutney that Martha had given her would hide that. She cut the slices of bread as thinly as she could, wondering whether she ought to spread the butter on them or not. In the end she decided that it was probably more correct to put the butter dish on the table and let everyone help themselves. She also put a pot of plum jam on the table, and in the very centre, the round fruit cake with almonds sprinkled all over its golden brown top that she'd bought that morning from the cake shop on the corner.

It all looked mouth-watering. She would have liked to have some watercress or lettuce, but with it being the end of November there wasn't anything like that in the corner shop. This was one of the reasons why she'd been so grateful to Martha when she'd offered her a pot of her home-made chutney.

Once everything was arranged to her liking, Sara picked Myfanwy up from her crib and took her into the scullery to change her soiled nappy and wash her little face and hands. She had already fed her a bowl of pobs so, with any luck, there wouldn't be a sound out of her until it was time to take her down the road for Janie Harries to suckle.

Her own toilet was rushed, as the hands of the clock seemed to be suddenly pointing to five minutes to the hour. If Miss Jones was as punctual as she expected everyone else to be they would be arriving at any minute.

Wiping her face with a flannel she removed her soiled skirt and blouse and put on the blue serge dress with the red collar that she'd worn at school. As she combed her straggly hair back from her face, Sara wondered if she ought to put on a pinny. It would protect her dress, but would it make her look childish, she wondered. Before she could reach a decision she heard the front door opening and her father's voice calling out to know where she was.

'Up there preening yourself again,' he frowned, as she ran down the stairs. 'You already know Miss Jones, of course.'

Sara smiled shyly.

'Well, say something, girl. Shake hands!'

Nervously, Sara complied. Gwladys Jones nodded as her gloved fingertips touched Sara's outstretched hand.

'I expected to see you in something more sombre so soon after the death of your mother, Sara,' she remarked.

She'd tried so hard to do what was right, yet Sara felt as if she was back in the classroom with Miss Jones deriding her in front of the rest of the children. She blushed scarlet, her eyes filling with tears. 'I'm sorry, Miss,' she gulped, 'this is the only dress I have!'

'Nonsense! You have a black skirt, I bought it for you for the funeral,' her father intervened.

'I . . . I know, but I was wearing that this morning when I was cooking and cleaning the house and I thought I ought to change.'

He shook his head sadly, his eyebrows lifting as his eyes met with Gwladys Jones's. 'Vanity before respect,' he intoned disparagingly.

She nodded. 'The young soon forget, I'm afraid.'

Sara felt mortified by the criticism. Wearing her blue dress was not vanity, nor was it a sign of disrespect to her mother. If anything it was the opposite since the dress was the last thing her mother had bought for her.

As her father led the way into the living-room she moved towards the grate to make the tea. The kettle standing on the iron trivet over the coals was already singing and she had put the big brown pot on the hob to warm in readiness.

'Aren't you going to offer to take Miss Jones's coat from her then, Sara?' her father demanded.

'Yes, of course.' Sara stopped and smiled nervously at Miss Jones, but there was no answering response. Nor was there a word of thanks from

Gwladys Jones as she handed over her black coat and black velvet cloche hat into Sara's keeping.

'Make sure you put those down somewhere very careful,' her father admonished as she headed for the stairs.

When she came back down, her father and Miss Jones were already seated at the table. Sara's heart lurched when she saw that Gwladys Jones had taken the chair she normally used, the chair that had always been her mother's.

'Come along, Sara, make that tea,' her father ordered impatiently as he sat drumming his fingers on the edge of the table.

The meal was far from being a success. As Sara had feared, Miss Jones found the ham a trifle salty, and the chutney far too sweet. She declined a slice of cake saying that she never ate shop-bought cake.

'It came from the cake shop down the road and it was made on the premises,' Sara assured her.

'It is still not home-made though, is it, Sara? I'm very surprised that with all the time you must have on your hands now that you are at home all day, you haven't mastered the art of baking a simple cake. I shall have to teach you.'

Ifor beamed. 'That would be very kind. You'd appreciate that, wouldn't you, Sara?'

No, I wouldn't, Sara thought rebelliously. I know how to mix up a cake, but it's making sure that the fire is at the right heat so that the side oven stays at the right temperature that is so difficult. Miss Jones probably had one of the new gas ovens where all you had to do was light it and turn a knob to control it.

Sara had been hoping that Myfanwy would sleep right through their meal, but she was disappointed. She had barely topped up Miss Jones's cup for the second time when a thin wailing cry came from the crib.

Sara saw a frown darken her father's face and she rushed to quieten Myfanwy, but nothing she could do would pacify her. She knew from the baby's cry that Myfanwy was hungry and needed a feed. In desperation she made her excuses to Miss Jones, wrapped Myfanwy in a shawl, and headed down the road to Janie Harries.

When she returned ten minutes later without the baby Miss Jones looked perplexed.

'She's gone to be fed,' Sara told her. 'Janie Harries has a baby of her own and she's letting Myfanwy suckle as well,' she added by way of explanation, her face scarlet with embarrassment.

Gwladys Jones looked shocked. 'Is that wise?' she frowned, looking directly at Ifor.

He spread his hands in a gesture of helplessness. 'It seemed to be the only answer,' he said almost apologetically.

'How old is the baby?'

'Almost six months.'

Gwladys Jones's frown deepened. 'Surely, Sara, weaning your baby sister is the answer?'

'I have started to do so,' Sara said quickly. 'Myfanwy only goes to Janie twice a day. I take her first thing in the morning and then just before I settle her down for the night.'

Gwladys Jones's mouth tightened to a thin line. 'You have a very bad habit of interrupting people when they are trying to tell you something for your own good, Sara. I noticed it before when you were one of my pupils!'

Sara felt the tears prickling in her eyes. She'd sensed Miss Jones didn't approve of Myfanwy being breast-fed by Janie Harris, which was why she'd wanted to assure her that it wouldn't be for very much longer. She waited for her Dada to speak up and take her side. Instead he said in a voice harsh with suppressed anger, 'Apologise to Miss Jones this instant, Sara, for being so rude! And then clear away these dirty dishes. I'm sure our guest doesn't want to sit looking at them all evening.'

Swallowing hard, Sara did as she was told.

As she washed up she thought resentfully how unfair it was that she was being criticised by Miss Jones and her father when she was trying so hard to please them both. She blinked away the tears of self-pity. Everything would have been so different if the fire had never happened. If her mother hadn't died then Miss Jones would probably never have stepped over their doorstep.

As soon as she had put everything away she excused herself to go and collect Myfanwy.

'It's enough to give a baby of that age a chill taking it out in the raw night air,' Gwladys Jones said disapprovingly. 'Make sure you keep her well wrapped up and don't loiter on your way home.'

'We're leaving soon for the Tabernacle Chapel, so we may not be here when you get back,' her father added, 'so don't forget to make up the fire before you go to bed.'

To Sara's relief the house was empty when she

returned with Myfanwy. After she'd settled the sleeping baby into her crib for the night, she made herself a hot drink, and sat by the fire with it, going over in her mind all that had happened during Gwladys Jones's visit.

It was quite plain that Gwladys Jones impressed her Dada. He hung on her every word and Sara had noticed the way his eyes lit up when they were both discussing the General Strike and the rising unemployment. He was almost as fanatical about politics as he was about religion, and it seemed to be something the two of them had in common.

The thought that they might be seeing quite a lot more of Gwladys Jones filled Sara with misgivings. If today was a taste of what it was going to be like in the future, then she was in for a hard time.

Already, in one afternoon, Gwladys Jones had disapproved about the way she was dressed, her cooking and the way she was looking after Myfanwy.

Sara's suspicions were well founded. In the months that followed not only was Gwladys Jones a regular visitor, but Sara was aware that the schoolteacher was influencing her father more and more.

It soon became apparent to Sara that the closer Gwladys Jones managed to get to Ifor Jenkins, the more Gwladys criticised her.

Sara felt angry and hurt by these remarks. She longed to answer her back, but her fear of her father made her keep a still tongue.

When she had crept off to bed, worn out from housework, and coping with Myfanwy who was now teething, Sara felt it was all too much for her to bear. She would struggle to remember the promise she had made to herself at her mother's funeral; to look after her sister and bring her up right, but sometimes even that wasn't enough.

If only she could have slept the whole night through without any disturbance then she might have been able to face each new day better prepared, but as it was she felt as though she was on a merry-go-round that never stopped.

When her father was on nights, no matter how many times she might have been disturbed by the baby, he still expected his tin bath of hot water to be ready for him in front of the fire. And he expected Sara to be up and downstairs, waiting to scrub the ingrained coal dust from his back.

Those mornings when he ate the breakfast which she had ready for him, and then went straight to his bed, Sara breathed a sigh of relief, and did everything possible to keep Myfanwy quiet so that he could sleep undisturbed.

It was when he finished his breakfast and then ordered her upstairs to his bed that fear made her heart thud so violently that she thought it would suffocate her. Her legs would tremble, and turn to jelly, so that she could hardly drag herself up the stairs.

It was even worse when he was on day shift. He would order her up to his bed the moment she had finished her chores and prepared everything for the next morning.

What happened after that she tried not to think about, but it haunted her like an evil nightmare. He was brutal, cold and ruthless. He handled her roughly, ignoring her tears and her pleas to leave her alone and let her go to her own bed. If she cried out, he clamped his hand over her mouth, hissing threats into her ear about what he would do to her if she didn't keep quiet.

Long after he was exhausted and snoring she would lie stiffly beside him, wanting to creep back into her own bed, but scared to do so in case any movement she made might disturb him. She knew that if he wakened, he'd repeat the whole horrible performance, or worse, all over again.

Sara felt sure that Martha Pritchard suspected that all was not well. She was too scared of what her father would do to her to confide in her neighbour, even though she longed for comforting words and understanding.

As she listened to her father and Gwladys Jones talking about the General Strike and how it had been the cause of so much unemployment and short time, or about how some chap called Lindbergh had flown an aeroplane called the *Spirit of St Louis* across the Atlantic, Sara was tempted to interrupt them. She wanted to tell Gwladys Jones about her father's behaviour.

Not that it would do any good. Miss Jones would be horrified, but Sara knew she wouldn't believe her. She'd probably send her to wash her mouth out with soap and water, like she'd made the boys do at school if they ever swore or answered her back.

And then, when Gwladys Jones had gone home, Sara knew her father would take off his strap and thrash her before subjecting her to even more pain and humiliation as he ravaged her body.

Chapter Seven

'One of your apple tarts, please, Mrs Morgan, and two loaves of crusty bread,' Sara requested.

'And what about one of my gingerbread men for that special little girl you've got there?'

Sara re-counted the money in her purse. 'No, not this morning, I'm afraid.'

Betti Morgan's round face puckered into a pout. She leant over the wooden counter and looked down at Myfanwy who was standing at Sara's side clutching tightly to her skirt.

'We can't have that now, can we, *cariad*,' she murmured, smiling down at Myfanwy. 'Not after you've toddled all this way. Lucky thing is I've got one put aside for you!' She dived under the counter and brought out a misshapen piece of confectionery. 'Special he is, see!'

Myfanwy's dark eyes lit up as she stretched out a hand to take the biscuit that Betti Morgan held out to her.

'There you are, my lovely. Don't drop it now, will you!'

'It's very kind of you, Mrs Morgan, but you really shouldn't spoil her like that,' Sara protested. 'She'll be expecting something every time she comes in here.'

'Of course she won't! Anyway, I wouldn't be able

to sell that one, it's too misshapen. Fat like me, see!' She gave a rumbling belly laugh that set her double chins wobbling. 'Now, what was it you wanted? An apple tart and two loaves. Got that Miss Jones coming to tea again then?'

Sara nodded.

'Twice this week that's been!'

'Yes. She and Dada are working out the plans for the special Sunday school party at the Tabernacle Chapel.'

'Are they indeed! Well, I hope you and Myfanwy will both enjoy it.'

'Oh, we won't be there. Myfanwy's too little. They have to be three, and they must have been going to Sunday school for at least six months. And I'm too old. The top age is twelve.'

'Since your Dada is the one organising it then surely he can arrange it so that you both can go?'

Sara shook her head. 'I don't think he would do anything like that, Mrs Morgan.'

'*Darw*! Christian charity should begin at home, I say. Never mind, though. Soon be out working yourself, and then you'll be able to do far more exciting things.'

'I don't think that's very likely, Mrs Morgan, not while Myfanwy is so young,' Sara sighed.

'Why ever not? Sixteen you are now, girl, and it's high time you were earning and had some money of your own to spend. What about the cinema, does your Dada pay for you to go?'

Sara shook her head.

Betti Morgan looked surprised. 'Dearie me! You

mean you've never seen any of those film stars like Mae West and Greta Garbo?'

'Only their pictures on the posters.'

'Not exactly one of the young flappers dancing the night away, are you?' Betti said with a teasing smile.

'My Dada would never let me wear one of those skimpy, floaty dresses,' Sara said wistfully.

Betti Morgan nodded sympathetically. 'All the same, I bet you wouldn't mind having some money in your pocket, even if you weren't allowed to spend it on the pictures or going dancing.'

Sara smiled and picked Myfanwy up in her arms. 'Say ta to Mrs Morgan for your gingerbread man, Myfanwy.' She put the child down and picked up her loaves and the apple pie that Mrs Morgan had put on the counter. 'I'd better be going or Miss Jones will arrive before I have everything ready for her.'

'Hold on a minute, girl.' Betti Morgan came from behind the counter, grabbing Sara's arm. 'Look, if you've a mind to do an hour or so working I could do with someone to help me out in the shop with Christmas only around the corner. What about on Saturday morning for the next three weeks, eh?'

Sara's dark eyes widened in disbelief. Then her face fell. 'Lovely idea it would be, Mrs Morgan, but there's Myfanwy to think about.'

'Wouldn't your Dada look after her for a couple of hours?'

'I could ask him, but I don't think he would.'

'What about Martha Pritchard then?'

Sara drew in her breath sharply. 'That's an idea, but it would be taking advantage of her kindness.

Good she is to me, so I wouldn't like her to think I was putting on her, it wouldn't be playing fair.'

'No, my lovely, I suppose you're right.' Betti Morgan's plump face was a study of concentration. 'Tell you what, *cariad,* why don't you bring Myfanwy with you? Look after her between us, we can.'

'You're just saying that to be kind,' Sara laughed.

'Not a bit of it! Be a lovely rest for my old legs to sit down and nurse her for half an hour, and let you do all the running about. And after that she'd probably sleep. Has a mid-morning nap, doesn't she?'

'Yes, usually. But . . .'

'No buts now, girl. If you turn me down then I shall think you are too lazy to do a morning's work!' Her loud cackle of laughter took the sting out of her words, and Sara joined in the joke.

'Come on then, give it a go,' Mrs Morgan urged. 'Let's make a start this weekend. Can you be here by eight o'clock, do you think?'

'I'll certainly try,' Sara grinned.

Her heart was singing as she made her way home, and her head was reeling with all the plans she'd have to make to be sure she was free on Saturday morning. This week would be easy because her father was on nights all week so he would be sleeping late on Saturday. As long as she made sure there was something hot for him to eat when he woke it should be possible.

Her mind buzzed. She'd prepare some cawl, the rich stew he relished, on Friday night, and leave it in the oven beside the fire to cook all morning. By one o'clock it would be piping hot, the meat tender as he liked it, and it would be all ready to dish up when she came in. He could even help himself if he woke up early and was hungry.

She was so excited that she felt she had to speak to someone so, as soon as she had put the bread and pie in the pantry, she went next door to tell Martha Pritchard about her good fortune.

'There's wonderful!' Martha beamed. 'Exactly what you need. A chance to meet a few people, too,' she enthused. 'Not healthy for a girl of your age to be spending all your time shut up in the house with a young baba.'

'Do you think Dada will mind?' Sara asked tentatively.

Martha took a deep breath and let it out very slowly. 'I'm not too sure about that, my lovely,' she said cautiously. Your Dada can be very difficult sometimes.'

'Mam would be so pleased if she was still here,' Sara murmured, tears blurring her eyes.

'She would indeed!' Martha agreed. She put an arm around Sara's shoulders and hugged her warmly.

'I tell you what,' Martha said thoughtfully, 'why don't you leave telling him until that Gwladys Jones is there. Keep your news until after he's had his fill of food and he's feeling mellow and in a good mood.'

Sara's face brightened. 'You're probably right, Martha. He is more likely to agree if Miss Jones is listening.' She giggled. 'He always tries to make sure she doesn't see him in a temper.'

'There you are then!' Martha hugged her again and planted a kiss on Sara's brow. 'Well, good luck, *cariad*. You go and make them a tasty meal so that you soften him up before you say anything.'

Sara could think of nothing else for the rest of the day. The idea of earning some money sparked off a hundred and one ideas for spending it. Silly, she'd been, not to ask Mrs Morgan what she'd be paying her, but it had never entered her head to do so. It wouldn't be very much, she reminded herself. She'd only be there five hours. And if Betti Morgan was helping to look after Myfanwy then she couldn't be expected to pay her a proper wage.

Still, she thought happily, whatever it was, it would be hers and she'd be able to spend it as she liked. She'd be able to buy Myfanwy something special for Christmas.

She wasn't sure whether she would buy her a toy to play with or something to wear. A lovely soft cuddly teddy bear that she could take to bed with her at night would be wonderful. Then again, a new dress, or a warm coat to take her out in, would be more practical. It would be nice for her to have something brand new instead of hand-me-downs, or things from the chapel jumble sale.

Having the patience to wait for the right moment was such a strain that when her father and Gwladys Jones eventually arrived home Sara was so nervous that she could barely speak or even keep her mind on what she was doing.

'Sara, I've told you time and again that I like the milk to be added after you've poured the tea into my cup, not before,' Gwladys Jones remonstrated.

'If you have to serve cold ham for our meal then for goodness' sake remember to put some mustard on the table,' Ifor Jenkins grumbled. 'On a bleak December day like this a hot meal would have been more appropriate.'

'You said it had better be something cold because you weren't sure what time your meeting would end,' Sara reminded him as she fetched the mustard pot and placed it in front of him.

'That will do!' Ifor's thin mouth hardened and his dark eyes blazed. 'I will not have you contradicting me in front of a visitor. Do you understand?'

Sara bit down on her lower lip. Things were not going at all as she had planned. She'd fed Myfanwy and put her to bed before her father and Miss Jones arrived back from the chapel meeting so that everything would be calm and peaceful when she told them her news about going to work. And now she'd made her Dada cross and ruined everything.

She ate her own food in silence, listening with only half an ear to their animated conversation about their plans for the Sunday school Christmas event. It always amazed her how much time the two of them spent discussing the welfare of other people's children when they took so little interest in either Myfanwy or herself.

When she saw that their plates were almost empty she excused herself and took the remains of her own meal into the scullery to finish eating while she made some custard to serve over the apple pie.

She knew Gwladys Jones refused to eat shop cake, but Betti's apple pies were so much better than anything she could make that even though it was cheating, she always warmed it up in the oven and then served it with hot custard.

Her hands were shaking when she brought in the apple pie and the jug of custard and set them down on the table. She waited until they had almost finished eating, and then said tentatively, 'Dada, could I ask you something?'

He frowned irritably. 'Not now, Sara, it can wait until later.'

Sara hesitated. Martha's advice drummed inside her head. If she left it until later he'd be too tired to listen, and then he would dismiss her idea as foolish without even considering it properly.

'Please, Dada,' she begged. 'It's important!'

'Very well, go on,' he said impatiently.

'Mrs Morgan asked me if I would like to work in her shop on Saturday mornings from now until Christmas because she will be extra busy.'

'She did what?' His tone was querulous and the veins on his forehead stood out alarmingly.

'She thought I might like to earn some money for Christmas . . .'

Sara's voice trailed into silence as her father put down his spoon and glared at her angrily.

'Charity! We don't need anything from her, or anyone else, and you should have told her so.'

Sara drew a deep breath. It was now or never, she thought resolutely. If she didn't stand up to her father, and put her viewpoint this time, then she would never be able to do so.

'It's not charity she's offering me, but money for my services,' she insisted bravely.

'Money for your services!' He laughed harshly.

'What sort of services can you give her? Tell me that? And what about Myfanwy? What are you going to do with her while you are providing Mrs Morgan with your services?'

'She said I could take her with me. We'd look after her between us. She said it would give her a chance to rest her legs if she sat down for half an hour nursing Myfanwy.'

'Absolute rubbish! She's looking for some cheap labour. What is she going to do, pay you with a bag of leftovers at the end of the day?'

'No, she is not. She's going to pay me properly. And that means I would have some money of my very own that I could spend as I like.'

'Aah! Now we have the real reason for you wanting to work for Betti Morgan on a Saturday morning. As usual it's Sara being selfish. Sara shirking her duty and thinking only about Sara.'

'No, Dada. I'm not just thinking about myself. I want some money of my own because I want to buy a present for Myfanwy for Christmas.'

Ifor's expression became thunderous. 'Are you implying that I don't give you enough housekeeping?' he snapped.

Sara shook her head vigorously. She couldn't speak. She'd exhausted every vestige of her willpower, and knew that if she tried to say anything more she would end up in tears, and he would have won.

'I think it might be quite a good idea for Sara to go and work at Mrs Morgan's shop on Saturday mornings,' Gwladys Jones intervened.

'You do?' Ifor looked startled. Sara could see that

he didn't want her to go, but neither did he want to argue with Miss Jones. 'It would mean Sara would be neglecting Myfanwy and I can't have that,' he said firmly.

'But I could ask Martha, Dada, and if it's not convenient for her to do it then Mrs Morgan said I can take Myfanwy . . .'

'That won't be necessary,' Gwladys Jones interrupted, 'because I'll look after the child.'

Sara listened open-mouthed. She couldn't believe that Gwladys Jones was speaking up for her, and to be offering to look after Myfanwy as well was quite incredible. Eyes shining with gratitude, she stumbled over her words as she tried to thank her.

Gwladys Jones ignored her. 'There is no school on Saturdays, you see, Ifor, so there will be no problem because I have the entire day at my disposal.'

'Myfanwy usually has a nap in the morning,' Sara told her, 'so if you put her in her crib at about eleven o'clock she will probably sleep for half an hour or more.'

'There is no need to give me instructions, Sara. I'm used to dealing with children of all ages and Myfanwy is almost three now, no longer a baby,' Gwladys Jones told her sharply.

'So can I tell Mrs Morgan that it will be all right?' Sara asked anxiously.

Ifor Jenkins looked from his daughter to Gwladys Jones and back again, then shrugged his shoulders and spread his hands in resigned acceptance of the situation.

Chapter Eight

On Saturday morning, Sara was up, dressed and had the tin bath waiting in front of the fire for her father at least half an hour before the usual time. She had decided to leave Myfanwy sleeping until the very last moment so that she would be in a happy frame of mind when Gwladys Jones arrived to look after her.

It would be the first time she had ever left her with anyone, apart from when she was a very small baby and she had taken her along to Janie Harries to be fed.

Those days were so far back in the past that she knew Myfanwy would have no memory of them, and she was worried in case the little girl was upset in any way.

Myfanwy didn't seem to understand when she'd tried to explain to her that she had to go to the cake shop and that Miss Jones was coming to look after her.

She felt very concerned as she got herself ready and wondered if, after all, she was doing the right thing or was she being selfish like her Dada said she was? She put on the blue serge dress she'd worn at school because it was the tidiest thing she owned. To hide the fact that she had grown, and filled out so much since then that it was uncomfortably tight, and too short for her, she'd covered it up with a flowered apron.

Perhaps, if she was working for the next three Saturdays, she would have enough money left after buying Myfanwy's Christmas present to be able to get herself a length of material from the market to make a new dress.

Martha Pritchard was a dab hand at sewing so she'd help her. She had already shown her how to cut the bodices off her mother's two winter dresses to make skirts for herself, and she'd helped her make a pinafore from her mother's summer dress. The skirts didn't fit very well because her mother had been such a short fat woman that although they would almost go round Sara twice they weren't really long enough.

As the hands of the enamel alarm clock on the mantelshelf approached a quarter to seven, Sara waited impatiently for her father to arrive home. Usually he was home well before seven, but this morning, because she was in such a hurry and so anxious to be at Mrs Morgan's on time, he seemed to have been delayed.

It was almost ten past seven before he walked in the door. Hurriedly she emptied the boiling water from the kettle and big iron saucepan into the tin bath.

'I'll have a cup of tea first,' her father told her.

She stared at him in dismay. He never had a cup of tea first. What was more, she had just emptied every vestige of boiling water into his bath, and it would take at least ten minutes to heat up some more.

'Something wrong, girl?'

'I thought you would want your bath first. I've used all the hot water.'

'Then boil some more!'

'Yes, Dada.'

He pushed the tin bath to one side with his foot, slopping water all over the floor. 'And clean that mess up,' he growled. 'I've been paddling through muck and water all night, and I don't expect to find my own home in the same state.'

By the time the kettle had boiled, and she had made his tea, the water in his bath was rapidly cooling. She refilled the saucepan and pushed it back over the fire.

When he eventually decided to strip off, and take his bath, it was too cold for him. She topped it up from the saucepan, but even then it was not to his liking and he grumbled incessantly.

As she scrubbed her father's back Sara kept one eye on the clock and one ear listening out for Myfanwy. If everything had gone as she'd planned, Myfanwy would have been up and dressed and had her breakfast by now.

While her father dressed in the clean clothes she'd laid out for him, Sara took the tin bath out into the scullery, and then dashed upstairs for Myfanwy.

There was no time to give her a thorough wash so she wiped her face and hands with a flannel, brushed her hair back from her eyes, then dressed her.

Sitting her down at the table she gave her a buttered crust to chew on while she cooked her father's sausages and eggs, hoping he wouldn't notice that she kept back half of one of the sausages for Myfanwy. Leaving her to eat it, she dashed round tidying up. She put her father's dirty pit clothes into the water he'd bathed in, leaving them to soak until she came home and had time to wash them.

'What's all this rushing about for?' Ifor grumbled. 'Enough to give a man indigestion.'

'I've got to have Myfanwy washed and dressed before Miss Jones arrives and I have to be at Mrs Morgan's by eight o'clock,' Sara reminded him.

His dark eyes gleamed as he stared at her. 'Determined to do it, are you, girl? Even though you know it's going against my wishes?'

Sara looked confused, hot colour blotching her cheeks. 'I thought you agreed I could.'

Ifor reached out and seized her arm in a vice-like grip. 'I didn't say that you could neglect your duties to your father, you ungrateful child,' he said in a low, menacing voice.

Sara's cheeks flamed. 'No, Dada, please! Not this morning,' she begged.

'Why should this morning be any different from any other? Take that child back to her bed, and then you go and get into mine. Do you understand?'

Sara squared her thin shoulders defiantly. 'I won't do it. Not this morning. You can't make me.'

His hand reached for the belt holding up his trousers, and with slow deliberation he began unfastening it. 'You need a thrashing first, do you?'

Sara flinched but stood her ground. 'Not this morning, Dada. Miss Jones said she would be here by quarter to eight so she'll be here any minute now . . .' She paused to draw a deep breath, keeping her huge dark eyes fixed on his steely dark ones.

Inwardly she was shaking with fright. She had never defied him in her life before, but some inner voice told her that this time it was possible. She was holding all the cards. He wouldn't want Miss Jones, or anyone else for that matter, to find out what went on between the two of them in his bedroom.

She watched fascinated as he refastened his belt and his hand dropped to his side. 'You'd best get round to Betti Morgan's. I'll look after Myfanwy until Miss Jones arrives.'

Everything was so strange to her in her first hour at the cake shop that Sara had no time to think of anything else.

'Come along now, *cariad*, put this on,' Betti told her, handing her a long white cotton coat that buttoned down the front. 'We don't want you getting that dress all messed up.'

After that they were both kept so busy serving that they didn't have time to talk. At mid-morning, Betti Morgan sent Sara out into the scullery at the back of the shop to make some tea. 'Enough for all of us, mind! And make sure you put two spoonfuls of sugar in the one for the baker,' she called after her.

'Have you taken one through to the bakehouse for Rhys Edwards, then?' she asked when Sara brought two cups of tea into the shop.

'No, but I've made him one, and put two sugars in it like you said.'

'Well, take it on through to him. Can't have him stopping work, not for another hour anyway, or we won't have enough cakes to see the morning out. Don't linger in there or you won't have a chance to drink your tea before the next rush. And pick yourself out a nice cake to eat with your tea, anything at all you fancy, *cariad*.'

It was the first time Sara had ever been in the bakehouse, and the heat from the two huge ovens, together with the overpowering smell of hot bread, made her feel dizzy.

Rhys Edwards, wearing only trousers and singlet, was unloading loaves of bread from one of the ovens. He was using what looked like a long-handled shovel, and he was deftly removing the newly baked loaves, and setting them down on a huge wire frame to cool.

Sara was so mesmerised by the speed and accuracy with which he worked that she was still standing there holding his mug of tea when he'd finished.

'Is that for me by any chance?' he asked, walking over to take it from her.

Her face scarlet, she handed it to him without a word. She had expected Rhys the baker to be a middle-aged man, probably fat and going bald, not someone only a few years older than herself, with crisp short curly hair, gorgeous blue eyes and a warm wonderful smile. He didn't look anything like a baker even though his trousers and singlet were coated with flour. In fact, she thought, he could have been an athlete or a boxer.

Back behind the counter she found it hard to keep her mind on what she was supposed to be doing. All she could think about was the man she'd just met, and who worked for Betti Morgan the same as she did.

The morning over, Betti packed up a bag of leftover cakes and a big apple pie for Sara, and then carefully counted out three shillings for her morning's work.

'Well, that worked very well now, didn't it, *cariad*? Coming again next week?'

'Oh, yes please. I do hope so. It . . . it depends on how Myfanwy has behaved, of course.'

'Very surprised I was that Miss Jones offered to look after her,' Betti Morgan commented.

'Good thing she did! I don't think we could have managed with her underfoot, do you?' Sara laughed.

'No, you're probably right,' Betti Morgan agreed. 'Busier than usual we were, see. Poor old Rhys was rushed off his feet. Nice young chap, isn't he?'

Sara blushed and nodded in agreement. 'I'd better be off,' she said. 'Miss Jones and Dada want to go to the Tabernacle Chapel this afternoon so I'd best not be late. Thank you for the cakes and everything, Mrs Morgan.'

'Off you go then, my lovely! See you down the week so you can let me know then about next Saturday.'

Sara walked the short distance home in a daze. She didn't know which was the most exciting, the money she had earned or meeting Rhys Edwards.

Remembering what her father had said about Betti Morgan paying her with a bag of leftovers, she put the apple pie and cakes in the scullery out of sight.

When she went into the living-room she was glad she had. Her father and Gwladys Jones were sitting at the table, their plates piled high with the cawl she'd prepared the night before.

'So what time is this then, girl?' her father greeted her. 'I thought you finished work at one o'clock?'

'I've come straight home, Dada,' Sara assured him. 'I had to sweep the floor and help Mrs Morgan clear things away after we put the closed notice on the door.'

'Now you see why workers need to belong to a trade union,' her father said, turning to Gwladys Jones. 'If they haven't got a strong union then the employers exploit them. If a working shift ends at one o'clock, then at one o'clock the workers should leave the premises.'

'It doesn't always work like that, Ifor,' Gwladys protested mildly. 'School finishes at four o'clock, but I rarely get away until almost five. And then I sometimes have to bring work home to prepare in readiness for the next day's lessons.'

Ifor merely smiled. 'Did you get paid?' he asked, turning back to Sara.

Proudly she showed him the three shilling pieces that she'd clutched in her hand all the way home.

'One towards your keep and one for chapel,' he commented as he took two of them from her hand.

'Dada!' There was both shock and anger in her voice. 'That's my money, I've earned it.'

'And I earn money every week and spend most of it on housekeeping.'

'I was planning to buy something for Myfanwy . . .'

'So you can, girl! I've left you a shilling to do just

that,' he said as he pocketed the rest. 'You'd better go and see to Myfanwy,' he added sharply. 'She's up in her bed and she hasn't had anything to eat yet.'

Sara turned away so that they wouldn't see the tears in her eyes. She knew she shouldn't be crying, not at her age. She had been so buoyed up with plans about what she was going to do with her money that the disappointment was like a knife turning inside her.

When she came back downstairs again, with Myfanwy in her arms, her father and Miss Jones were putting on their coats ready to leave. 'We'll leave you to clear up, and we'll be back for high tea at six o'clock,' Ifor told her, 'so make sure it's ready for us.'

Not for the first time, Sara thought sadly about the days when her mother had been alive and they used to attend chapel together, leaving her father to go up to the front. It seemed that he and Miss Jones weren't too pious now to neglect her chapel-going in favour of skivvying for them.

Myfanwy still seemed to be sleepy so Sara propped her up in the rocking-chair while she went out to the scullery to make her a milky drink and prepare something for her to eat.

The cawl was all gone, so she opened the bag of cakes Mrs Morgan had given her and took out one for herself, and one that she thought Myfanwy would like, then settled down in the rocker cuddling the little girl in her lap.

She managed to persuade her to take a few sips of the hot milk, but Myfanwy seemed disinclined to eat. Snuggling into the warmth of Sara's arms she drifted off to sleep again as if she was completely worn out. Sara felt uneasy, wondering what Gwladys could have been doing with her to make her so tired.

Sara sat there for almost an hour, day-dreaming about their future. Once she was working properly she'd save every penny she could and when she had enough she and Myfanwy would run away. She had no idea where they could go but it would be as far as possible from Ponty. Somewhere Dada couldn't find them, somewhere he could never use her little sister as he had her.

But even while she was day-dreaming about leaving Ponty for ever, Sara couldn't put Rhys Edwards out of her mind. He was so good-looking and he'd smiled as if he had been really pleased to meet her. She tried to work out how old he was and wondered if he had a girlfriend, or if he was married.

She hoped that when she went into Mrs Morgan's shop down the week for bread she'd see him and not have to wait until next Saturday before she could talk to him again.

From now on, she thought dreamily, every mouthful of bread, every slice of apple pie, and every cake that came from Mrs Morgan's shop would taste all that much better because she knew that they'd been baked by Rhys Edwards.

Chapter Nine

Sara was so looking forward to working at the cake shop the following Saturday that when Gwladys Jones arrived unannounced on the Friday evening she felt a frisson of alarm in case she'd come to say she wouldn't be able to look after Myfanwy the next day after all.

'Dada is on night shift,' she said tentatively after she had invited Miss Jones in.

'Yes, Sara, I am well aware of that fact. It's you I've come to see.'

Sara waited numbly, expecting her to say their arrangement for Saturday morning had been cancelled. She had been dreaming of her next stint at the cake shop. She hadn't seen Rhys Edwards this week as she'd hoped, and it was her chance to meet him again.

All week she had been rehearsing the things she would talk to him about. She held imaginary conversations in which she'd told him all about herself and Myfanwy, and in return he told her everything there was to know about himself. He would also say that he liked her working there, and that he'd been looking forward to seeing her again.

It was all make-believe, of course, like the stories in Martha's magazines, but that didn't matter. It brought a ray of happiness into her life, and kept her mind off the more serious matters that gnawed away inside her head until she felt sick with guilt.

Each time she was pinned down by her Dada's long scrawny frame, and his calloused hands had invaded her body, she knew she ought to tell someone so that they'd make him stop. But who would believe her?

Gwladys Jones's voice brought her out of her reverie. 'It's about your working at Betti Morgan's shop.'

'Please ... please don't say you can't come tomorrow,' Sara begged.

'Of course I can come tomorrow. That's no problem at all. What I was going to suggest, Sara, was that if Mrs Morgan needs you any other day between now and Christmas I will be available to look after Myfanwy.'

'You will!' Sara's huge dark eyes shone like twin orbs in her small face. 'Oh, Miss Jones, that is so kind of you. I ... I don't know what to say.'

'Yes, yes,' Gwladys Jones said briskly, 'but remember Mrs Morgan might decide she doesn't need any additional help except on Saturdays.'

'Thank you for offering, though,' Sara said gratefully. Her face clouded. 'But I'd better ask Dada for permission before I speak to Mrs Morgan about it.'

'There's no need for you to do that, Sara. I have already discussed it with him. He won't raise any objection. He agrees with me that you should be out earning money, not messing around at home all the time.' She moved towards the door. 'I'll be here tomorrow morning at quarter to eight. Make sure you have breakfast on the table for your father and me, and make sure you have fed Myfanwy.'

Sara couldn't sleep for excitement. Her mind went round and round. Suddenly life seemed to have so much to offer that it was almost too good to be true.

Her Dada was on night shift, which meant she was able to sleep in her own bed, unmolested. Myfanwy had been as good as gold all day. Her little face had beamed and she'd clapped her hands in delight when Sara told her that she would be bringing home a gingerbread man for her the next day. But Myfanwy didn't seem to understand that Miss Jones was going to be looking after her.

'Me come to shop with you, Sara,' she'd insisted.

That was the bit Sara didn't like, having to leave Myfanwy with Gwladys Jones and her Dada. She knew Gwladys was used to children, after all she was a teacher. The children she taught, however, were a lot older than Myfanwy. She was still little more than a baby.

'She can't be tied to your apron strings for ever, my lovely,' Martha had said when Sara mentioned how worried she was about leaving Myfanwy. 'Time you started having a life of your own. It'll only be for a few hours. Pass in no time, you'll see.'

Betti Morgan was delighted when Sara told her that she would be able to help out in the days running up to Christmas if she was needed.

'That's splendid news!' Her round face beamed. 'That Miss Jones is turning out to be much better than you thought she was.'

'It's wonderful, isn't it, Mrs Morgan. I can hardly believe my luck,' Sara agreed rapturously.

'You can come in every day next week if you can manage it, and that will take us right up to Christmas Day. It's on a Sunday this year and that means I'll be keeping the shop open on Saturday afternoon for last-minute customers. Do you think you will be able to stay the whole day? There will be plenty for you to do.'

Sara nodded enthusiastically, too overcome to reply. A whole week of work! If she got three shillings for a Saturday morning then that would mean she'd go home on Christmas Eve with at least one pound!

It would also be a whole week of seeing Rhys Edwards every day, and that brought a glorious feeling that was worth even more than money.

Sara found it also meant a great deal of adjustment at home as Gwladys Jones spent more and more time at Taff Court. Gwladys had her own ways of doing things which were often quite different from Sara's, and this seemed to confuse little Myfanwy. In many ways she was really only a baby still, but Sara found they expected her to behave like a child of six or seven. She was shocked to find that they demanded Myfanwy say grace before they would let her have anything to eat or drink, and that she had to help put the dishes on the table and then clear them away afterwards.

'She seems to be very strict with the poor little mite,' Martha told Sara. 'Still, she is going on for three so I suppose you've got to start making her do as she's told.'

'I've never had any problems with her,' Sara frowned. 'Very obedient I'd say she was.'

'Being a schoolteacher I suppose it's second nature for Miss Jones to expect the child to understand right from wrong.'

By the time the last customer had left on Christmas Eve, Sara felt so tired that she could have gone to sleep standing up. It had been the most hectic week of her life. Even Betti Morgan said she'd never known it so busy, and that she couldn't wait to put her feet up.

'I'd never have managed without you, *cariad,*' she said as she handed over three pound notes. 'A little brick you've been, and no maybe.'

Sara looked down at the money in her hand and gasped. 'You've given me three whole pounds, Mrs Morgan, have you made a mistake?'

'Not a bit of it, you've been worth every penny!'

Sara's mind spun. She'd never had so much money of her own before. Remembering the way her father had taken two of the three shillings she'd earned on her first Saturday morning, she determined not to let him or anyone else know how much she'd been paid. She'd try and think of a safe place to hide it so that later on she could buy things for herself and Myfanwy.

'But what about all the other things you've given me down the week? All the pies and so on to take home, and the sausage rolls and meat pies and cakes you've fed me on here. I haven't paid you for any of them.'

'My way of saying thank you for working right

through the day without a grumble,' Betti smiled. 'Ray of old sunshine you've been, *cariad*. I know it's not been too easy for you, working here and seeing to things at home as well.'

When she got home at six o'clock each evening Sara had been expected to get a hot meal on the table for her Dada and Miss Jones, as well as feed Myfanwy, and then wash and undress her and put her to bed.

The first couple of nights she had been working flat out until midnight. Betti Morgan had commented on how tired she looked, and when she told her the problem Betti advised she should cut a few corners.

'Ask Rhys to make you up a big meat pie and an apple pie, and to have them piping hot when you are ready to leave for home. Then all you'll have to do is pop them in your oven to keep warm while you prepare some vegetables. And while those are cooking you can be seeing to Myfanwy.'

'Won't it be cheating, though?'

'Cheating? What are you on about, my lovely?'

'Miss Jones won't eat shop pies and such.'

'Oh, indeed! She eats my apple pies, doesn't she?'

Sara nodded. 'I cheat over those,' she admitted, her colour rising. 'I always wait until she arrives before I make the custard and so she probably thinks I've made the pie as well.'

'Well, if she sees you taking the meat pie indoors, tell her it's been cooked here instead of at home, *cariad*. Anyway, if Rhys makes it especially for you then it's the same as being home-cooked now, isn't it? The only difference is that he's baked it here in one of our ovens instead of in your kitchen one.'

When she went home on Christmas Eve, Sara was loaded down with good things for the family. Betti Morgan gave her a rich dark plum pudding, and Rhys had baked a wonderful fruit cake and topped it with white icing and placed a snowman in the very centre of it. There was also a gift each for her and Myfanwy from Mrs Morgan, wrapped up in pretty shiny paper with snow and Christmas scenes all over it. Sara's heart danced with happiness.

The most exciting present she received, though, was from Rhys, a silver chain with a round silver medallion on it. On one side there was a fiery dragon and the words *'Cymru am Byth'* were engraved on the other.

He didn't wrap it up; he slipped it round her neck when she went into the bakehouse to wish him a happy Christmas, a few minutes before they closed.

'There you are, *cariad*, now that makes us twins,' Rhys told her, pointing to an identical one hanging around his own neck.

Sara flushed scarlet. 'Thank you!' she whispered. 'I wasn't expecting to get a present from you, or from anyone else here. I haven't got anything for you or Mrs Morgan,' she said awkwardly.

Rhys frowned darkly at her. 'That's terrible, *cariad*!' He caught her by the shoulders and spun her round to face him. 'And I thought you liked me?' he said in disbelief, looking down into her upturned face.

'Oh, I do, Rhys. I like you a lot,' Sara said earnestly, then blushed even more deeply when she saw that his blue eyes were twinkling, and she realised he was teasing her.

Overcome with embarrassment, she wriggled to escape his hold, but Rhys only held her more firmly.

'I must demand a present from you before I set you free,' he said forcefully, and before Sara realised what was happening he was holding her face between his two hands, and planting a warm kiss on her pursed lips.

She closed her eyes; he was standing so close to her that she could feel the heat from his body and she wanted the two of them to stay like this for ever.

'Happy Christmas, Sara,' he said softly as he released her. 'It's been great having you here all week. I hope to see you back again in the New Year.'

Then before she could make any answer at all he handed her the special Christmas cake he had made and decorated for her. Her eyes filled up with tears, and she was too choked even to thank him properly.

When she got home, she unwrapped the cake and set it on a dinner plate, and placed it in the centre of the table. Myfanwy let out a squeal of delight when she saw it and reached out to touch the snowman in the centre. Gently Sara stopped her doing so in case she spoilt it.

'This is a very special cake, Myfanwy, and we must keep it for tomorrow, Christmas Day,' she explained. 'After it's been cut, and we've all had a taste, then you can have the snowman to keep for your very own,' she promised.

Sara told no one about the medallion. She wasn't too sure what her father would say about her accepting such a personal present from a man she barely knew. He would probably quote from the Bible and demand to know all about Rhys, and Sara knew there was nothing she could tell him that he would find acceptable. She had no idea where Rhys lived or even how old he was, although she was sure he was only a few years older than herself.

If her Dada asked her to describe Rhys and she said he was handsome, broad shouldered and muscular, and that he had strong tender hands, he'd tell her she was a brazen hussy even to notice such things. And if he ever found out that Rhys had kissed her he would probably take off his belt and thrash her.

The present from Rhys, she decided, must definitely remain a secret. She kept it tucked away inside the neck of her dress, but every few minutes her hand would stray towards her neck, and her fingers would work along the chain until she was holding the medallion.

In her mind's eye she was reliving the precious moment when his lips had joined with hers, and she wondered if his feelings for her were even a fraction of what she felt for him.

Chapter Ten

Even though Sara was well aware of the close friendship between her Dada and Miss Jones she was still very taken aback when early in 1928 they told her they were going to be married.

At first she felt resentful that he had been able to put her Mam out of his mind and out of his heart. Then the longer she brooded about it the more she realised that probably she had more to gain than to lose by their marriage.

If he marries again, and Gwladys Jones moves in with us, then he will have to leave me alone, Sara reasoned. She shuddered with relief. Her summonses to his bed had been so frequent lately, and his demands so outrageous, that she felt her stomach churn every time she heard his voice calling her name, or he came near her.

The thought of Miss Jones submitting to his physical demands astounded her. Perhaps it would be different with her, Sara thought, he'd have to be more reasonable because she was sure Gwladys Jones would stop him from doing anything she didn't like.

He'll have to stop taking off his belt to me, as well, Sara thought optimistically. Sometimes, when he was in one of his tempers, he would give her a thrashing for no reason at all except to relieve his own feelings. He always took care to make sure it was on her back or thighs where the weals weren't visible to others, but he wouldn't be able to do that even with sharp-eyed Gwladys Jones around the place.

The wedding date was fixed for the middle of spring. It would be a very quiet affair because it would be Ifor's second wedding, and although Gwladys Jones was a spinster she was well into her forties.

Sara realised that there would be changes at home, but she had not expected the tremendous upheaval that went on prior to the wedding. Miss Jones believed in new brooms sweeping clean, and she wanted most of the existing furniture and furnishings out, and replaced by those that had belonged to her own parents.

The only thing that it seemed was to remain untouched was Sara and Myfanwy's bedroom, but then, Sara reflected, all that was in there was her bed and Myfanwy's crib.

'It's high time she was in a proper bed,' Gwladys Jones decreed about a week before the wedding. 'She'd better have my single bed and we'll get rid of that old crib. Eyesore, it is!'

'There isn't enough space really in such a small bedroom for two beds,' Sara pointed out. 'We won't be able to move!'

'A bedroom is a place for sleeping, not to hold a party in. Of course you will have enough room. Put one up against each wall or push them together, you'll manage somehow,' Gwladys said dismissively.

'Myfanwy's still only three, she's too little to sleep in a big bed on her own.'

'Stop being difficult, Sara,' Gwladys told her angrily. 'From now on we do things the way I want them done. Do you understand?'

Sara's resentment increased, but she knew it was no good antagonising Gwladys. She bit down on her lower lip. 'I'm sorry, Miss Jones, but I have run things here since well before my Mam died. It's not easy to take orders from anyone else.'

'Then you had better get used to it, Sara, because that is how things will be from now on,' Gwladys snapped, a determined expression on her long face. 'And it's no good running to your father behind my back because he's bound to agree with me.'

Sara burned with indignation. Who did Gwladys Jones think she was? She was using the same tone and manner as she had when she was my teacher at school, and I never liked her then, Sara thought furiously.

Well, at least Gwladys would be out at school most of the day, five days a week. When she was at home, though – as Miss Jones had already pointed out – Dada will be taking her side not mine, Sara thought resignedly.

As if reading her mind, Gwladys Jones announced, 'Oh, and by the way, Sara, I shall not be teaching any more!' She gave a triumphant smile that seemed more like a grimace. 'After I marry your father I shall be at home here all day so I will be taking charge of Myfanwy; and remember, I do not want any interference from you.'

The words struck Sara like a blow, and she felt

resentment deep inside herself. 'I am quite capable of taking care of Myfanwy. I've looked after her from the day she was born,' she replied quickly.

'Yes, well, there are going to be changes. There will be plenty of other things for you to do, but Myfanwy needs proper supervision or she will be growing up a little hoyden. I don't want her playing out in the gutter, and running up and down the pavement, screaming her lungs out and kicking tin cans with a gang of other children.'

'She certainly will not be doing any of those things!' Sara retorted.

'Don't argue with me, Sara! I know you have grown up completely undisciplined, but we don't want your little sister to end up the same way.'

This was by no means the only change Gwladys Jones intended to make, as Sara discovered when she went off to work at the cake shop the following Saturday.

'Well, now, my lovely, what's all this tale I was told by your new Mam-to-be yesterday?' Betti Morgan greeted her.

Sara looked puzzled. 'Gwladys Jones has been along to see you? What about?'

'About you, of course, *cariad*. No other reason why she should call in here, now is there? She doesn't eat shop cake, as she was quick to tell me.'

'What did she want then? She isn't going to stop me working here, is she?'

'On the contrary, *cariad*, she wants me to employ you full-time.'

Sara gaped open-mouthed. 'She said that?'

'True as I'm standing here! Gave me an ultimatum, in fact. Either I employ you full-time, she says, or you'll have to go and look for a job somewhere else.'

Sara shook her head, bemused. 'I'd love to work for you full-time, Mrs Morgan, that is if you wanted me to, but how can I possibly do that until Myfanwy is old enough to go to school?'

'Well, *cariad*, as I understand it that is all taken care of, see. Gwladys Jones is giving up teaching so she will be there all day to look after your little sister. There's nice it's going to be for you!'

'Is it?' Sara looked dubious. 'She's making so many changes, Mrs Morgan, that I don't know where I am. Turfed all my Mam's furniture and things out, she has, and brought along all her own stuff. Awful, some of it, leastwise it is to me.'

'Well, *cariad*, you've just got to expect it. A new wife doesn't want to be saddled with too many memories of the old one, now does she?'

'I suppose you're right,' Sara agreed reluctantly.

'Look on the bright side, my lovely. Like I said, she's been asking if you can work here.'

'You don't need anyone full-time, though, do you, Mrs Morgan,' Sara sighed.

The thought of no longer working at the cake shop was a depressing one. She loved being there on Saturday mornings. The smell of baking bread and newly made cakes, the bright busy atmosphere, and meeting so many people, were the high spot of her week.

It also meant she saw Rhys. They had become really close since Christmas, and bit by bit she had learnt about his life in Tonypandy which was where his family lived.

Tonypandy was also a pit village, and he had grown up in a house and street very similar to the one she lived in. He had gone to the local school, and at fourteen his father had taken him to the pit to start work alongside him at the coalface.

Ever since he had been a small boy Rhys had known that this was where his intended future lay. After growing up in a street where more than half the men had been maimed or killed by underground explosions or accidents of some kind, and where most of the others were suffering from silicosis caused by coal dust, he hated the idea.

'It's the family tradition to work down the mine, see,' he told Sara. 'My Da's been there since he was a boy and his father before him. My Da's brothers were down the pit and so, too, were Mam's two brothers. Lucky, they've all been. A couple of them have been buried, like, when there's been explosions, but they've suffered nothing worse than a broken leg and crushed ribs.'

He paused to ladle the hot loaves from the deep oven on to the wire tray to cool. 'It wasn't the thought of being hurt that bothered me, it was the atmosphere you work in,' Rhys went on. 'Pitch black, acrid smell of coal dust, lying cramped while you chiselled out a seam, and the cold dank atmosphere that went into your very bones, all sent shivers through me.'

Sara stared at him wide-eyed and spellbound. 'So what did they say when you wouldn't work down there?' she breathed.

'Furious, they were. Even my Mam and she usually stuck up for me when I was in any sort of trouble.' He grinned. 'I had to threaten to run away to sea before they would see sense. That's when they said I'd better find myself some other sort of a job then.'

'And you did?'

'That's right. My family never forgave me for turning my back on the pit, mind you. Said I was breaking with tradition. No other son, see, to step into my Dad's shoes. Ashamed of me, they were!'

'So you became a baker?'

Rhys nodded. 'It wasn't easy. In the end I managed to get myself apprenticed to a baker. One-man business he had, see, and he wanted a lad to hump the sacks of flour, sweep the floor, and generally make himself useful. When he saw I was keen to learn he started letting me mix the dough and gradually, bit by bit, he taught me all he knew.'

'And then you came here?'

'Not right away. I'd always wanted to go to sea so I got myself taken on as a ship's baker, but before we could put to sea there was the Strike and the owner of the ship went bankrupt. I was on my way back home to Tonypandy, I'd walked all the way from Cardiff, I had twopence in my pocket and I was starving hungry. I stopped off here in Ponty because Mrs Morgan's my Da's sister. We got talking and she said her baker was waiting to retire so if I wanted the job I could have it.'

Rhys straightened up, and wiped the flour from his hands down the sides of his check trousers.

'Seemed like Fate to me.' He grinned. 'Great believer in destiny, I am!'

'So you stayed on here and you've been working for Mrs Morgan ever since?'

'That's right. She said I could have her spare bedroom and turn it into my own quarters. Nice, it is now. You should come and see it some time,' he added, his blue eyes twinkling.

Sara blushed and looked away. She liked Rhys so much, and she thought he felt something for her, but when he teased her she didn't know how to handle it.

It was several weeks before Sara heard the rest of the story and understood why Betti Morgan treated him more like a son than a nephew. Her own boy had died over ten years before. He and his father had been killed when the seam they'd been working on in Pentre Mine had caved in. Neither of them had been brought up. Along with the bodies of twenty of their colleagues they had been left at the site, and the seam had been sealed off.

Betti had always had a strong independent streak. Determined to make the best of her life, she turned her front parlour, where she sold cakes and pies that she made herself, into a proper baker's shop.

The house stood on a corner, and it was not only larger than those in the rest of the terrace, but it also had a big back yard, so she extended it, and had proper ovens put in.

At first, she had relied on an old retired baker coming in each morning to bake the bread for her, but when Rhys had appeared on the scene it was almost like an answer to her prayers.

Unlike the rest of his family, Betti was able to understand his hatred of the mines. She didn't think for one moment that he was letting the family tradition down by wanting some other kind of life. She was more than happy to have him not only working for her, but sharing her home as well.

Even so, although she was sprightly, despite being overweight and almost sixty, she sometimes felt that if it wasn't to help keep Rhys in employment she would happily sit back and take things easy.

When Gwladys Jones had offered her the alternative of taking Sara on full-time, or losing her altogether, she had been shrewd enough not to appear to be too keen, but in fact it seemed to her that once again Fate was playing into her hands.

If she employed Sara full-time in the shop then she would be able to take things quite a bit easier. Sara was a hard worker, honest and very bright. The customers all liked her, and she got on so well with Rhys that there wouldn't be any problems at all from that quarter.

It meant, Betti Morgan reasoned, that all she would need to do was keep a supervisory eye on things, take care of the ordering and the books, and be there to give Sara a hand when they were extra busy.

It was the end of the morning, before Sara and Betti got a chance to talk about it again. 'Well, girl,' Betti said, 'what's it to be then? Are you coming to work here full-time or are you going to leave me altogether?'

'Work here full-time if you'll have me, Mrs Morgan,' Sara replied without a second's hesitation.

'Good! There will be one or two changes, of course.'

Sara's face fell. Changes! Everyone wanted changes. Why couldn't life simply go on as it was?

'Did you hear what I said, Sara?'

'Yes, Mrs Morgan,' she said resignedly. 'What sort of changes did you have in mind?'

'I'll expect you here at eight o'clock each morning, and after we close at five o'clock you'll be expected to sweep the floor, and stack away any bread or cakes that are left over. Think you can manage that?'

'Yes, of course I can, Mrs Morgan. Is that all?'

'No! I shall expect you to sit down with Rhys and me for a half-hour break at midday, and eat whatever I put on the table in front of you.'

'That sounds lovely!' Sara laughed. 'That certainly won't be any hardship!'

'And there's one more thing. From now on, when we are on our own, I expect you to call me Betti. Still address me as Mrs Morgan in front of the customers, mind, but it's Betti when we're on our own. You understand?'

Sara's smile broadened so much it almost covered her face. 'Yes, Mrs . . . Betti, I do understand. And thank you . . . Betti!'

Chapter Eleven

Despite its grandeur, the Tabernacle Chapel was so dark and gloomy inside that Ifor Jenkins's marriage to Gwladys Jones seemed more like a funeral than a wedding ceremony.

Ifor had refused to spend out on any flowers to decorate the place; he said that he didn't deem it necessary and that it was a form of popery to have them.

Gwladys had agreed with his sentiments although she had said that the white lilies that had been placed there earlier for a funeral service could remain where they were.

Ifor was dressed in his best navy blue three-piece suit, the same as he always wore when he attended chapel. The heavy gold chain stretched across his front, from the second buttonhole of his waistcoat to where his solid gold hunter was safely secreted in the right-hand pocket; that was the only difference. It had been his father's and he wore it only on very special occasions.

Gwladys Jones wore a light grey, high-necked dress with a matching three-quarter jacket. Her dark grey hat was trimmed with a light grey band. She carried a brand new black leather bible and wore black shoes and black gloves.

Sara had suggested that Myfanwy should walk

either behind her or alongside, carrying a posy of spring flowers, but both Gwladys Jones and Ifor Jenkins had been strongly against this idea.

'It's your father's second marriage and I'm not a frivolous young girl,' Miss Jones told Sara reprovingly. 'Marriage is a serious business, not a light-hearted event. In fact,' she went on in censorious tones, 'it might be a good idea if Myfanwy didn't come to chapel at all, but stayed home with Martha Pritchard.'

'You can't make her do that!' Sara protested. 'I've bought her a new dress for the occasion. She's looking forward so much to wearing it to chapel that it would break her heart if you stopped her now.'

'She can wear the dress without coming to the service,' Gwladys stated firmly.

'She ought to be there,' Sara protested stubbornly. 'It's only right that if our Dada is getting married then Myfanwy and I should be at chapel for the ceremony.'

'Ridiculous! I would prefer you both to stay at home. You could lay out the sandwiches and make the tea and lemonade for those members of the Tabernacle Chapel who may wish to come home with us after the ceremony and partake of some refreshments.'

'I've already arranged with Martha Pritchard that she will see to all that,' Sara told her.

Gwladys Jones's face hardened. 'Indeed, I would appreciate it if you would remember that I'm the one who gives the orders or permission on any matters to do with the running of my home. Do you understand?'

Sara did. She wanted to tell Gwladys that it wasn't her home yet, not until after the ceremony, but she knew she would only make matters worse by doing so. Even so, she was determined that Myfanwy should wear her pretty white muslin dress with its pink and blue smocking and that she should attend the wedding at the Tabernacle Chapel even if they both had to creep in and stand at the very back.

Both Martha Pritchard and Betti Morgan agreed wholeheartedly with Sara on this point when she asked their opinion.

'Have a quiet word with your Dada,' Martha Pritchard advised. 'Even if the old hypocrite always keeps you so busy skivvying and minding his child that there's no time for you to attend chapel in the normal way of things, I'm sure that even he would make an exception just this once if you put it to him in the right way.'

But what was the right way, or the right time, Sara wondered? It would have to be when Miss Jones wasn't within earshot or she would quickly persuade him that it was better if neither of them were there.

Perhaps it would be better if I told him that Myfanwy and I won't be there because I'm afraid Myfanwy is too young to sit through the service and might make a noise and cause a diversion. If I do that he will doubtless order both of us to attend and tell me to make sure that Myfanwy behaves herself.

Right up until five minutes before they were ready to leave the house Sara was still in a quandary about what to do for the best.

She dressed Myfanwy in her new dress, brushed her dark hair until it shone and tied a lovely white bow in it. Then she put on her own new blue dress with the white lace collar: Martha Pritchard had run it up for her on her sewing machine from a length of material she'd bought in the market. Martha had told her she thought it was a lovely shade and that it would suit her. Sara wondered what Martha would have said if she'd told her that she'd chosen it because the colour was the exact shade of Rhys Edwards's eyes?

She thought her Dada had already left the house for the Tabernacle Chapel when she came downstairs with Myfanwy and was surprised to find him still in the hall.

'Good heavens, girl, what are you doing dawdling here?' he rasped. 'I'll be there before you if you don't hurry. Don't you know that it is good manners to be in your pew well before the service starts? Hurry along now. And make sure your little sister behaves herself. No crying, calling out or chattering, mind.'

'Yes, Dada. We're just leaving,' Sara said quickly and set off at as fast a pace as she could, almost dragging Myfanwy down the street in her haste to get away before her father changed his mind and stopped them.

She wondered whether Miss Jones had suggested that she and Myfanwy should stay at home and her father had vetoed the idea, or whether she hadn't mentioned it to him at all.

Perhaps she was hoping I would stay away so that she could say I couldn't be bothered to attend and then he would be terribly cross with me, Sara thought.

Keeping in the good books of both of them was like jumping between two fires. It had all been so much easier when her mother had been there to take the brunt of his moods and smooth away any differences between them.

Sara pushed those memories to the back of her mind. Today, minutes before her Dada was to go through a ceremony that would make Gwladys Jones his new wife, was not the right time to be thinking about her mother or those distant happier days.

So many awful things had happened in the past but Sara was determined to put them out of her mind and concentrate on the future. She wanted this to be a fresh start for so many reasons and she didn't want to do or say anything that might jeopardise that hope.

The Tabernacle Chapel was packed. The regular members of the congregation were there to support Ifor Jenkins because he was renowned for his religious fervour and was a stalwart in their ranks. At the back of the chapel there were a great many ex-pupils from the school where Gwladys Jones had taught, who had sneaked in purely out of curiosity. They hadn't been able to believe their ears when they heard the rumours that the grim-faced schoolteacher was walking out with the widower Ifor Jenkins.

Sara felt herself going scarlet as she recognised the faces of some of her old school associates and suspected that she knew exactly what they were thinking and why they were there.

They wanted to see with their own eyes what sort

of man it was who would tie himself to a harridan like Gwladys Jones for the rest of his days.

Sara knew there would be gossip in plenty afterwards and most of it would be expressions of sympathy for her and for little Myfanwy. Like her, most of them would be well aware what a martinet Gwladys Jones was and the rigid discipline she imposed.

Myfanwy seemed to be overawed by her surroundings. She clutched Sara's hand tightly all through the service. Sara didn't think she understood anything of what was going on, but that was not the point. The important thing was that in later years, if she looked back, she was bound to have some dim recollection of what took place.

Afterwards, when they emerged on to the steps outside the Tabernacle Chapel, there were no smiles from the newly married couple, only a look of smug satisfaction on Gwladys's face as she showed off her thick gold wedding band.

As people came up to her and Ifor, offering their congratulations and wishing them every happiness for the future, it was as much as Sara could do to keep her tears in check and a still tongue in her head. The wedding ring that her father had slipped on to Gwladys Jones's finger, and which she was displaying in such a self-satisfied manner, was the one that had belonged to her mother!

Sara found it hard to believe that her father was so stingy that he had used her dead mother's wedding ring again instead of buying a new one for Gwladys.

She wanted to speak out and tell him what she

thought of him but she was too scared to do so. As if reading her mind he drew her to one side and hissed in her ear, 'What on earth do you think you are doing, dolling that child up in those glad rags and parading her like that in front of all my friends and acquaintances?'

Sara hurried back to Taff Court with Myfanwy, to the comforting presence of Martha Pritchard who had arranged the food as attractively as possible.

'Not really what you'd call much of a spread,' she grumbled. 'If it wasn't for that cake that you brought home from Betti Morgan's it would look no better than a rugby scrum tea.'

Sara looked at the cake that took pride of place. Betti had asked Rhys to make one of his special fruit cakes and he had taken it upon himself to ice it in white with an edging of pink flowers and had wrapped a silver paper frieze around it. He'd wanted to put a bride and groom in the centre, but Sara had said she didn't think they would like that. It would remind them of the cake she'd brought home at Christmas, which they'd both thought was in bad taste.

'Well, shall I write their names on it in the centre in pink icing, "Gwladys and Ifor", how about that?'

Sara had shaken her head. 'No, you'd better not. Dada would think that was ostentatious,' she'd murmured.

'Not going to be a very jolly celebration party, is it?' Rhys had laughed. 'I'm glad you haven't invited me! I bet there won't be any dancing afterwards, either.'

'There certainly won't be any dancing and there

won't be anything intoxicating to drink. Tea or lemonade only,' Sara had replied.

Rhys had rolled his eyes as if in despair.

Now, when she saw the frown of disapproval on her father's face as he came through the door and his gaze fixed on the white cake with its silver frieze for the first time, she was glad she hadn't let Rhys decorate it any other way.

For the next hour or so, immediately after her father had said grace, Sara found herself kept busy handing out the bloater paste sandwiches, Welsh cakes and *bara brith* to those friends of Ifor and Gwladys who had come back to Taff Court after the ceremony at the Tabernacle Chapel.

Finally there was only the wedding cake left on the table and Sara began to wonder if they were ever going to cut it. Her father ignored the cake completely but in the end Gwladys picked up the big kitchen knife, plunged it into the centre and then handed round slices to everybody.

After the visitors had all left, Ifor picked up the plate containing the remains of the cake and handed it to Martha.

'Throw this rubbish away, Mrs Pritchard,' he ordered.

'Throw it away?' Martha queried in surprised tones as she saw the colour drain from Sara's face. 'Do you know what you are saying, Ifor Jenkins?'

'I always know what I am saying, Martha Pritchard. It should never have been brought into this house or placed on my table. Sinful, such extravagance. Now do as I say, woman!'

Martha was about to argue but Sara shook her head in time to silence her.

'Very well, if that's the way you want it,' she agreed. 'You won't mind if I take it home then, and me and my Alun has a slice of it with our tea tonight. Likes a bit of iced fruit cake, does my Alun.'

'Do what you like with it only get it out of my sight,' Ifor thundered. 'And you, Sara, don't stand there gawping, get this place cleaned up. A right pigsty, so it is.'

'Right, well, I'll give the girl a hand before I go home then,' Martha offered.

'No need for that, Mrs Pritchard. Sara can see to it. We'd like to be on our own now!'

'As you wish,' she told him huffily. 'Ask Sara to bring my dishes back to me then as soon as she's washed them.' As she walked out of the kitchen door, Martha winked at Sara and gave her an encouraging smile.

After she'd cleared everything away and washed up, Sara made use of the excuse and said she was returning Martha's dishes and would take Myfanwy with her.

'Don't stay there very long, mind,' Gwladys told her. 'It's time that child was in bed.'

'Very well,' Sara promised. 'No need for you to worry, though, I'll wash her and put her to bed.'

'Of course you will,' Gwladys smirked. 'It's an early night for us. Your father is on early shift in the morning.'

At Martha's house, Sara found a special tea was on the table waiting for them. Martha had made a strawberry jelly and a raspberry blancmange and there was a huge slice of the iced cake apiece.

'There's still plenty of cake left so I'll pop it into my pantry and you can bring Myfanwy round again tomorrow night for another treat,' Martha told Sara. 'Lovely it was, you tell your Rhys that. No need to tell him how ungracious those two were, mind. Telling me to throw it away and saying that it was sinful, indeed! I've never heard anything like it in my life.'

'Remember, we're always here if you need us, or we can do anything to help,' Alun Pritchard told Sara. 'Not going to be an easy ride for you with those two, *cariad*.'

'They deserve each other if you ask me,' Martha added. 'A pair of religious cranks and mean minded with it.'

When Sara finally took Myfanwy home their house was in darkness. The thought of Gwladys lying upstairs in her Dada's bed overwhelmed her with sadness.

She'd loved her Mam so much. She'd been so sweet and gentle, the exact opposite of Gwladys, and despite her years of poor health she had always been smiling and patient.

Speaking only in whispers, she got Myfanwy ready for bed and together they tiptoed up to the small back bedroom.

Myfanwy, worn out by all the excitement, was asleep in seconds. Sara lay there in the darkness, her mind a cauldron of disturbing thoughts, until eventually sleep claimed her as well.

Chapter Twelve

From the moment Gwladys Jones became Mrs Ifor Jenkins, Sara's life seemed to be divided into two separate compartments.

There were the working sessions from Monday morning to Saturday midday when, dressed in one of the smart white coat-style overalls Betti Morgan had bought her, she ran the cake shop with such efficiency that the number of customers almost doubled.

People liked her friendly manner, the cheery greeting she gave them when they came into the shop, the way she remembered not only their names but all about their aches and pains as well. They liked the fact that she knew what sort of loaf they preferred, which cakes they liked and countless other small details, as well as the efficient way she served them.

'Nothing is ever too much trouble for that girl.'

'You got a little treasure there, Betti Morgan, and no mistake.'

'Smile like a ray of sunshine.'

'It makes my day just to come in here.'

'Pity her Mam isn't still here to see what a fine girl she's turned out to be.'

'Make someone a good wife one of these days.'

'You'd better keep an eye on her, Betti Morgan, or someone will be snapping her up.'

Sara would smile, and take their praise and their jokes in her stride. When Betti Morgan praised her as well then it was indeed a bonus. Best of all, though, was when Rhys said something flattering, or whispered a private word in her ear when he brought through a fresh tray of bread or cakes.

Sara loved it when he said they made a good team. Her heart would skip a beat and then race like mad, and the colour would creep up into her cheeks.

'You look quite pretty when you blush,' he would tease, and that would make her go redder than ever.

Her other life, from six in the evening until eight the next morning, was not nearly so idyllic. Gwladys was a harsh taskmaster. She still expected Sara to do most of the cleaning, and looking after Myfanwy became her responsibility as soon as she arrived home.

Sara didn't mind this. She adored her little sister; Myfanwy was filling out and growing prettier by the day. She was quite a chatterbox, and her quaint expressions delighted Sara.

What Sara didn't like were all the rules and restrictions imposed on the little mite by her stepmother.

Right from the day she had come back to Taff Court as Mrs Jenkins, Gwladys had started to discipline Myfanwy in earnest. Although Myfanwy was still barely four, Gwladys insisted she must sit at the table with the grown-ups for all her meals. If she spilled anything, or misused her knife and fork,

Gwladys would rap her sharply across the knuckles with the back of her own knife, or whatever else she happened to have in her hand.

Myfanwy was not allowed to chatter while she was at the table, and she was not allowed to get down until all the others had finished eating and were ready to leave. Sometimes it seemed to Sara that Gwladys deliberately took as long as possible over her meal in order to make Myfanwy sit there, even though she was often so tired that she was almost dropping asleep.

When Sara pleaded with her father to have a word with Gwladys, and remind her how very young Myfanwy was, he flew into a rage.

'It's time you learnt more respect for your elders,' he barked. 'My wife is bringing up your sister the way she should be brought up. The reason Myfanwy needs so much correction is because you were too lax with her. Spoilt the child, so you did. Pandered to her from the day she was born, so no wonder she doesn't know right from wrong or the proper way to behave.'

Their arguments became more and more acrimonious and Gwladys encouraged the animosity between them. It was almost as if Gwladys had bewitched Ifor. Everything she said or did was right in his eyes. Her father was a changed man. He had never treated her mother with any respect, or ever tried to please her. Yet he couldn't do enough to please Gwladys.

He even insisted on Myfanwy calling her Mama, because this was what Gwladys wanted. This pained Sara almost more than anything else.

Gwladys had insisted that any photographs of their Mam should be destroyed so that Myfanwy would never know who her real mother was.

'No point in confusing the child, she never knew her mother so it is better that she grows up thinking I'm her mama,' Gwladys stated.

'Far better and very sensible in my opinion,' Ifor agreed.

'Surely she ought to be told the truth,' Sara protested.

'It is the truth. The Good Lord has sent Gwladys to us and she is the perfect mother for Myfanwy,' Ifor said pompously. 'I don't ever want to hear you telling the child anything different, mind, Sara.'

'Perhaps you should call me Mama as well,' Gwladys suggested.

Sara looked aghast. 'Me? Never!' she declared emphatically. 'No one could ever take my Mam's place! Different from you as *bara brith* from a bread roll.'

'That's enough!' Ifor roared. 'Any more back answers like that, girl, and I'll take my strap to you.'

'No, Dada. I'm too big for the strap. You take it to me ever again and I walk out of that door and never come back.'

He gave her a contemptuous look. 'Those are fine words, girl! And where do you suppose you'd go? Who do you suppose would take you in?'

'I'd find somewhere.'

'Shack up with that chap who works for Betti Morgan no doubt,' Gwladys said stingingly. 'I've heard the rumours that are going about. Shut my ears to them, mind you, but it makes me ashamed that my husband's daughter should carry on in such a wanton way.'

'What's all this?' Ifor's face was alert as he looked from Sara to Gwladys and back again. 'You been carrying on with some chap behind my back? Why haven't I been told about this?'

'Not my place to carry tittle-tattle,' Gwladys said smugly.

'You may think you are behaving in a Christian manner, and being charitable,' Ifor said softly, 'but if Sara is misbehaving behind my back then I should have been told. I will not have sinners under my roof. Is that understood?'

'There's no sin been committed,' Sara said defensively. She turned towards Gwladys. 'I don't know what rumours you may have heard, but they're all lies.'

'Oh, they are, are they!' Gwladys licked her thin lips. 'All this talk about you nipping out into the bakehouse at every whip stitch to see him, that's all lies, is it?'

Sara went pale. 'I have to go into the bakehouse to tell Rhys Edwards what we need, and to collect special orders.'

'And do you have to spend your lunch break in the back room of the shop with him?'

'We go in there to eat the food Mrs Morgan has prepared for us, but she is always there as well.'

'And when this Rhys Edwards is working in the bakehouse I hear he is stripped right off! His arms and chest completely bare!'

'Of course he's stripped down to his singlet! It's a very hot place to work.'

'Admire his physique, do you?' Gwladys said scornfully.

Colour surged into Sara's cheeks. She wasn't sure what Gwladys was trying to insinuate. 'There is nothing going on between us,' she protested. She stared straight at her father. 'I'd certainly know if he was doing anything he shouldn't be doing.'

'That will do, I've heard enough,' Ifor snapped. 'You'd better tell us everything you know about him, Sara.'

'Rhys Edwards is Betti Morgan's nephew. His father is her brother and he lives in Tonypandy.'

'How old is this Rhys Edwards?'

Sara shrugged. 'About twenty-four, I think.'

'Twenty-four! And you are only seventeen! He's far too old for you,' Gwladys intervened.

'Which does he attend, chapel or church?'

Sara bit down on her lip. 'I don't think he goes to either, Dada.'

Gwladys and Ifor exchanged exasperated looks.

'What sort of chap can he be if he doesn't attend either church or chapel?' Ifor exclaimed, aghast. 'Doesn't he believe in the Lord and his teachings?'

'I've never asked him, Dada, but he's a very nice sort of person,' Sara defended. 'He's kind and helpful and good-looking.'

'Good-looking!' Ifor exclaimed in derisory tones. 'When has a man's looks ever been a deciding factor in the eyes of the Lord? The Good Lord doesn't judge a man by his looks, Sara, but by what is in his heart and soul!'

Sara stared at him blankly. How could her father sit there and make such a statement! How could he profess to be so righteous and holy after the unspeakable things he had subjected her to in his bed after her mother had died? Or complain about Rhys not attending chapel or church when he never let her go, in case she should neglect any little bit of cooking or scrubbing at home?

She wondered what Gwladys would say if she spoke out and told her how he had abused her. Would she believe how right up until his wedding night her father had made her go to his bed? Would Gwladys even listen if she tried to tell her about the terrible demands he had made on her?

If anything was wicked, then the way he had behaved towards her was, but Sara was pretty certain that Gwladys wouldn't believe a word of it even if she swore on the Bible that it was all true.

She had never told a living soul, though she had often thought that Martha Pritchard had suspected all was not well. She remembered the look on her face when she had told her that her Dada was marrying Miss Jones. It had been a mixture of surprise and relief although all she had said was, 'That will make things better for you, Sara.'

And it had. Since they'd been married she didn't have that particular burden any more. She was still haunted by the memories, though. She wondered if they would ever go away. She sometimes felt guilty when Rhys sneaked a kiss. Would he feel the same way about her if he knew the truth?

It was something she tried not to think about. She kept telling herself that it hadn't been her fault. She had hated every moment of it, but she hadn't known how to stop him. Perhaps she should have told someone. It was so easy to contemplate what she should and shouldn't have done now that it was all behind her and too late.

If telling Rhys, or anyone else, meant that she might lose Rhys then she would sooner keep the truth hidden. Now that it was all in the past perhaps it didn't really matter. If the Lord was as kind and loving as her father always said He was then He would know that she wasn't the sinner, but the one who had been sinned against.

And if she believed in what the Bible said then she must forgive her father for the sins he had committed against her. Yet that was something she didn't think she would ever be able to do, no matter how long she lived.

Chapter Thirteen

It was a long hot summer. There were flies and wasps everywhere, and Sara was stung several times as she picked up one of the sugar-topped buns, or jam-filled cakes, whilst serving customers.

It was even worse for Rhys in the bakehouse. The heat from the ovens was overpowering, and even though he was working stripped off to the waist he was sweating so profusely that he still found it exhausting.

'Drinking gallons, I am,' he laughed when Sara brought him in mug after mug of tea. 'Perhaps you should put it in a jug instead of a mug.'

'This mug is as big as a jug,' she laughed. 'Betti says it holds nearly half a pint!'

During their half-hour lunch break, Betti encouraged Sara and Rhys to take some food with them and go and sit down by the river Taff to eat it.

'The sight of all that water will cool you off,' she told them. 'Go on, the pair of you. I'll keep an eye on things here if you're a few minutes late back. Off with you now, and get a breath of fresh air.'

At first Sara had been worried that someone might see them and tell Gwladys or her Dada, but Betti told her not to be so silly.

'You're eighteen now, old enough to have a life of your own, *cariad*. And old enough to have a regular boyfriend if it comes to that. Time you were married, in fact, not living at home. It isn't as if that Gwladys is your proper Mam, now is it?'

Sara looked uncomfortable. 'I couldn't leave home, not until Myfanwy is older.'

Betti Morgan's eyebrows shot up. 'Not even if Rhys popped the question and asked you to marry him?'

'Ssh! He might hear you,' Sara grinned. She wondered if Betti Morgan knew that Rhys had already asked her to marry him.

'We could share Betti's house, for a while,' he'd suggested. 'You two get on well enough, and she's always saying you're like a daughter to her. So what about it? You do care for me, Sara?'

'Of course I do! I more than care for you,' she'd whispered shyly. 'You're never out of my thoughts for one moment, Rhys Edwards!'

'There you are then, *cariad*. What's holding us back? Shall we ask Betti if she's agreeable to us living with her and then we can fix the day?'

'It's not that simple, Rhys. I couldn't leave Myfanwy. She needs me.'

'Bring her with you. She's a lovely kiddie, I wouldn't mind her living with us, really I wouldn't!'

His generosity brought tears to Sara's eyes just thinking about it. It never failed to amaze her that he was so wonderfully understanding and interested in her and her problems. She was younger than he was, inexperienced and not even pretty. He was handsome, and had such charm that he could have captured the heart of any girl.

Betti looked at her strangely when Sara broke the

news that Rhys had already proposed, her plump round face alert with curiosity. 'Why can't you go ahead and marry him then? Most girls would think him a fine old catch, I can tell you, and jump at the chance.'

'Myfanwy needs me,' Sara mumbled, going red and avoiding Betti's quizzical gaze. How could she explain that Rhys probably wouldn't want her if he knew what had gone on between her and her father.

'Bit harsh with her, that Gwladys, is she?'

Sara nodded. 'Something like that.'

'And your Dada. Doesn't he speak out, then, *cariad*?'

Sara bit her lip. 'I don't think he notices it like I do,' she confessed. 'He seems to think that Myfanwy needs disciplining.'

'Mmm!' Betti's small mouth clamped into a firm line. 'Once a schoolteacher always a schoolteacher,' she intoned disparagingly.

Silently Sara agreed with her. She couldn't bring herself to list the many ways in which Gwladys disciplined Myfanwy. Somehow, in themselves they seemed to be almost trivial. It was only when you saw the fear on the child's face when Gwladys raised her voice, or the way Myfanwy cowered whenever Gwladys approached her, that it became apparent that the little girl was terrified of her.

Sara had to admit that she had never seen Gwladys hit her, except across the knuckles, and there were no bruises on the child's small body, but she knew only too well that Gwladys had other forms of chastisement; ones that left no visible scars.

One of Gwladys's favourite forms of punishment

was to strap Myfanwy into her high chair, and leave her there for hours at a time. Often Myfanwy would fall asleep, slumped over her straps.

On one of the hottest days of the summer Sara had returned home just after five o'clock and found that Myfanwy had been left sitting out in the back yard in the full glare of the sun.

The child had been burning hot almost as if she had a high fever. And when she had taken her indoors, and given her some water to drink, Myfanwy had gulped it down almost as thirstily as Rhys downed his great mugfuls of tea when he was working in the heat of the bakehouse.

When Sara was getting Myfanwy ready for bed that night, she found that the back of her neck and the tops of her little arms were covered in watery blisters.

Worried, she went to ask Martha Pritchard's advice about what she ought to put on them.

Martha was shocked. 'I'll give you something to dab on to soothe the burning. It's been caused by the poor little mite being left out in the hot sun without any kind of covering or shade.'

'She's been out there all afternoon, crying her eyes out, the poor little thing,' she added angrily, 'and that lazy baggage Gwladys has been sitting in a chair in the shade reading her bloody bible!'

'I called over to her, and said that Myfanwy would fry if she left her there much longer, and she told me to mind my own business. She said the Good Lord sent the sunshine so it could do no harm to the child. Did you ever hear such nonsense?'

'If it had been rain, or snow even, she would have said the same thing,' Sara said morosely.

'It's enough to put you off religion for life to see the way she and your father carry on,' Martha said indignantly. 'The compassion of the Lord, indeed! There's not a spot of milk of human kindness in that woman.'

Sara nodded in agreement.

'I'm sorry, my lovely, I shouldn't go on like this. Only make you all the more worried. But do have a word with your Dada and see if he can make that Gwladys look after the child a bit better.'

When Sara told Rhys about what had happened and her concern over Myfanwy's welfare, he was even more indignant than Martha Pritchard had been.

'She could have died of sunstroke,' he exploded. 'A little one like that needs keeping in the shade, and she needs plenty to drink in weather like this. She'd be better off if you brought her to work with you. I'm sure Betti wouldn't mind.'

Sara sighed. 'Betti's feeling the heat pretty badly herself. Most of the time it's as much as she can do to get around. Her feet and legs are terribly swollen. It wouldn't be fair to add to her problems.'

'You said Myfanwy will be going to school at the beginning of September so it would only be for a few weeks,' Rhys persisted.

'Well, I could ask Betti, I suppose. I'll see how Myfanwy is when I get home tonight.'

When she did get home, though, there were much more serious matters to deal with. There had been an explosion at the Trehafod Mine where her father worked.

'Who told you about it, Gwladys?' Sara asked.

'That fat woman, Martha, from next door. It seems her husband Alun works there as well, but he wasn't hurt, only a few cuts and grazes and a bit of shock.'

'Come on, Gwladys!' Sara lifted Myfanwy up in her arms. 'We'd best get up there, see if there is anything we can do.'

'Put Myfanwy down this instant, we're not going anywhere,' Gwladys said firmly. 'We'll wait here and pray to the Lord.'

'What good is that going to do?' Sara blazed.

'If your father is in any sort of trouble the Good Lord will protect him, Sara. We'll just sit here and pray and wait for someone to bring us the news. Your father will probably walk in the door at any minute.'

Sara shook her head vehemently. 'I want to be there to find out what has happened.'

'Very well. You go if you want to. I shall stay here and offer up prayers to the Lord knowing that he will protect him,' Gwladys repeated placidly.

News of the explosion had spread. The road from Taff Court up to the pit was packed with people who, like Sara, were anxious for news of their loved ones.

Holding Myfanwy's hand tightly, her heart pounding with mixed emotions, Sara hurried up the steep hill that led out of the town towards Trehafod. Much as she feared her father, she didn't want him dead. She would never forgive him for the way he had treated her in the past, but the thought of him being trapped underground sent shivers through her.

'Walking much too fast, you are, my lovely, for such little legs to keep up with you,' a familiar voice exclaimed, and she found Myfanwy's hand being taken from hers.

'Rhys! What are you doing here?' she gasped as he swung the child up on to his shoulder.

'I heard the news and I guessed this was where I'd find you. Betti said she'd stay home and have some hot food waiting for us when we got back. Have you heard any details yet?'

'Not really. Only that there's been a big explosion, and that most of the men on Dada's shift are trapped underground.'

'Does Gwladys know?'

Sara nodded grimly. 'She's at home praying.'

They exchanged expressive looks, but said no more. As they reached the pit gates the crowd stopped moving and became an impenetrable wall. They watched as rescue parties went down into the darkness, and waited anxiously as teams already down there came to the surface bringing up the dead and injured.

As each rescued miner was identified, and his name called out, a small knot of people would move forward to claim him and if he was capable of moving would help him away home.

There were seven dead, and their bodies were laid out on the ground some distance away. Nothing more could be done for them, and so all help was focused on the injured.

The waiting seemed to be interminable. Myfanwy

became restless, and Rhys suggested to Sara that perhaps she should take her back home, but Sara refused to move from the spot.

'Tell you what, *cariad*, why don't I take her back and you stay on here until you have some news?' Rhys suggested.

'No!' Sara shook her head emphatically. 'That Gwladys will be too busy praying to give Myfanwy a thought. She's better off here with me.'

'I intended taking her to Betti's place, not your house,' Rhys told her. 'The poor little mite's probably hungry. Betti will feed her and take care of her and keep her amused until we get back.'

Sara looked up at him, her eyes filled with tears. 'That sounds a splendid idea,' she agreed.

'Right. You tell her then, Sara, so that she's not frightened when I walk off with her. You stay here and I'll be back again as soon as I can.'

As she waited on her own, Sara thought what a lovely chap Rhys was. He was so kind and considerate that she wished they could be married. She knew he was willing to have Myfanwy to live with them, but she was almost certain that her Dada would never agree to such an arrangement.

It was strange, she thought, as she waited at the pit-head for news, that Rhys was the one who had come to find out what had happened to her father while Gwladys, his new wife, showed no concern whatsoever, but had stayed at home. Could her faith in prayer really be so immense, or was it a case that she couldn't be bothered to stand around at the pit head?

It seemed ages before Rhys came back, but when

he did he had a bottle of hot tea for her, and Betti had sent along a huge bag of cakes and buns in case anyone waiting was desperately hungry but afraid to leave the site without news.

'Hang on to these two buns for us, and I'll pass the rest round the crowd,' Rhys told her. 'Some of these people have been waiting here for hours and they must be starving by now.'

It was almost midnight before they brought Ifor out. He had been protected by a protruding lump of rock and was not too seriously injured. One of his legs was either completely broken, or just slightly fractured, and his face and chest were badly cut by falling debris, but he was alive and breathing.

'The Good Lord looked after me,' he told Sara as she knelt beside the stretcher. 'I knew there was nothing to fear.'

'It will take a couple of hours probably to clean him up, set his leg in plaster and dress his cuts,' the doctor told Sara as they waited for an ambulance to take him to hospital. 'After that you'll have to take him home. All the beds in the hospital are full with those who've been seriously injured.'

'We'll be at the hospital to collect him,' Rhys told the doctor. He took Sara's arm and led her away.

'I'd better let Gwladys know that he is safe,' Sara muttered.

'Rubbish! The Good Lord will already have told her,' Rhys joked. 'Let's go and have the food that's waiting at Betti's place first and then we'll let Gwladys know the news.'

After they'd eaten a great bowlful of hot cawl that Betti had simmering away on the range, and Sara had checked that Myfanwy was tucked up sound asleep, they went to Taff Court to tell Gwladys that they were on their way to collect Ifor.

Gwladys was not only in bed, but she was also sound asleep. Having bolted the door from the inside before retiring, she was more than a little annoyed at being disturbed by Rhys thumping on the door and calling out her name until she opened the bedroom window and agreed to come downstairs.

The rumpus brought Martha Pritchard to her front door.

'Your Dada all right then?' Martha asked Sara.

'A broken leg and some cuts and grazes. He was one of the very last to be brought up, but he was in good spirits nevertheless.'

'Alun had only a few scratches. Lucky he was. Suffering from shock, mind. They insisted he should come home right away and told him to go to bed.'

'Yes, so I heard. Pleased I was. One of the first brought out, wasn't he?'

'That's right. Ten dead and twenty-three injured, so we heard.'

'A terrible night that no one in Ponty will forget in a hurry,' said Alun, joining his wife at the door. 'It's been a sleepless night for most of the town.'

'Not for everyone,' Martha said acidly, lifting her eyes up to the bedroom window.

'Well, she'll have to get up again now,' Sara said grimly. 'We're off to the hospital to bring my Dada home. The doctor said they would see to his injuries, but then it was up to us to nurse him. Packed out, they are, in there. Every bed is taken!'

Chapter Fourteen

Ifor Jenkins was still at home three months later. His broken leg had healed quite well, but things were going from bad to worse in the coal industry, and there was rumour and speculation that the Trehafod pit would be shut down.

It was now October, and too cold for Sara and Rhys to walk along the banks of the Taff so they usually spent their lunch break in Betti's back room. It was where Betti lived most of the time so it was warm and cosy. There was a large carpet square on the tiled floor, and as well as a round table and upright chairs where they sat down to their meal, there was a comfortable leather sofa and an armchair.

These days, Betti, sensitive to their desire to be alone together, would absent herself as soon as she had dished out the bowls of cawl or whatever else she had prepared for midday.

'I had mine earlier on,' she'd tell them. 'Lovely, it is so make sure you mop up every scrap. I'm going up to my bed for half an hour so sing out when it's time to open up again.'

Aware that Betti was finding the working day too much for her, Sara left her to rest until about four o'clock when they started to get busy. It was the time when women collecting their children from school came into the shop on their way home for pasties or bread and cakes for their evening meal.

'There's wicked you are, girl, letting me stay up there all this time,' Betti would scold. 'Turn me into a lazy old woman if you had your way, wouldn't you?'

Her warm smile belied the ferocity of her words. The understanding between them these days was every bit as close as mother and daughter. The only thing they ever disagreed about was over Rhys and Sara getting married.

Betti thought that they should and said they could move in with her, but Sara still felt she couldn't simply walk out on Myfanwy and leave her to be brought up by Gwladys and her father. She'd vowed she'd care for Myfanwy and make sure her father never behaved towards her little sister as he had towards her. But even though that seemed to be all in the past, he and Gwladys could still make Myfanwy's life miserable in so many different ways.

'She's at school now, so Gwladys doesn't have all that much say over the way she's brought up,' Betti would argue whenever the subject was discussed.

'Gwladys doesn't look after Myfanwy like a mother, or even a stepmother, should,' Sara would point out. 'She's strict over prayers and manners but careless over her general welfare. She's always so shabbily dressed and Gwladys doesn't even feed her properly.'

Betti sighed. 'If I've said it once I've said it a thousand times, move out! Marry Rhys, like he keeps asking you to do, and then come here and live, and bring little Myfanwy with you. She'd be no trouble, and I'd be here to keep an eye on her when you and Rhys wanted some time on your own.'

'I know, Betti, and believe me I am very grateful, but I just can't bring myself to do it. If I so much as suggested it Dada would fly into a rage. Since his accident the least thing riles him.'

'Only because you pander to him, *cariad*! He's better now so you go ahead and tell him what you intend to do.'

'Betti is right,' Rhys agreed. 'Tell you what, I'll come round to your house tonight, and we'll tell him together.'

This time Sara agreed. She knew she had kept Rhys waiting long enough and she wanted to marry him so desperately. As Betti had said, Myfanwy was at school now and so there was less opportunity for Gwladys to mistreat her. Sara still doubted very much that her Dada would let her take Myfanwy to live with her and Rhys, but if they were at Betti's then they wouldn't be far away.

I'll be able to see Myfanwy every day if I want to, Sara reasoned, and I can keep a sharp eye out for any sign that things are not as they should be at home.

Yet, as she cleared the table and washed up that evening, all the while listening out for Rhys, Sara felt on tenterhooks. It was a dark wet night and the wind was blowing a gale, and she felt more and more uneasy as she listened to the storm.

It wasn't just that she was terrified of how her father would react to the news. He would probably be outright rude, even aggressive, but she was sure

Rhys could deal with that. Once he'd sent Rhys packing, though, would he take off his belt and thrash her as he had done in the past? She wondered if Gwladys would do anything about it, or even if she would be able to stop him?

What worried Sara even more than this was her own uncertainty over whether she was doing the right thing. Was she being selfish and putting her own happiness above protecting Myfanwy? She might be able to see her every day but they would no longer be sharing a room every night. And what about her and Rhys? Sara still hadn't told him, would never be able to tell him, about what her father had done.

In some ways, Sara half hoped that perhaps Rhys wouldn't come at all and things could stay exactly as they were.

Sara was tucking Myfanwy into bed when she heard the knock on the front door. Before she could get downstairs her father had answered it, so she waited nervously at the top of the stairs to see what would happen.

At first she thought he wasn't even going to let Rhys over the doorstep. Then she heard Gwladys call out to know who it was and her father answered, 'It's that fellow from the cake shop where Sara works.'

Plucking up her courage, Sara went down the stairs.

'I asked Rhys to come round, Dada, because we have something to tell you.'

'You'd better make it quick because I'm off down

to the Tabernacle Chapel in half an hour,' her father told them.

'Well, let him come in then!'

Reluctantly her father moved aside and let Rhys into the hall.

'You're half drowned,' Sara exclaimed. 'Shall I take your jacket, it's soaking wet?'

'It's raining cats and dogs and blowing a gale,' Rhys smiled as he handed it to her. 'Tipping it down, in fact.'

'Well, you'd better come and sit by the fire and get dried out then,' she invited.

Her father had moved back into his armchair at one side of the grate and Gwladys had remained where she was in her armchair on the other. Neither of them made any attempt to make room for their visitor as Sara pulled two straight-backed chairs closer to the fire.

'So what do you want to tell me?' Ifor Jenkins scowled. 'Not got my daughter into trouble, have you?'

'Dada!' Sara blushed beetroot red with embarrassment. 'Of course he hasn't!'

'No of course about it,' her father ranted. 'A man who is not a believer in the Good Lord is hardly likely to have any morals.'

Rhys looked very affronted. Ifor's abruptness shocked him, and Sara could see that he was struggling to hold his temper. 'Will you tell him or shall I?' she said quickly.

'He's got a tongue in his head so let him speak for himself, can't you?' her father said irritably.

Sara bit her lip and looked pleadingly at Rhys.

She wasn't sure what she wanted him to say but all the misgivings she'd had earlier seemed to be justified. This was not going well at all, she thought uneasily.

'I've come to tell you that Sara and I are going to be married,' Rhys stated firmly.

'Getting married, are you? And on whose say-so is this?' Ifor asked. His tone was mocking, his mouth stark with distaste.

'She's eighteen. She doesn't need your permission,' Rhys told him bluntly.

'And where do you think you are going to live, then?' Gwladys butted in. 'There's certainly no room for the pair of you here and I wouldn't have you here even if there was!'

'We have somewhere to live, thank you,' Rhys told her politely.

'You mean you've fixed yourself up with rooms without ever saying a word to me about your plans, Sara?' her father barked.

'We wanted to make sure we had everything arranged before we said anything, Dada,' she said meekly, fighting back the sour taste in her throat.

'Everything arranged? So where is this marriage going to take place? You're not a chapel man, are you?' he asked, fixing Rhys with a steely glare.

'Nor do you go to church from what I've heard,' Gwladys stated sharply.

'We're planning on a registry office wedding if that's all right with you,' Rhys told him.

'All right with me? All right with me!' Ifor Jenkins struggled to control his anger. 'Have you any idea what you are saying? I am a man who believes in the Lord. A man who attends the Tabernacle Chapel with all due regularity. A man who devotes himself to serving the Lord, and you have the audacity to sit there and tell me that you are going to marry my daughter in a registry office. That's not a marriage. That's a travesty in the eyes of the Lord. You may as well live together in sin as consider that to be a marriage.'

'It's all perfectly legal,' Rhys defended.

'It's not a true marriage in the eyes of the Lord,' Ifor stated emphatically. His eyes bulged, his features became distorted. 'You'd be sinners, both of you! Now get out of my house, Rhys Edwards, and let's hear no more of this nonsense.'

'Selfish you are, the pair of you,' Gwladys intervened as if anxious to add her weight to the discussion. The fact that they might marry without the benefit of chapel didn't worry her nearly as much as the realisation that if Sara married and moved away she would have to do a lot more work herself around the house.

In addition, there was the matter of Sara's wages. As things stood, because of Ifor's accident, she had been able to insist that Sara handed over her entire pay packet, each week. If she had to manage without that then there would have to be drastic economies.

Without Sara's money she would no longer be able to indulge herself in so many of the little luxuries that she enjoyed so much. Not unless she went back to teaching and she didn't like the idea of doing that again one bit.

'Look, our minds are made up, Mr Jenkins!' Rhys

said balefully as he rose to his feet and groped for his jacket that Sara had spread over the back of a nearby chair.

'And so is mine!' Ifor roared, his face mottled with anger. 'Now get out of my house!'

Chapter Fifteen

The next day was Sunday so Sara did not have an opportunity to see Rhys, and she worried all day about what he must be thinking. However, when she went into the bakehouse on Monday he seemed to be quite amiable. Betti was there with him and Sara sensed they had been talking about her.

'Was everything all right after I left your place on Saturday?' Rhys asked diffidently.

Sara hesitated. She didn't want to talk about the rage her father had been in all weekend or the way he'd been watching her every movement.

She'd seen that speculative look in her father's sloe-dark eyes before and sensed what he was thinking. She knew he was waiting for an opportunity to get her on her own and if that happened she was apprehensive of what he would do to her. If only she could divulge the whole story about what had happened in the past and reveal the real reason why he was so determined she shouldn't leave home.

If only it was possible to confide in someone, tell them of her fears and sense of impending disaster because of the way he had treated her in the past, and ask them to protect her. But what would Rhys, or even Betti, think of her if they knew the truth?

'I love you, Rhys, and I really do want to marry

you,' she said wistfully, 'it's just that I am so worried about leaving Myfanwy.'

'Then why not agree to Betti's offer? Marry me, we'll move in here and Myfanwy can come and live with us. That will solve your problem and everything will be wonderful,' he urged.

Sara shook her head doubtfully. 'My Dada would never let Myfanwy come and live with us.'

Rhys stared at her in bewilderment. This had been Betti's reaction when they'd talked over her plan and it baffled him.

'Sara won't leave that poor little dab Myfanwy behind to face that pair of Holy Joes on her own,' Betti had told him, her round face troubled.

He'd felt dumbfounded. 'You mean she intends to ruin both our lives in order to look after Myfanwy?' he'd asked.

'I don't think she sees it quite like that, boyo,' Betti had told him. 'She feels responsible for her little sister, see.'

He had frowned irritably. 'I know that, but she does have her own life to live.'

'So what are you going to do about it then, boyo? You can't simply leave things up in the air as they are now.'

'I want Sara to move in here, but it seems to be impossible to get her to agree. Sometimes I'm not even sure if she loves me.'

'As far as I can see there's only one thing you can do to find out,' Betti Morgan told him.

'And what's that?'

'Tell her you've decided to leave Ponty and that if

she doesn't want to go with you then you're going on your own.'

At the time he'd laughed at Betti's suggestion, but now he felt so desperate that he blurted it out without giving a second thought to the effect his words might have.

Sara looked stunned. The colour drained from her face and her lips trembled.

How could she make sure Myfanwy was safe if she moved right away from Taff Court? She hesitated, struggling with her conscience, wanting to explain the situation to him, but when it came to the final moment words failed her. Instead, all she could do was insist that she loved him and that she wanted to marry him more than anything else in the world.

'I want you to come with me,' Rhys said firmly. 'If your Dad is against our getting married here in Ponty then the only thing we can do is elope. Betti agrees with me that we need a fresh start,' he added quickly. 'It's the only way you'll make a clean break, Sara, and get right away from your father.'

Sara looked bemused. 'How can we manage to do that?'

'Leave here and go to Cardiff,' Rhys grinned.

She looked shocked. 'That would be letting Betti down! She'd have no baker and no one to run the shop.'

'She knows that and understands why we're doing it. I've talked it over with her and she's already making plans to replace us.'

Sara sighed. 'It's still a big step,' she said cautiously. She reached up and pulled his head down so that she could kiss him. 'I do love you Rhys, it's just that I need more time to think it over.'

'We both want to get married so if we elope now it will save having any more rows about it with your father,' Rhys persisted.

'It would be very upsetting for Myfanwy though if I simply disappeared,' Sara argued. 'She's too little to understand. Anyway, I can't leave her behind,' she added stubbornly.

'It won't be for very long. As soon as we are on our feet and have a decent roof over our heads then she can come and live with us.'

Still Sara hesitated. She longed to do what Rhys suggested more than anything else in the world, but she felt so guilty about leaving Myfanwy.

'Give me a little more time to get used to the idea,' she begged.

Rhys's face clouded and when she reached out to hug him he drew back and busied himself at one of the ovens as if he couldn't bear for her to touch him.

Sara bit her lip to stop herself from saying anything that might make matters between them any worse. She had never felt more miserable in her life. The atmosphere here at work was now almost as tense as it was at home, she thought unhappily.

For the next few days Gwladys devoted as much time to trying to think of ways to stop Rhys and Sara marrying as she normally devoted to reading her bible. Somehow she had to find a way to discredit Rhys Edwards in Sara's eyes, or better still, in Betti Morgan's eyes as well. If Betti sacked Rhys and he left Pontypridd then there would be no further problem, she reasoned. Sara was young and this was her first boyfriend so she would soon forget about him, Gwladys told herself.

Ifor was also grappling with the same problem, but for quite different reasons. Sara was his property; he had raised her, fed her and clothed her. Now that she was old enough to work it was only justice that he should reap the benefit of her labours. It was right in the eyes of the Lord. It said as much in the Bible.

There was another factor, too. He had been surprised at the anger that had churned up inside him when Rhys had said that he wanted to marry Sara. Although he'd no longer had any need to take her to his bed since he had been married to Gwladys, he liked to know that Sara was still there under his roof, and readily available should he want her.

Lying with Sara, he reflected, had brought him much greater satisfaction and pleasure than anything that he ever experienced with Gwladys. He didn't intend to let some other man take her away when he might desire her himself some time in the future. It was all a matter of patience. The Good Lord would show him a way, and give him a sign telling him what he must do, when the time was ripe.

Over the next few days the atmosphere between Sara and her father became more and more fraught with tension. She was aware that he was watching her closely, a strange glare in his eyes, almost as if he suspected she was planning something.

When a couple of nights later he came into the bedroom she shared with Myfanwy she pretended to be asleep. Keeping her breathing slow and regular, and hoping he couldn't hear the thundering of her heart, she watched him through half-closed eyelids. He stood motionless at the bottom of her bed staring down at her for what seemed like an eternity.

Suddenly he leant over the bed, a frightening dark spectre, and she cowered back, her feeling of distress and impending danger increasing, as he gave a low growl and his hand shot out, pulling back the bedcovers.

Afraid of what might happen next, she was unable to suppress her scream of terror. As his calloused hand clamped instantaneously down over her mouth she bit into the flesh as hard as she could. With a cry of rage he attacked her so swiftly and savagely that she was stunned into submission.

And then he was gone.

Stifling her sobs into her pillow Sara knew she had to get away from Taff Court. It was imperative for Myfanwy's sake, as well as her own, that she took some action.

She couldn't take Myfanwy with her, not right away, but while she was still little more than a baby she'd be safe enough. Her father was not that perverted, she told herself over and over again. She had to believe that Myfanwy would be safe for the moment, long enough for her and Rhys to get a home of their own together. The moment they'd managed to do that she could redeem her promise and Myfanwy could come and live with them.

The next day, the minute she arrived at Betti's shop she headed straight for the bakehouse, anxious to make a commitment before her courage failed.

'Rhys, I've thought over your suggestion and I think you're right. I'm ready to fall in with your idea about us leaving Pontypridd for Cardiff,' she gabbled.

For a moment he stared at her as if he couldn't believe his ears.

'Do you really mean that, *cariad*?' he asked, grabbing her by the shoulders.

She nodded. 'I've just said so, haven't I?'

Rhys gave a whoop of delight, crushing her to him in a bear-like hug and dancing round the bakehouse with her in his arms.

Betti was equally pleased for them both. 'Mind you,' she said reflectively, her plump face wreathed in smiles, 'I'm making a tremendous sacrifice letting you both go like this.'

'We know that, Betti, and we'll never forget your kindness,' Sara assured her soberly.

Betti sniffed. 'I still can't see why you couldn't get married and live here. Your Dada and Gwladys would get used to the idea in time.'

Sara smiled sadly. 'He's a hard man, Betti, he doesn't forgive easily.'

'Well, I'm sure you know best, *cariad*. If you don't like Cardiff then you know there's always a home here for you both.'

Remembering her vow to care for Myfanwy, it broke Sara's heart having to leave her behind in Pontypridd, but she knew there was no alternative. All she could do was to promise that she would come back for her as soon as ever she could.

'Once we've got our own place, my lovely, I'll be back for you,' Sara promised. 'And if you ever need me you can always tell Martha Pritchard next door, remember, and she will send me a letter to let me know.'

Myfanwy looked bewildered. 'Won't Mama and Dada know where you are?'

'Probably. But they might be too busy. Or you mightn't want to ask them. Martha will listen to you and she will let me know, so you will remember that, won't you?'

Myfanwy looked puzzled. 'Don't you know where you are going then?'

'Of course I do, *cariad*! I'm going to Cardiff with Rhys. We are both going to find work there and the minute we have found somewhere nice to live I'll come back for you.'

Myfanwy stared at her wide-eyed, still not fully comprehending. 'If you go away, Sara, you might forget all about me,' she said wistfully.

'Forget about you! How could I ever forget my precious little sister?' She pulled the little girl into her arms, burying her face in her dark hair. The pain inside her at the thought of leaving Myfanwy almost choked her.

'No, my lovely,' she whispered, 'I'll not forget you, not for a single minute!' She took a deep breath, and said with forced cheerfulness, 'I'll be back before you know it, you'll see.'

'Do I have to pray for you every night, Sara, and ask the Good Lord to look after you?'

Sara's eyes clouded with unshed tears. 'Yes, you can do that, *cariad*, but I'll be back for you very soon. I've promised, and you know I always keep my promises to you.'

Chapter Sixteen

Cardiff, three weeks before Christmas 1928, was a mixture of brilliant festivity in the city centre and abject poverty around Tiger Bay.

When they arrived at Cardiff Central station, Rhys and Sara had twenty-three pounds between them. At any other time they would have thought themselves well off, but they both knew that once they began paying out for somewhere to live and for their food, it would vanish like snow in summer.

As soon as they stepped off the train they set out to find the registry office so that they could be married.

'Perhaps we should have done this in Pontypridd, probably it would have been easier and much cheaper,' Rhys said as he humped the battered old cardboard suitcase holding his and Sara's belongings.

'How do you make that out? Surely it's the same price everywhere, isn't it?'

'Even so, it would be better if we already had a certificate to prove we're man and wife. Make it easier when we try to find lodgings.'

Sara frowned. 'Do we have to tell them? Can't we simply call ourselves Mr and Mrs Edwards?'

'There's wicked you are,' Rhys grinned. 'We could do that, and if they believed us then we needn't bother with all the fuss and expense of going to the registry office at all. Only a bit of paper when all is said and done!'

Sara pondered on this for a minute. 'It wouldn't be right, though, would it?'

He shrugged. 'It wouldn't bother me, but I can see you wouldn't be too happy about it.'

'That's because I want to be legally Mrs Edwards,' she smiled, slipping her hand through his arm. 'Come on, let's go and look for this old City Hall, and find out what we have to do to make it all legal.'

Cardiff City Hall took their breath away. They'd never seen anything quite like it. It had not long been built and was a magnificent edifice in gleaming white Portland stone, set in a leafy landscaped setting, with a huge frontage that seemed to go on for ever in two directions. On one side there was a lofty clock tower that soared upwards, dominating the skyline. Over the main entrance was an immense dome surmounted by an enormous Welsh dragon. Looking at it brought a lump to Sara's throat as she remembered the trip to Cardiff she and her mother had planned.

As they went up the broad stone steps to the enquiry office, Sara was half afraid that the doorman, resplendent in his top hat and gold-trimmed livery, would turn them away. Instead he directed them to an office where a clerk asked so many questions, that she felt bewildered.

Sara felt even more bemused when he told them how much it would cost them and when the actual ceremony would take place. She'd thought they'd simply walk in, give their names and sign a piece of paper.

She was even more confused when Rhys thanked the man for his time and said they would think it over.

'Christ!' he exclaimed once they were outside, 'I had no idea it would cost that much. If we go ahead we'll have nothing left for food or somewhere to stay!'

Sara squeezed his hand. 'Never mind, we can leave it until you get a job.'

'Bloody well have to,' he muttered, his mouth tightening.

She felt shocked. She had never heard Rhys swear before. He seemed to be so angry that she felt uneasy and a little scared, wondering if leaving Ponty had been the right thing to do after all.

She looked sideways at him, noting the aggressive jut of his jaw. It was as if the happy, carefree Rhys she had fallen so much in love with had been left behind in Pontypridd. This was a harder, harsher man who was churlish and on edge.

He's worried about what is going to happen to us, she told herself. He'll be fine again once we are properly married and have a place to live.

She hoped they'd find somewhere soon. She'd looked forward so much to being married to Rhys, who she loved more than anything, but things all seemed to be going wrong for them. And though he had never been anything but gentle and affectionate in their embraces so far, the tension between them now brought all her fears of going to bed with him for the first time flooding back. On top of that, she was so afraid that he might realise he wasn't the first man she'd known in that way. She felt guilty for not telling him about what had happened in the past between her and her Dada, but it was too late to do so now. She prayed fervently that all would be well.

Finding somewhere to live proved harder than either of them had expected. They tramped around the streets of Cathays and Canton, where a lot of the terraced houses had 'Room to let' signs in their front windows, until Sara was footsore and weary. No one wanted to take them in, even though they called themselves Mr and Mrs Edwards.

'Looking for a single bloke,' they were told. 'Married couples can be trouble. In next to no time we'll be having to put up with a screaming baba. Not worth it, see!'

In desperation they made their way to Tiger Bay, the dockland slums where people of all nationalities lived. Here, as long as they could pay in advance, it seemed there was plenty of accommodation available.

Even so, their search seemed to be endless. It was the state of the rooms they were offered which made finding a place to live so difficult. Very few of them were clean; cockroaches, mice and even rats were rampant, and the mixed smells of cooking and worse choked them as soon as they went inside a front door.

Worn out and hungry, they went into a café in James Street. It was the cleanest place they had seen, and on impulse, as he ordered a meal for them,

Rhys asked the owner if he knew of anywhere they could get a room.

The man shook his head, but as he handed Rhys his change he leant over the counter and said in a hoarse whisper, 'Daisy Street. Number three. Her name's Polly Price. Tell her Jack sent you. I'm her brother, see!'

When he brought their meal he pushed a brass curtain ring towards Sara. 'You'd better wear this, Missus,' he muttered, 'she mightn't take you in otherwise.'

The terraced house in Daisy Street looked no better than any of the others they had tried and Rhys didn't hold out much hope.

The woman who answered the door was in her late thirties, smartly dressed in a low-waisted green dress, with her straight brown hair caught back in a loose knot. Her hazel eyes regarded them suspiciously when Rhys mentioned renting a room, and she shook her head emphatically. When he added, 'Jack sent us,' she seemed to relax and invited them inside.

The room was upstairs, and at the back of the house. It was not very big and had only one small casement window which looked out on to the back yard and the house next door. There was a small double bed, a straight-backed chair, a washstand and a storage cupboard at one end. The really good thing about the room was that it was spotlessly clean.

'Five shillings a week, and the use of the kitchen once a day,' she told them firmly. 'There's a gas ring and your own meter so you can heat the room and boil a kettle on the ring if you want to do so.'

'Five shillings?' Rhys said speculatively.

Her thin lips tightened. 'That's what I said, and I want two weeks' up front, boyo. Not having you vanishing in the middle of the night owing me rent.'

Rhys looked questioningly at Sara and she nodded eagerly. She would have settled for almost anything. Furthermore, the room and the inside of Mrs Price's house were palatial compared to everything else they'd looked at. Mrs Price was rather forbidding, but at least she was clean and smart, even if she wasn't very friendly.

To their relief, Mrs Price didn't ask to see any proof that they were married. After they'd paid her the ten shillings they unpacked their few possessions and tidied them away.

'It's too late to go looking for a job, so let's take a tram back up to the city centre and have a good look round at all the shops,' Rhys suggested.

'We ought to buy some bread and whatever else we'll need for our breakfast tomorrow morning,' Sara said worriedly. 'Only where do we keep it? Mrs Price never mentioned if we could keep food in her kitchen, did she?'

'We'll sort that out tomorrow. Come on, or all the shops will be closed and they might put their lights out.'

'No, I'm sure they'll leave them on in the windows this close to Christmas.'

There was only one large department store in Pontypridd, but here in Cardiff, as Martha Pritchard had told Sara, there seemed to be a great number.

Two of them, James Howell's and David Morgan's, were so immense they took Sara's breath away. There was also the Bon Marché, and the glass-roofed Arcades which linked one main street with the next and were full of smaller shops. Each of them specialised in something different, so that it was like an Aladdin's cave of treasures.

As they emerged from one of the Arcades on to St Mary Street, Sara caught her first glimpse of Cardiff Castle, and gasped in wonder. She stood there entranced by the sight of the long stone curtain wall and the great stone clock tower until Rhys grabbed her by the arm and hurried her back to the main shopping area in Queen Street.

'Come on, *cariad*, there's a lot more still to see than that pile of old stones,' he joked.

Together they wandered from one shop to the next, like excited children, exclaiming over the displays, the vast array of goods on offer and, above all, on the prices that were being charged.

'Who can afford to buy all this stuff when so many people are out of work?' Sara asked in disbelief.

'Those people who have jobs and who are earning regular wages,' Rhys told her. 'With any luck we'll be amongst them very soon. First thing tomorrow morning I'm going to look for a job. With such a lot of shops selling bread and cakes, and so many hotels and other eating places, I shouldn't have any trouble at all in finding work as a baker.'

'I wonder if I could get a job in one of those posh shops?' Sara asked wistfully.

She felt the blood rush to her face as Rhys slipped

his arm around her waist and pulled her close. 'You can find out tomorrow if you want to.' His voice dropped to a whisper. 'There's more important things to do first.'

He grabbed her by the hand and hurried her towards a tram stop. 'Come on, why are we wasting time, you've made me wait long enough for this night.'

The room in Daisy Street seemed cold and uninviting when they got back there. It certainly wasn't the cosy love-nest of her dreams, but Rhys seemed oblivious to his surroundings. The moment they closed the door he led her towards the bed. When she tried to pull away he pinioned her beneath him.

'Come on,' he urged, 'this is what we've waited for. Forget the bit of paper, we'll sort all that out later on. I want you, Sara, I'm burning up for you.'

His mouth covered hers hungrily, his breath was hot on her neck as he started to undress her. She knew she was trembling. Her heart was racing as she felt Rhys's hands moving eagerly over her body. Her breath caught in her throat as she tried to blot out the dire memories of past encounters from her mind.

Then as Rhys began murmuring endearments, the black fear ebbed away and her intense love for him became the only thing that mattered. Her need matched his. Everything else was forgotten, even their dismal surroundings.

Afterwards, as she lay cradled in Rhys's arms, she knew that the memories that had haunted her would never completely disappear, but making love with Rhys had been such a wonderful experience, so very different from what had happened before.

This was love, not lust, she thought triumphantly. Something so precious that she felt bewildered by her own good fortune. A future filled with the love they had for each other brought with it a promise of blissful contentment. In time they would be a real family with children of their own.

The thought jolted a niggling doubt into her mind. A baby was what intimacy between a man and a woman usually resulted in, so why had she never become pregnant before? Was there something wrong with her? Or had she simply been fortunate? She shuddered, but then as she looked up at Rhys's sleeping face, she felt confident and secure. Her experiences with Dada had all been so brutish and short, nothing like this gentle love-making, and surely that's where the difference lay. A baby would grow from love, she reasoned.

Sleep claimed her before she could decide on an answer.

Rhys's optimism was short-lived. No one needed a baker, not even a skilled and experienced one. After two weeks of hopeless searching he became moody and sullen.

Sara wasn't faring any better. The big stores in the centre of Cardiff turned her down because of her lack of experience. The fact that she had been a counter hand in a small cake shop in Pontypridd was not the sort of background they were interested in.

Polly Price advised her to try at some of the

smaller shops in Splott, Butetown, Canton, Cathays and Grangetown. Each day she tried a different area, but no one showed the slightest interest.

'Plenty of local girls looking for work, see,' she was told time and time again. Those in the smaller, family-run businesses told her, 'I've daughters of my own that I can call on if ever we get busy.'

Sara also quickly discovered that sharing a kitchen with Polly Price wasn't going to work out. Their landlady resented Sara's presence in her shiny little kitchen. She made sure that Sara kept to the 'one visit a day' rule as though her life depended on it.

Even that seemed to annoy her and she stood in the doorway of the tiny room with her arms folded aggressively over her spotless print apron, waiting impatiently for Sara to complete whatever she was doing.

When Sara, trying to win favour with Polly, suggested she would take turns in scouring the front step and black-leading the grate, Polly bristled as though she had been insulted.

'I don't like interference of any sort in my home,' she said pointedly. 'You stick to keeping your room clean and tidy, and don't leave any mess behind in my kitchen when you use it. Keep out of my way, that's all I ask of you. Take yourself on out, don't hang around in your room all the time.'

'I'll be out all day once I can get a job,' Sara told her.

'If you can't get work in a shop, then why don't you try one of the factories?' Polly asked. 'Curran's employ a lot of girls. None of them ever seem to stay long so you should get taken on there. It's along the Taff Embankment, you can't miss it. It's the biggest building along there, you can see it and smell it a mile away.'

Polly was right. Sara was taken on straight away. The first day she started work at Curran's, she thought she was in the hell her Dada had always threatened she would end up in.

The noise, the dust, the smells, and the vast number of people working there, were all overpowering. All the workers were kitted out in regulation overalls and caps that completely hid their hair. At first Sara couldn't tell who was the charge hand, who was the forewoman, or who was one of her fellow workers.

'You go by the colour of their overalls, stupid!' the girl next to her on the assembly line told her. 'Anyway, instead of looking round and trying to make out which is which, try keeping your mind on the job. We're on piecework, you know, and we don't all want our pay docked because you're too bloody slow to keep up.'

Rhys wasn't too pleased that Sara had found work and he hadn't, even though their money was running out fast, and he was becoming more and more impatient over Polly's strict rules about the kitchen.

'Perhaps you should give us a regular time when we can use your kitchen,' he suggested.

Polly's face flushed with anger. 'You cheeky young fellow!' she exclaimed, affronted. 'Are you trying to dictate to me when I can and cannot use my own kitchen?'

'No, of course I'm not. I simply want you to tell us when we can use it.'

'When I say,' she scowled.

'That is exactly my point, Mrs Price, you don't say,' Rhys said exasperatedly.

'*Darw*! What's wrong with you, boyo? Are you deaf or daft? You can use it when I'm not in there. Now do you understand?'

In a last attempt to find work, Rhys began frequenting the pubs around the docks in the hope of hearing of any jobs going. At the Hope and Anchor in Adelaide Street he made a point of chatting to Barbie Buckley, the landlady. She was a voluptuous blonde, good-looking and a great flirt. They enjoyed each other's banter, and he tried to talk her into serving meals for her regular customers.

'I'd come and cook for you,' he offered, leaning on the counter and watching her polishing the glasses.

She raised carefully arched brows. 'I thought you said you were a baker, not a chef?'

'Well, I am, but I can turn my hand to general cooking as well. I made meat pies, apple pies, sausage rolls and all that sort of stuff when I was working in Pontypridd.'

'Well, you might, boyo, but take a look round this bar and tell me how many of this lot would eat those? Our customers come from every part of the globe and most of them hate our food.'

'They seem to like the beer, or is it you they come to see, Barbie?'

'Best way you can earn a living at the moment,

you cheeky young bugger, is to get yourself some casual labour on the docks. I'll put in a word for you with one of the gaffers, if you like.'

Rhys's face brightened. 'Oh yes? What sort of casual labour would that be?'

'Loading and unloading the boats, of course.'

His face fell. 'You mean working as a navvy?'

'And what's wrong with that? Isn't it good enough for you?' she teased.

Rhys downed his beer. 'I'll do anything that's honest.'

'Good. Well, you see that bald-headed cove over in the corner, the one with tattoos all up his arm, he's one of the gaffers. Do you want me to put in a good word with him for you?'

Chapter Seventeen

Sara couldn't stop worrying about Myfanwy. Her wistful little face haunted her continually. Her promise that she would be back to collect Myfanwy as soon as she and Rhys had somewhere to live had a hollow ring.

The chance of her sister coming, even for a visit, while they were living in Polly Price's house was right out of the question.

Sara's dream was that once they were both working they'd move into a flat or small house of their own. A place with at least two bedrooms so that Myfanwy could join them and have her own room.

The possibility of that happening was so far away that Sara felt a deep sense of despair. They had already spent the money they had left Pontypridd with and what they had earned since they'd been in Cardiff had been quickly absorbed in day-to-day living.

She'd written to Myfanwy twice. She sent a picture postcard of Cardiff Castle and one of Roath Park, with a promise to take her to see them for herself when she came to stay.

There had been no reply. Suspecting that neither Ifor nor Gwladys would take the trouble to write to her, before she'd left Pontypridd Sara had arranged with Martha Pritchard that Martha would write back whenever she wrote to Myfanwy. Now Sara was worried in case Myfanwy was ill. There were so many things a child of that age could have, anything from a head cold to bronchitis, from a sore throat to diphtheria.

Or, of course, she reasoned, it could be that Gwladys had stopped Myfanwy from seeing Martha.

In the end, she was so concerned that she sent a letter direct to Martha asking for news.

Martha wrote back to say she was coming to Cardiff to do some last-minute special shopping for Christmas so why didn't they meet.

Sara was overjoyed. She could think and talk of nothing else.

'It's only a couple of weeks since you left Ponty, for God's sake,' Rhys said irritably when Sara told him she was planning to take a day off work so that she could spend it with Martha.

'I know, but it feels like a lifetime!'

'There'll be nothing new for you to talk about, *cariad*. What do you think can have happened in that short time?'

'Martha will be able to tell me how Myfanwy is. She's bound to be missing me. I'm worried about her, Rhys. She's still not much more than a baby and I feel I've betrayed her leaving her to the mercy of Gwladys and my Dada.'

'He's her Dada as well, for Christ's sake!'

'I know that, but Gwladys isn't her real mother.'

'Neither are you!'

'Not physically, perhaps, but I feel I am in every

other way. I've been the same as a mother to her ever since my Mam died. Myfanwy was only three months old when that happened, remember.'

'I know.' Rhys held her face between his hands and kissed her gently. 'You did a wonderful job, Sara. You've loved and cared for Myfanwy but you don't own her. They're her family as well, *cariad*.'

Sara shook her head sadly. 'You don't understand, Rhys. They're both so hard. You've met them, you could see that Gwladys has no heart, no softness about her, no real understanding of how a little child should be treated.'

'Your Dada will watch out for her. He's brought up a daughter before, remember!'

Sara shivered. She was fourteen again and back in Taff Court, lying in her Dada's bed, her eyes tight shut as she heard him undressing. Shivering because she knew only too well what was going to happen. Trembling as she felt his hard calloused hands touching her body. Quivering with fear as she tried to make her mind a blank and shut out the inevitable.

When Sara met Martha off the train at Cardiff Central station, the first thing she thought as she saw the plump familiar figure coming towards her was why hadn't she asked Martha to bring Myfanwy to Cardiff with her.

It was too late now, of course, she thought disconsolately as she greeted Martha with a warm hug and a kiss.

As they walked from Westgate Street towards St Mary Street Martha talked nineteen to the dozen about Myfanwy, relaying all the loving messages she had sent to her big sister.

'She's missing you, *cariad*,' Martha sighed. 'I talk to her as much as I can, but that old Gwladys hates it. If ever she catches us talking to each other then she always finds some reason why Myfanwy has to go back indoors.'

'Is she treating Myfanwy all right?' Sara asked worriedly.

Martha hesitated. 'Well, she keeps her spotlessly clean and I suppose she feeds her well enough but the poor little dab has such sore knees, red raw they are.'

'How does that come about?'

'All the praying, *cariad*. Kneeling on that old coconut matting praying. That's what does it. Harsh it is, see. Rubs the little mite's knees red raw.'

Sara frowned. 'And you say she's praying?'

'Well, praying and learning from the Bible, like.'

'Myfanwy can't read properly yet!'

'No, well, she doesn't have to, does she. That Gwladys makes her say the same text over and over again. Chanting it, see, so that it's drummed right into her head. Last week it was "The good Lord is watching over me", and the week before that, "I'm a little sinner but the Good Lord will forgive me".'

'That's terrible, Martha. How can such a little girl be a sinner?'

'Load of old rubbish if you ask me. I doubt if she even knows what the words mean. That Gwladys calls herself a teacher yet she's taken all Myfanwy's picture-books away from her and every night Gwladys tells her a Bible story. No fairy stories or tales about animals like you used to tell her, only Bible stories.'

Sarah shook her head. 'Poor little mite. Still, I suppose it could be worse. At least Gwladys is not ignoring her.'

'No, far from it. Might be better if she did. Obsessed with seeing she's always doing something so that she won't get into any mischief.'

'You mean cleaning and helping in the house?'

'Oh, there's always chores for the child to do but now she's teaching her to sew. Embroidering samplers with religious texts on them.'

'She's far too young to do that sort of thing!' Sara exclaimed.

'Of course she is,' Martha agreed. 'She stabs herself with the needle time and time again. If she gets any blood on the work she's doing then that old Gwladys carries on something alarming.'

'What about my Dada? Is he treating Myfanwy all right?' Sara asked tentatively.

'Dour, he is these days, *cariad*. Very down in the mouth. Talks of your evil ways, deserting your family, and that he hopes you will never darken his door again, but if you turned up tomorrow he'd welcome you with open arms and all would be forgiven.'

'Forgiven! I've done nothing wrong, Martha!'

'I know that, *cariad*. It would be a face-saver for him if he could say you came back home and he forgave you.'

Sara's face tightened. 'Maybe, but it's not going to happen, Martha. The only time I'll come back to Taff

Court will be to collect Myfanwy and bring her back here to Cardiff to live with me.'

'That's the sort of fighting talk I like to hear,' Martha smiled. 'So when do you expect it to be? The sooner the better, I'd say.'

Sara sighed. 'I wish I knew. Not yet awhile, I'm afraid.'

'Finding things hard down here in Cardiff, are you?' Martha asked shrewdly, studying Sara's shabby appearance. It was a bitterly cold day and she had wrapped herself up warmly with a thick scarf and woollen gloves, yet Sara had neither.

'Finding work hasn't been easy, leastwise not the sort of work either of us want to do,' Sara admitted. 'I wanted to work in a shop, but they all said I hadn't enough experience so I'm working in a factory. Rhys wanted a job as a baker, but the best he has been able to get is labouring at the dockside.'

'Never mind! It's early days, *cariad*. Once you've got a job you always hear of something better going, so don't get despondent. Anyway, we're going to enjoy ourselves today so let's start with a pot of tea at one of the cafés in Morgan's Arcade.'

It had been one of the best days of her life, Sara reflected, as she waved goodbye to Martha later. It had been wonderful to see her and catch up on all the news, even if some of it about Myfanwy wasn't to her liking; and she hadn't been able to bring herself to confide in Martha about the past or to tell her that she and Rhys still weren't married.

Seeing Martha had given her a chance, though, to send a pretty doll back as a present for her little sister and to know that it really would be given to Myfanwy.

'Tell you what, my lovely, why don't I keep it at my place for her to play with whenever she manages to come round,' Martha had suggested when they came out of the shop. 'If she takes it home the chances are that Gwladys won't let her have it. Or, worse still, she'll take it off her as a punishment every time she does some silly little thing wrong.'

Sara frowned. 'Won't Gwladys think it strange if she knows we've seen each other and I haven't sent anything back for Myfanwy, though?'

'That's a point,' Martha agreed. 'I tell you what, *cariad*, why don't you buy her some cheap little toy or other, something that it won't matter too much if Gwladys does confiscate it.'

'She'd probably love to have a whip and top, or a wooden hoop,' Sara suggested.

'Well,' Martha looked doubtful. 'She's not allowed to play out in the street, remember.'

'So that's out of the question!'

'It had better be something she can play with indoors,' Martha mused.

'What about a picture-book?'

Martha shook her head. 'Like I told you, that Gwladys takes them all off her.'

They searched for something they thought Gwladys would let her have and in the end decided on a knitting set. Two little wooden needles and several balls of brightly coloured wools all packaged in a box with a pretty picture on the top of it.

'It seems perfect to me,' Martha enthused. 'Even

Gwladys will have to admit it is practical and if she won't teach Myfanwy to knit then I will. Knitting will be far better for her than stabbing herself with a sewing needle all the time.'

'I wish I could be there to give her both her presents,' Sara said sadly.

'Well, don't you worry about it. I'll pack them both up in some pretty Christmassy paper and make sure she knows they are from you.'

'It would be so nice to see her little face when she unwraps them,' Sara said wistfully.

'By next Christmas you'll have her living with you, I'm sure,' Martha told her confidently.

Chapter Eighteen

As the newest casual labourer in the gang, Rhys found he was given all the dirtiest, messiest, smelliest jobs there were. The men he worked alongside were casual labourers like himself, but they were old hands and knew all the short cuts and scams. Most of them were also very light-fingered.

When they levered open a case, and extracted a couple of hands of bananas, or dropped a crate of oranges, accidentally on purpose, so that it burst open and they could pocket half a dozen each to take home for their kiddies, Rhys turned a blind eye. He told himself that since he wasn't involved it was best to mind his own business.

As Christmas itself approached the filching became more serious. Whisky, brandy, rum and cigarettes were targeted and this worried him. The loss of a few oranges was one thing; the loss of a dozen or more bottles of spirits was something else again.

Rhys tried to steer clear of what was happening. The rest of the men were afraid this was a sign that he would grass on them, and so they did everything they could to involve him.

The last boat they unloaded on Christmas Eve was carrying a very mixed cargo. There was both tobacco and spirits, and the men were determined to purloin whatever they could before the Customs men arrived.

'Bloody fools, if you get caught it will be the end of your job and what sort of a start will that be for the New Year?' Rhys said with some exasperation.

'We'll have enjoyed ourselves first, though, won't we, boyo?'

'Think about it, boyo, plenty to drink and smoke over the Christmas holiday, what more could you ask for?'

'A clear head and a clear conscience!'

'Christ, bloody secret Bible basher, are you?'

'No!' Rhys defended. 'I don't even go to church, but I don't want to end up blacklisted.'

'Is that right, brother?' A burly negro with knotted biceps took Rhys by the throat, and pinned him up against the bulwark. 'Are you saying you never take a bloody drink?'

Rhys tried to pull apart the thick fingers that held his throat in a vice-like grip. 'Of course I do,' he panted. 'I like a pint the same as the next man.'

'A pint?' His assailant looked round the faces of the crowd that had gathered to watch. 'This bugger likes a pint,' he grinned, 'so shall we give him one?'

There was a rumble of assent, and from somewhere one of the men in the crowd produced a bottle of whisky. Knocking the neck off it against the side of the boat he held the jagged opening to Rhys's mouth.

'Drink then, you asshole,' the negro ordered.

Rhys tried to turn his head away, but the bottle was so close to his mouth that the jagged edge ripped his lower lip open.

The coarse laughter from the crowd drowned his anguished scream of pain as the raw whisky ran into the deep cut.

'Sounds as though he bloody well enjoyed that,' his tormentor laughed. Releasing his hold on Rhys's throat he grabbed him by the hair and tipped his head back. 'More?'

Lifting the bottle high, he poured the fiery liquid down Rhys's throat in a continuous stream, shaking his victim's head from side to side each time Rhys gagged and gulped for air.

When the bottle was empty, the man tossed it overboard into the murky dock waters. Releasing his hold on Rhys he watched him slump to the deck, completely incapable.

'You can't bloody well leave him there, the gaffer will find him and know what's happened!' one of the others said anxiously.

'Throw him over the side then!'

'Drown the bugger?'

'Perhaps not. Stick him down in the hold until he comes round.'

When Rhys didn't arrive home from work that night, Sara became more and more annoyed. It was Christmas Eve, and she began to wonder if he had gone on a drinking spree. In the end she was so worried that she put on her hat and coat and went to look for him. First she tried the Torbay at the junction of Daisy Street and Margaret Street since it was nearest to home. He wasn't there so she went to the Hope and Anchor in Adelaide Street, knowing that was his favourite pub.

It was a cold dark night with scurries of snow

sweeping in off the Irish Sea. There were a lot of people about and she found herself jostled from one side of the pavement to the other.

Most of the people who were coming off the trams had been shopping in the city centre and were laden with bags and parcels. Sara envied them the gatherings they would be enjoying the next day, Christmas Day, with relatives or friends.

She thought of Myfanwy and the presents she had sent for her and hoped Martha would have a chance to see her on Christmas morning and give her the lovely doll. She'd tried over and over to persuade Rhys that they should go back to Pontypridd for a couple of days, but he would have none of it.

'Knowing your bloody father he'd find out that we aren't legally married even though we're living together, and then the fat would be in the fire.'

'How can he find out if we don't tell him?' Sara asked, puzzled.

'I don't know, but he's such a crafty bastard he's bound to ask you so many questions that you'll give the game away.'

'Then perhaps the best thing we can do is get married properly,' Sara snapped.

'Go through all that bloody questioning all over again? Grow up! What difference does a bit of paper make? I look after you and pay my way, don't I?' Rhys snarled.

'I know,' Sara sighed, 'but the sort of life we're leading isn't exactly what I imagined it would be like.'

'Life ain't all lovey-dovey and kisses and cuddles, you know,' Rhys told her.

'I've found that out for myself,' Sara smiled. She slipped her hand in his and squeezed it lovingly. Despite everything she hated it when they argued. 'You don't really regret it all, do you?'

'Not as long as you don't keep going on about us getting married. We live together, we sleep together, so what more do you want?'

Sara smiled, but said nothing. How could she explain that even though she wasn't religious like her father she still felt it was a sin simply to live together as they were doing? Every day she was afraid that Polly Price would find out they weren't married, that her ring was just a brass curtain ring, and tell them they must leave Daisy Street. Or that someone at the factory where she worked would guess the truth and she'd be the butt of their scorn and jokes.

She wondered if it was because she was a woman that it mattered so much to her. Rhys never seemed to give it a second thought. She sighed. Rhys had changed so much in the few months since they'd left Pontypridd that there were moments when she wondered if he was the same man.

He still looked the same. He was still so tall and handsome that at times her breath caught in her throat when she looked at him. Sometimes she had to pinch herself even to believe that he cared for her. It was his manner that had changed so drastically.

When he had worked for Betti Morgan he had been so happy and carefree; now he seemed to be bad-tempered and discontented most of the time.

He was constantly criticising her, and grumbling about Mrs Price and all her restrictions.

In the past she'd never heard him swear or say anything derogatory about anyone. Now, he cursed and swore freely, which she supposed was understandable considering the sort of men he was mixing with every day on the dockside.

Sara was prepared to accept all of that, and blame it on the way they were living, but it was the way he treated her nowadays that really upset her. At first, Rhys had been tender and thoughtful, and she had been happy to put the past behind her believing she had found true love at last. His loving words, and gentleness when they made love, had helped her to erase the harrowing memories of her father's assaults on her body. Now, though, he'd begun drinking more and more and after he'd been on one of his boozing bouts she hated him coming near her: he was so rough that after they'd made love she felt sore and bruised and dreaded him touching her.

She had tried to talk to him about it, but he didn't want to listen. He jeered at her prissiness. 'You don't expect all that love mush now that you're broken in, do you?' he'd say. 'That's the way I am, the way all men are, so you'd better get used to it.'

Sara bit her lip and kept silent. It was like being back with her Dada all over again. When she'd left home she thought she'd escaped from the indignity of being used whenever a man needed her body for his own lustful pleasure.

Was she to blame? Was it something about her that made men behave like this towards her? Perhaps Rhys would have more respect for her if they were married. But lately whenever she mentioned going back to the City Hall it seemed to start a row.

Or maybe it was fitting in with Polly Price's fanatical dictates that was causing the tension between them?

Sara couldn't use the kitchen in the morning before she went off to work because it was too early; in the evening when she got home from work it was too late.

On Sundays when they were all at home all day Polly Price insisted that Sara should make a casserole and leave it for her to put it in the oven. When it was ready, Polly would place it on the stairs, and shout upstairs to them to come down and collect it.

There was no table in their room so they were forced to sit on the edge of the bed and balance their food on their knees. Rhys hated this and often, halfway through his meal, he would slam down his plate and stomp out.

When he returned, often hours later, his walk would be unsteady and his breath reek of beer. Sara found that if she asked him where he'd been he would fly into a rage so she said nothing, even when he sprawled across the bed in a drunken sleep.

Christmas Eve, though, was different. When she found Rhys wasn't in the Hope and Anchor she instinctively felt there was something wrong but she had no idea where else to look for him.

'All his mates came in here tonight after they'd finished work,' Barbie Buckley, the landlady, told her. 'Boisterous, they all were. Think they must have been drinking before they left the dockside, or else they'd been given a Christmas bonus and made a few stops before they got here. Perhaps he's gone shopping to buy you a present,' she teased.

Sara smiled. She thought it highly unlikely, but she wasn't going to fuel any gossip if she could help it.

'The gaffer from his shift is over in that corner, want me to ask him if he knows where your Rhys is?'

Sara shook her head. 'No, don't bother,' she said quickly. She knew Rhys would be incensed if he even heard she'd been at the Hope and Anchor looking for him. If he ever found out she'd asked his boss where he was she dreaded to think what would happen.

Barbie Buckley was not to be put off. 'Jake,' she shouted across the crowded bar, 'any idea where young Rhys is tonight?'

'Who's asking?'

'Young woman, here. His wife!'

A hush fell on the crowded bar and Sara felt herself going scarlet as all eyes turned to look at her.

'You mean he's not come home?'

'Sleeping it off,' a voice sniggered loudly.

'Sleeping what off?' Jake rasped.

Again there was silence, but Jake was determined to get to the bottom of it. When he discovered what had happened to Rhys he was livid.

'You bloody fools!' he stormed. 'If one of the ship's officers finds him we're all for the sodding high jump. Go on, all of you, get back there and find him!'

He turned to Sara. 'Where do you live then, my lovely? Don't worry, we'll have him back home and tucked up in bed in next to no time.'

'Daisy Street, number three.'

'Right!' He turned back to the half-dozen men who had downed their beer and stood waiting for his orders. 'Off you go then, you silly buggers, and get him home in one piece. Understand?'

'Want me to see you home, Missus, and keep his bed warm till he gets there?' one of the men leered, putting his arm round Sara and pushing his face up close to hers.

As Sara shrank away there was the sound of fist meeting flesh, and the next moment the man was sprawling in the sawdust on the floor of the pub.

'Thank you!' Sara whispered as Jake wiped the blood from the back of his hand down the side of his trousers.

'Probably best if you let me walk back with you as far as the corner of Daisy Street, at any rate,' he said gruffly, picking up his glass and draining what was left in it in one gulp. 'There's plenty more buggers in here with the same idea.'

By the time they reached Daisy Street, Sara was so worried about what Polly Price would say if Rhys was brought home drunk that she insisted on waiting outside for him.

'Thank you for walking back with me,' she said shyly to Jake. 'I really am grateful.'

'Get along indoors then, you don't want to be out on your own in this area after dark,' he warned. 'You never know who's loitering down some of these dark alleyways.'

At that moment the men he had sent to collect Rhys appeared at the corner of the road. Two of them were propping Rhys up between them as though he was incapable of walking. Sara had never seen him so drunk. He wasn't boisterous or even aggressive. His face was a greenish grey and he was almost comatose. Sara wondered how she was ever going to get him up the stairs to their room.

As if sensing her problem, Jake stepped forward, hitched one of Rhys's arms around his neck and half carrying, half supporting him, walked towards her.

'Go on then, my lovely, you lead the way,' he said quietly.

Luck was on their side. Jake managed to lug Rhys upstairs, and plonk him down on the bed, without disturbing Mrs Price.

'Leave him to sleep it off,' Jake advised. 'He'll be like a bear with a sore head tomorrow, and he'll probably be off his food for a couple of days. Happy Christmas,' he grinned as he made his way out.

Christmas Day was the most miserable one Sara had ever known. Rhys either snored, or was sick, for the entire day. It took most of the next day as well for him to sober up completely, and all the time he was so bad-tempered that she was glad to go back to work.

Rhys refused to talk about what had happened. The only thing she could get out of him was that he didn't intend to work as a labourer on the dockside ever again.

'So what are you going to do then?' she asked worriedly.

'Find something else, of course!'

'You tried to find work as a baker when we first arrived in Cardiff, and there was nothing available,' she reminded him.

'Not here in Cardiff, but I can get a job as a ship's baker.'

'And leave me here on my own?' she gasped.

'It will only be for a couple of months. I'll be able to save all my pay, and then when I get back we can move out of this hell-hole to somewhere better.'

'But it's all right for me to stay in this hell-hole, as you call it, on my own?'

Rhys shrugged. 'There's no choice. It's the best I can do. You can either stay here or go back to Ponty.'

'You've already fixed it up, haven't you?' she asked suspiciously.

Rhys looked slightly shamefaced. 'Yes! I've signed on as ship's baker on the *SS Tasmania* this morning. We sail at the end of the week,' he admitted.

Sara stared at him, aghast. 'You've done that without even telling me?'

'I'm telling you now, aren't I,' he blustered, avoiding her eyes.

'So where will you be going, and how long will you be gone, or don't you know?'

He looked exasperated. 'Of course I know where I'm going. We're sailing to Australia.'

Sara stared at him in dismay. 'You said you'd be away for a couple of months. I didn't think you could sail to Australia and back in that time?'

'The round trip will probably take six or seven

months. Depends on how many stops we make on the way,' Rhys muttered.

'And you're going to leave me here all on my own for that long. You do know that it's not safe to walk in the streets around here after dark?'

He shrugged. 'The time will soon pass. Now we've got Christmas over, it won't be long before it's better weather and then it will be lighter at nights. Anyway, you never go out anywhere at night so what are you worrying about?'

'I don't go out because you never take me anywhere!' Sara exclaimed angrily. 'You are always at the Hope and Anchor boozing.'

'So? Nothing has changed then, has it? You'll probably never even notice I've gone!' He pulled her into his arms. 'Look at it this way, *cariad*, neither of us likes living here. You've got a job so you're out of the house for most of the day. Without me cluttering the room up when you get home from work it won't seem so bad. You'll be able to have it just as you want it. I'll be back home by the end of the summer with a mountain of money, and then we can move.'

'I'll be so lonely, Rhys,' Sara sniffed. 'It's not much fun working at Curran's, and I'll have no one to talk to in the evenings. Please don't go,' she pleaded.

'You can always make friends with some of the other girls,' he told her. 'Think about it, you'll be able to go off to the pictures as often as you like.'

'On my own?'

'Well, go with one of the girls from work. How

about that Chinese girl you talk about so much, she only lives a couple of streets away.'

'I don't want to go out with her, I want to come home at the end of the day and spend time with you,' Sara argued.

'Then you're going to be disappointed. If you don't want to stay on here in Cardiff then go back to Pontypridd. Betti will probably take you in if your father and Gwladys won't let you live with them.'

Sarah sighed. 'I'd like to do that for Myfanwy's sake,' she admitted, 'but I couldn't face all the gossip and recriminations. I'd feel such a failure. It wouldn't be so bad if you came back with me, Rhys.'

'That's out of the question,' he stated adamantly. 'I've already signed up as ship's baker, and we sail for Australia on Friday.'

Chapter Nineteen

Rhys had been away at sea for almost a month before Sara went to the doctor. At first she had thought that her general feeling of not being at all well was because she was pining for Rhys. Living in Cardiff on her own she felt desperately lonely most of the time. Her life had changed so drastically since she'd left Pontypridd that she felt unsettled and on edge. She'd hoped after Rhys had gone to sea that Polly Price would become more approachable and that perhaps they could be friends, but she remained as cool and distant as ever.

After the first couple of weeks, when her efforts to be friendly were rebuffed, Sara avoided Polly as much as possible. She hardly went into the kitchen. Instead of cooking herself a meal when she came home from work, or at the weekends, she lived on buns and chips and anything else that she could take up to her room to eat but which didn't need to be cooked.

She knew that such food wasn't very good for her, and it certainly didn't seem to be agreeing with her because she felt sick most mornings nowadays. She must be putting on weight, too, because her skirt was getting tighter around the waist, although with Rhys away that didn't really matter. It wasn't until her face became puffy that she wondered if there was something seriously wrong with her.

When the doctor questioned her and examined her and then told her she was at least three months' pregnant, she stared at him in disbelief.

'I can't be! Rhys has sailed for Australia, and he won't be back for at least six months!' she said in a shocked voice.

'Then you will have a nice little surprise waiting for him when he comes home,' the doctor smiled.

Sara stared at him blankly. How could he joke about such a matter when she was alone in Cardiff, and living in one room? The only people she really knew were her landlady, Polly Price, and Anna Wong, a Chinese girl she worked with and who lived two streets away.

Sara walked out of the doctor's surgery in a daze. How was she going to manage to live when she had to stop working? Rhys had made no plans to send her any money. He had promised to save every penny he earned so that when he came back they would be able to move, and find themselves a bigger better place to live.

If she wrote to him right away it would be several weeks before her letter reached him, and goodness knows how many more before she would receive his reply.

How long would she be able to go on working at Curran's, she wondered? The work was so heavy that they would probably sack her as soon as they saw she was pregnant in case she had a miscarriage.

For a brief moment she pondered on whether that was the answer. Conceal the fact that she was pregnant from everyone, go on working and then if she did have a miscarriage and there was no baby, all her problems would be solved.

How low was she sinking even to consider such a wicked thought? It was Rhys's baby she was carrying; she should be over the moon. Except that she had no idea if Rhys would be happy when he heard the news. He had never said he wanted children, but he must have known there was always that possibility, she told herself.

Rhys couldn't have given it any thought, she realised, or he would have insisted on them being married before he sailed. They still weren't man and wife, she thought uneasily, and that meant that their baby would be a bastard in other people's eyes as well as according to the law.

What would the people back home in Pontypridd think if they heard that? Even Betti, who had encouraged them to elope, would be horrified. She probably thought they were married now, anyway.

For a moment she felt a wave of relief that she hadn't confided in Martha about what had happened when they'd gone to the City Hall. It seemed so trivial to say they hadn't married because it had cost too much. That might have been true once but there had been plenty of time since then for them to put matters right.

As she walked home from the doctor, worrying every step of the way about the future, Sara kept asking herself that selfsame question over and over again. Why hadn't they got married? Why hadn't she insisted? Once she started work she herself could have found the money to do so. Was it because she'd been afraid that Rhys might refuse?

He loved her, he really did, she was quite sure. When he hadn't been drinking he was kind and tender and a wonderful lover. It was only when he'd had too much to drink that he became rough and uncouth.

He'd never once, in all the time they'd been together, ever said he regretted leaving Ponty and coming to Cardiff with her. Even when he'd been despondent because he'd been unable to find work, he'd never blamed her in any way.

No matter how black things had seemed in those early days before either of them had found work, they had found comfort in each other's arms.

She stopped abruptly on James Street Bridge and looked down into the swiftly flowing Taff. She wished she had the courage to jump off, let the grey swirling water claim her, and carry her right out into the Irish Sea.

Polly Price looked at Sara suspiciously as if she guessed that something was wrong the moment she walked in the house.

'You're home early. What's happened? Not stood you off at Curran's, have they?'

Sara shook her head. 'No, nothing like that. I've just had a bit of a shock, that's all.'

'Oh yes?' Curiosity got the better of Polly Price. 'You'd better sit down then, and I'll make us a cuppa while you tell me all about it.'

Sara slumped dejectedly into one of the hard-backed kitchen chairs and covered her face with her hands.

Polly looked at her shrewdly as she pushed the kettle over the glowing coals. 'You'd better tell me what's happened then,' she said as she collected cups and saucers from the sideboard and put them on the table.

Sara took a deep breath. 'I'm pregnant. Three months at least, possibly more.'

'*Duw anwyl*!' Polly looked both shocked and angry. 'What a fool you are, girl, to let that happen!' she exclaimed bitterly.

'It might even be born before Rhys gets back into port,' Sara added glumly.

'Have you thought of the consequences of being saddled with a little one? All the cost! And, above all, the mess. Filthy little beggars, babies are, there's no doubt at all about that!'

Polly was so irate in her condemnation of babies and children that for a brief minute Sara found herself smiling. Then the full impact of the seriousness of the situation was brought home to her when Polly said, 'There's only one thing for it, isn't there, and that's an abortion.'

Sara stared at her in disbelief, wondering if she had misheard what Polly had said. 'You mean get rid of it?'

'Of course!'

'I couldn't do that!'

'Well, what are you planning on doing then?' Polly asked as she poured boiling water into the teapot.

Sara shook her head wearily, her dark eyes full of doubt and uncertainty. 'I'm not sure,' she admitted. 'If only Rhys was here to advise me.'

'Well, he's not and from what you've told me it's unlikely he will be back before it's born. Get rid of it now and he need never even know a thing about it,'

Polly stated firmly as she poured out their tea. 'There's a woman in the next street who is a dab hand at that sort of thing. You'll have to hurry and make your mind up, though. She likes to get rid of them before you're too far gone.'

Sara looked shocked. 'I couldn't possibly do something like that. It's a human being, after all.'

'Rubbish. There's daft! It's not human until the day it's born.'

'Even so, I couldn't do it, Polly. Really, I couldn't. What would Rhys say?'

Polly Price looked cynical. 'What he doesn't know about needn't concern him,' she said pointedly.

'I've already written a letter telling him that I am pregnant, and the date when the baby is due. I'm hoping he'll be able to get home before it's born.'

'Then write him another letter and tell him it was all a mistake, a false alarm, and that you're back to normal. Or if that bothers you then you can always tell him you've had a miscarriage.'

Sara shook her head vehemently. 'No, it wouldn't be right.'

'Then you'd better make arrangements right away to go back home to Pontypridd, either to your family or to his, and let them look after you, hadn't you,' Polly told her crisply.

'I don't think I want to do that, either,' Sara said slowly as she sipped at her tea. 'No, I'll stay here and wait until Rhys comes back.'

Polly Price's mouth tightened.

Over the next couple of months it became obvious that Polly wasn't prepared to give houseroom to a new baby. Whenever she saw Sara she nagged her continuously to think about going back home.

Their arguments over this became more and more intense. When Sara came home and said she'd been stood off at Curran's because of her condition, Polly took a hard line.

'It was only to be expected, Sara, I did warn you. So how are you going to manage?'

'I've saved something each week from my pay packet, so I'll be able to cope for a while. Anyway, I might be lucky enough to get another job, something different where the work isn't so heavy.'

'Chance would be a fine thing,' Polly sniffed. 'More and more people are out of work, you know, and there seems to be no sign of any let-up.'

Three weeks later, when Sara had still not managed to find any other work, Polly delivered her ultimatum.

'Look here, Sara, I like you well enough, but I won't tolerate a baby around the place, so the best thing you can do is find yourself somewhere else to live or go back home to your own family in Pontypridd.'

Sara shook her head. 'I can't do that!' she said ruefully, a tremor in her voice.

'Why not? Doesn't your Mam like kids either?'

'My Mam died about five years ago. My Dada has married again.'

'And his new wife wouldn't have you living there with them? Lovely world, isn't it? Well, if your own folks won't take you in then you can hardly expect me to house you, can you? We're not even blood relations. You shouldn't have been so damn daft as to get yourself pregnant,' she added tartly.

Sara felt too upset to answer. She really had made a mess of things, she thought unhappily. She seemed to let everyone down. Rhys would be thinking that, like him, she was working and saving towards them getting a better place. Betti Morgan thought she and Rhys were happily married and making a life for themselves in Cardiff. And she had built up poor little Myfanwy's hopes that as soon as she and Rhys managed to get a home together she could come and live with them.

Her whole life seemed to her to be a mass of broken promises. How could she possibly have Rhys's baby and care for it and bring it up, as a mother should, when she couldn't even redeem the promise she had made to her own little sister?

Sara felt such a failure that, desperate to find someone to help her, she asked Anna Wong, the only other person in Cardiff she felt to be her friend, if there was any room at her place.

Anna looked at her blankly, her slanting dark eyes inscrutable. 'You are asking if you can live at my house?'

'It will only be for a few weeks, until I can find somewhere permanent,' Sara said quickly.

'What is wrong with your room in Daisy Street?'

Sara told her about Polly's objections to her having a baby there.

Anna shook her head. 'That would also present a problem with my family. I have many brothers and sisters. Our house is small. We sleep three and four to a bedroom. They all work right round the clock in my father's emporium, and they sleep at all kinds of hours. A crying baby would not be welcome in our house.'

Sara sobbed herself to sleep. If only Rhys had been able to find a job as a baker in Cardiff. If only his first trip hadn't taken him to Australia, so far away that it would be at least six months before he was back home again, she railed.

Next morning, exhausted and feeling decidedly unwell, she knew she had to take some positive action. Polly was becoming more and more hostile. Sara suspected that if she didn't find somewhere soon Polly would be putting her few belongings out in the street and locking the front door so that she couldn't get back in.

She considered going to Betti Morgan. Betti had been so very understanding about them taking off suddenly and leaving her in the lurch. When they'd arrived in Cardiff, though, Betti had written to Rhys telling him that she wasn't sure if she'd been right to encourage them to do so. Running away as they'd done had made people talk.

'Some people think you had to leave because you'd got Sara into trouble,' she'd written. 'I think it was Gwladys who started the rumour.'

Rhys had laughed about it but Sara had felt really upset. Betti had been so kind to her that she'd wanted to go and see her right away and reassure her that it didn't matter what Gwladys or anyone else had said about them, but Rhys refused to do so.

Now, though, if she did go back to Ponty, alone and pregnant, it would only give strength to those rumours. No, Sara decided, she couldn't do that and no matter what happened to her she'd never go crawling back to Taff Court. Which left only one other alternative, Rhys's family in Tonypandy.

She debated with herself all day as to whether she should go and see them, or if she ought to write to them first and ask if they would help her.

In the end she decided to compose a letter. If Rhys's parents didn't want to help her then it would be easier for all concerned if they wrote back and said so. If she went there, and they turned her away, she would feel even more miserable and defeated than she did now.

It took her a long time to write a suitable letter. She didn't want to grovel for help, but she didn't want to antagonise them in any way either. She explained about Rhys taking a job as a ship's baker because he was unable to find any suitable work in Cardiff. She stressed the fact that she hadn't realised she was pregnant until after he had sailed.

Although they were not as strict about religion as her father was, Rhys had said that his parents did attend chapel regularly and upbraided him because he never did.

Sara wondered what Lloyd and Olwen Edwards's reaction would be if they knew that not only had she and Rhys been living in sin, but they were also bringing a child into the world who would be regarded as a bastard.

After a great deal of soul-searching, Sara decided not to tell them that she and Rhys were not legally man and wife. She'd leave that for Rhys to do when he came home. Or perhaps when he came ashore the two of them could sneak off and get married without anyone else knowing anything about it.

Chapter Twenty

Olwen and Lloyd Edwards took so long to reply to her letter that Sara began to think they weren't going to write back at all. Whenever she caught sight of her reflection and saw how ungainly she had become, or felt the child inside her moving, she felt a sense of panic because time was defeating her.

Polly Price was almost as frosty as the March weather so Sara spent a lot of her time in bed, huddled under the blankets, trying to keep warm and worrying her heart out about her promise to Myfanwy and her own future.

Martha Pritchard had written to her shortly after Christmas to say how delighted Myfanwy had been with the lovely doll and that she was calling it Sara. She'd enclosed a drawing Myfanwy had done at school with coloured pencils, showing the doll wearing a brightly striped woollen scarf that Martha said Myfanwy was struggling to make from the knitting set Sara had also sent her.

Martha hadn't said very much about how Myfanwy was, or whether she was happy at school. Martha had been too full of her own problems. Her father had died and so her mother had been given notice to quit the terraced house she'd lived in since the day she first got married. The pit owners wanted her out right away because they needed the house for another employee.

Since her mother had no money and nowhere else to go but the street, Martha had been forced to offer her a home and so now she was living with them.

The news depressed Sara. Even though she'd already resolved that she wouldn't go back to Pontypridd and that staying next door to Ifor and Gwladys had never been an option, it was one less person to turn to if she was desperate.

Some days Sara felt so ill that she wondered if she should go and see the doctor again, but the thought of spending money unnecessarily when she had so little of it, and her future was so uncertain, made her put it off.

When the letter from Lloyd and Olwen Edwards eventually arrived it was couched in such restrained terms that Sara could hardly read it for crying.

Olwen Edwards made it quite plain that she held Sara responsible for Rhys going away to sea, and for taking him away from them. She agreed to her visiting them, but made it quite clear that it was only to talk about the possibility of her staying with them until after the baby was born.

She doesn't really want me there, Sara thought bitterly. She's not even said she's pleased at the prospect of having another grandchild.

Yet what alternative did she have but to go and see them and find out if they would help her? Her savings were almost gone, and in her condition there was no way she could find a job. Anyway, she thought morosely, even if she could afford to pay the rent for her room in Daisy Street, Polly Price had made it quite clear that she wanted her out before the baby arrived.

It was a sunny day in early April when Sara finally set out for Tonypandy. At the very last minute she wondered whether perhaps it would be better if she went to Pontypridd first to see if she was welcome there. It would be an ideal opportunity to see Myfanwy.

Letters from Martha were all very well, but it wasn't the same as seeing her little sister for herself. For a moment she even contemplated asking her father if he would help her. After all, he was her own flesh and blood whereas Olwen and Lloyd Edwards were complete strangers and not even related to her.

She went hot and cold at the thought of their reaction if they ever discovered the truth, that she was not even legally their daughter-in-law.

I'm simply being a coward, she told herself as she left Daisy Street. At least Olwen and Lloyd know I'm pregnant, but I've still got to break the news to Dada and Gwladys.

Olwen didn't kiss Sara or show any kind of pleasure in meeting her. Sara noticed, though, that she was wearing a very smart dress and had even put on a pearl necklace and matching earrings as if she felt that their first meeting was important.

'You decided to come then,' she said, speculatively eyeing Sara's bulging shape under her shabby dress. 'So when's it due?'

'I'm not sure of the actual date,' Sara puffed, leaning against the doorpost.

Olwen patted her newly marcelled blonde hair

and sniffed disparagingly. 'You'd better come in and sit down, I suppose. You look all in.'

'I get short of breath very easily,' Sara gasped. 'Could I have a glass of water, please?'

'Water?' Olwen looked annoyed. 'Yes, I suppose so. I'll be making a pot of tea for us as soon as the kettle boils. Can't you wait?'

Sara shook her head, fighting for her breath.

Grudgingly, Olwen filled a glass from the kitchen tap and handed it to her. 'Here you are then.'

She waited until Sara had gulped down most of it, then snapped, 'When's our Rhys coming back?'

'He said he'd be away about six months. It depends on how many stops the ship makes on its return journey.'

Olwen's mouth tightened. 'Will he be back before the baba is born?'

'I'm not sure,' Sara smiled wanly. 'I certainly hope so!'

'Are you still living in that one-room place in Cardiff docks, then?' Olwen frowned.

'I am at the moment, but not for very much longer.'

'Oh, and why is that then?' Olwen's eyes sharpened.

Sara shrugged helplessly. 'Polly Price has told me to go. She doesn't like the idea of there being a baby in the place. Much too messy for her.'

'Well, I'm with her on that one.'

'I won't be able to stay there for more than another week anyway, my money has run out.'

'Huh! Been living it up, have you, girl, since our Rhys has been away?'

Tears welled up into Sara's eyes. 'No, nothing like that. I was turfed out of my job at Curran's when they saw I was pregnant, and I haven't managed to get a new job since then so I've been living on the few pounds I'd managed to save up.'

'Oh yes? And what about the money our Rhys sends you?' Olwen asked sharply.

'He doesn't send any money home. We agreed that he'd save every penny he earned on this trip so that when he came back we could move to somewhere a bit better.'

'Are you telling me that he left you in the family way with no money?' Mrs Edwards sounded sceptical. 'I can't believe my Rhys would do a thing like that!'

Sara's shoulders slumped. 'He didn't know I was expecting.'

Olwen Edwards looked her up and down, fingering her pearls as if they were worry beads. 'And when did you say he sailed? How far gone are you now?'

Wearily Sara went over all the dates once again, but she could see that Mrs Edwards still seemed to be puzzled.

'So you were expecting before he sailed! And you didn't tell him?' Her lip curled. 'Funny sort of carry-on if you ask me. What do you want us to do about it?' she asked as she stood up to make the tea.

Sara bit her lower lip to stop it trembling. 'I was hoping that perhaps I could stay here with you until after the baby was born.'

'*Duw anwyl*! You're asking a lot, girl.'

She spooned tea into a big brown pot and poured

the water on to it. 'I've already brought up one family, I don't want my life and home cluttered up with another!'

'It will only be for a few weeks, Mrs Edwards. Once Rhys comes home we'll be able to sort ourselves out.'

'You're sure he's coming back to you, then?'

'Of course he is! We haven't quarrelled or anything. It was just that he couldn't find any work in Cardiff as a baker, and this chance of a job on a ship came up so he grabbed it.'

Olwen Edwards poured out the tea and pushed a cup across to Sara. 'Drink that while I have a bit of a think.'

The silence seemed ominous. Sara was afraid to look at Rhys's mother for fear of what she might read on her face.

Finally, unable to stay quiet any longer, Sara blurted, 'You don't seem very pleased about having a new grandchild?'

'Pleased?' Olwen Edwards bristled. 'I've got eight of them already so what difference does one more make? I certainly don't like the idea of our Rhys being saddled like this before you've got a proper home together. Not a stick of furniture between you!'

'We'll be sorting all that out, see, when Rhys gets back,' Sara told her quickly. 'He'll have the money to do it then.'

'Not even a roof over your heads,' Olwen Edwards went on implacably as if Sara had never spoken. 'What has your own father got to say about all this?'

'He doesn't know. I haven't told him yet.'

Olwen's eyebrows lifted in surprise. 'Not told him! You're nearly eight months gone, girl!' she shrieked.

Sara went red. 'He's remarried, see, so I don't think they'd want me there.'

'So you come to us instead,' Olwen sniffed.

Awkwardly Sara stood up, finding it difficult because of her bulk to move her chair back far enough from the table in the overcrowded room. 'I know when I'm not wanted, Mrs Edwards, so I'll be on my way. Thanks for the tea.'

Olwen flushed. 'Stop being so tetchy, girl. Sit back down, and let's thrash this out between us,' she said briskly. 'You know how I feel about having a baby in the house. So now that's out in the open let's see what we can do about the mess you're in.'

Sara squared her shoulders and looked Olwen in the face. 'You don't have to inconvenience yourself, I'll manage.'

'*Darw*! You're a stubborn girl! Let's hope the baby takes after our Rhys, not you!' Olwen Edwards snapped. 'Wait until Lloyd gets home, and then perhaps we can sort something out between the three of us, see.'

Sara dreaded the thought of having to tell her story all over again, but she found that telling Lloyd Edwards was surprisingly easy. He was such a kindly man, and with his sharp blue eyes and warm smile he reminded her very much of Rhys.

Rhys would probably look like him when he was older, when he, too, was turning grey and his hair receding and when, perhaps, he had a grizzled moustache like Lloyd.

She hoped he would never have a cough like Lloyd, though. Lloyd blamed it on the coal dust. 'Gets in the old lungs, see,' he told her after one of his distressing bouts of coughing that had him gasping for breath and brought the tears to his blue eyes.

Lloyd was sympathetic, and far more conciliatory than Olwen. 'Shame you didn't know about the baby before our Rhys went off,' he murmured. 'If you had then he might have been able to get a boat doing some short trip, and be home again in next to no time.'

'It was a chance in a million getting a job on this ship so I don't think he would have turned it down,' Sara told him. 'He couldn't find a baker's job in Cardiff for love or money. Cutting back everywhere, see, so there's not that many jobs going.'

'You mean he was out of work?'

'No, not all the time. He had a job labouring on the dockside. Hard work it was, mind, but he stuck at it until he heard about this job as a ship's baker.'

'He should have stayed in Tonypandy and gone down the pit like we all wanted him to do,' Olwen interrupted.

Sara was aware that Lloyd was looking at her keenly as if he sensed that she was only telling him half the story. She didn't think, though, that there was any point in worrying them still more by telling them about the drunken episode at Christmas time.

'So have you written to Rhys to tell him about the baba?'

'Yes. I wrote him a letter as soon as I'd seen a doctor and I knew for sure.'

'And he's not written back?'

Sara smiled at the surprise in Lloyd's voice. 'I don't even know when he'll get it. Perhaps not for months. Even if he answers right away he may be home before I receive his letter. Australia's the other side of the world.'

'Six months he said he'd be away?'

'That was what he was told, but he said there was every possibility it might be longer. A lot depends on how many stops the boat makes on its way back,' she told Lloyd as she had Olwen.

'*Duw anwyl*! What a silly old mess. Still, never you mind, you did the right thing in coming to us, didn't she, Olwen? We'll take care of you, my lovely, until our Rhys gets back,' he assured her. 'Collect your things from Cardiff, then, and move in with us as soon as you like. Olwen will have our Rhys's room ready for you, won't you, *cariad*?'

Olwen sniffed disparagingly. 'Have you thought about this properly, Lloyd?' she asked her husband sharply. 'A new baba is a lot of hard work, you know. Not to mention all the crying and disturbed nights.'

'A few nights' inconvenience, and then Sara will be strong enough to look after the baby herself, so it won't disturb us one jot. You'll probably never hear it,' he chuckled. 'Olwen sleeps like a log, Sara! Even my old cough doesn't disturb her!'

His jovial acceptance of the situation heartened Sara. She thanked them both for their kindness, and asked if it would be all right if she came back the next day.

'No need to rush yourself, is there?' Olwen asked, as if hoping to put off the evil moment.

'Whenever you're ready,' Lloyd told her. 'Take your time, my lovely. We're not going anywhere so we'll be here, ready and waiting, whenever you turn up. Can you manage on your own or do you need one of us to come down to Cardiff to help you bring your stuff back up here?'

'No, I can manage fine. I've only the one suitcase, and everything will go into it,' Sara smiled confidently.

When she returned two days later she was so exhausted that she could barely stagger through their front door.

'Too much for you with that case,' Lloyd scolded. 'I knew I should have come down to Cardiff to help you.'

'Go to Cardiff indeed!' Olwen said scathingly. 'The last time you went there you got lost and that was in the centre of the city! How do you think you would manage to find your way around Tiger Bay? You wouldn't be safe there, for one thing.'

'Then if it's all that wicked down there it's a good job Sara is safe here with us. Now let's get some food and a hot drink inside her before she passes out.'

The food and hot drink did very little to make Sara feel any better. Every few minutes she doubled over with stomach cramps, and when those eased off her back was aching so much that she couldn't sit up straight.

Olwen looked worried. As the stomach cramps gripped Sara again she told Lloyd to go up the street and fetch Nerys Palmer. 'Put her in the picture so that she comes prepared, and tell to be as quick as she can.'

'You mean you think the baby's coming?' he challenged.

'Either that or she's about to miscarry. Get on with you then, mun! Don't stand there gawping with your mouth open like a fish!'

She turned to Sara. 'As for you,' she said curtly, 'you'd better get yourself upstairs. I'll come with you and cover up the bed with some newspapers and old blankets so that you don't ruin it for me.'

'I'm sorry to be such a nuisance,' Sara gasped. She felt frightened; the pain seemed to rack her body from top to bottom leaving her utterly exhausted.

'I wish Mam was still alive and was with me now,' Sara whimpered, as she was gripped by another onslaught of pain.

'Yes, well, it's too late to be thinking like that. What's done is done and we've got to make the best of a bad job. Come on then, girl, get up the stairs before the pain gets so bad you can't make it.'

Although she spoke sharply, Olwen's mood softened considerably as she saw the discomfort Sara was enduring. She'd borne four children herself and she had helped all three of her daughters when their babies had been born, and could understand the pain and anxiety Sara was going through.

'Come on then, up those stairs, and let's get the whole thing over as quickly as we can,' she murmured encouragingly. 'Another couple of hours and you'll be nursing your baba, think of that.'

'I won't be able to stand this agony for another couple of hours,' Sara told her as perspiration dripped from her forehead.

'Of course you will!' Olwen said brusquely. 'And once it's all over, and you're holding your baba in your arms, you'll forget all about the pain. Believe me, I know what I'm talking about so come on now, and stop making such a fuss.'

Chapter Twenty-one

Averyl Edwards was born on 15 April 1930. A small puny baby, premature and only a little over four pounds in weight, she gave some cause for concern.

The minute she was born Nerys Palmer handed her to Olwen. 'You look after this little scrap, and I'll do what I can for the mother. Fair exhausted, she is, and bone thin. You want to tell that Rhys of yours to see she eats more. Out of work, is he?'

'No, not at all,' Olwen said sharply. 'He's been at sea for the last four months. He's working as a baker on board ship. Probably being on her own she's not taken proper care of herself.'

'Where's Rhys gone then?'

'Australia!'

Nerys chuckled. 'Well, there's not much chance of getting the news through to him if he's that far away. This will be a nice surprise for him when he gets back, and no mistake.'

Sara made a very slow recovery. There were times when she felt so weak and listless that all she wanted to do was sit in a chair by the fire, staring into its glowing heart, lost in a world of her own.

She kept wishing she had gone back to Pontypridd to see Martha and Myfanwy, and made her peace with Betti Morgan, before Averyl had been born.

Myfanwy weighed heavily on her mind. She'd had no news of her for months now and she knew it was her fault for not going to Ponty to see her. Martha had stopped writing since her mother had moved in with her. In her last letter she'd explained that her mother was not at all well and so she found all her time taken up with caring for her.

'Going dotty, she is,' Martha had written. 'Moving to Ponty hasn't been good for her. Half the time she doesn't know where she is. She wanders off and gets lost if I don't keep an eye on her. Talks a load of rubbish, too, most of the time. Always on about when she was a young girl, yet she can't even remember to wash her face when she gets up in the morning. She constantly loses things, or else hides them away under her bed or beneath her pillow. Some days I'm so vexed with her that I rue the day she ever moved in here.'

Sara was ashamed that she hadn't written back. Each day she'd intended to do so. Somehow she would have to tell Martha and her Dada and Gwladys about the baby, but whenever she thought about it the tears would stream down her cheeks, and then, when she went to bed, there would be terrible nightmares.

Curled into a ball, her heart thudding against her ribs, she would find herself waiting with bated breath for the sound of her father's footsteps, fearful of what would happen next. Next morning she would be filled with morbid thoughts about Myfanwy, afraid that she, too, might be in danger.

There were times when Olwen despaired of her gloomy despondent manner. 'Come on, girl,' she would say sharply, 'stir yourself, this babby of yours needs seeing to.'

Sara fed Averyl whenever Olwen handed the baby to her, but it was an automatic reaction without any of the love and enjoyment for the task that most new mothers express. Afterwards Olwen would change Averyl's nappy and settle her back into her crib to sleep.

The crib and its little sheets and blankets, like the napkins and baby clothes Averyl was dressed in, were all ones that Olwen had borrowed from her own daughters.

'You mean she hadn't anything at all ready for the baba, our Mam? Not even a shawl to wrap it in?' Mari, her eldest daughter, exclaimed in surprise.

Mari was a younger version of Olwen with shoulder-length fair hair, flaring eyebrows, deep-set hazel eyes and pale complexion. She had her father's generous mouth, though, and she was taller than her mother, and had a trim figure despite having had three children.

'Not a thing! There was nothing in the suitcase she brought with her from Cardiff except a few shabby bits of her own. If they were mine I'd be using them as cleaning rags, they were so worn out.'

'*Darw*! The girl must be mad or something. You start putting things together in readiness the moment you know you are caught. Leastwise, I do,' she grinned.

'She said she had no money to do that because she needed every penny she'd saved to live on, see!'

'Waiting for our Rhys to get back and buy everything, I suppose,' Mari sniffed. 'I've heard about these Cardiff girls. Take a man for all he's got if they can.'

'Sara's not a Cardiff girl, she's from Pontypridd. Worked in your Aunt Betti's cake shop. The one where our Rhys was the baker.'

Although all three of Olwen's daughters tried to talk to Sara when they called to see the new baby, she had very little to say to them. She seemed to be too weak to care about what went on around her, or the fact that Olwen was looking after the baby.

Even the family celebrations in May for Olwen's birthday seemed to pass over her head. She wouldn't have joined in at all if Lloyd hadn't persuaded her to do so.

'This is no way to spend your life, my lovely,' he cajoled. 'Come on, enjoy yourself with the rest of the family.'

Averyl was two months old when Rhys came home. He turned up quite late one suffocatingly hot evening in June. He had been so surprised when he knocked on the door in Daisy Street, and Polly Price told him that Sara had gone to live with his family, that he hadn't even asked her why.

That shock was mild compared to the one he got when he arrived home in Tonypandy, and found that not only had Sara been there for two months, but that here was a two-month-old baby as well.

His arrival acted like a tonic on Sara. It was as if it gave her something to live for. Her lethargy vanished almost overnight, and she was suddenly full of life, and anxious to help with the baby.

'Best leave her to me, girl,' Olwen told her time after time. 'You're still not very strong, so save your energy, and get as much rest as you can or you'll be running short of milk. You feed her and then pass her back to me, and I'll see to her after that. More used to me handling her than you, see, so she'll settle better.'

'But I want to do things for her,' Sara would protest.

'Spend your time with your husband, girl. He'll be going back to sea again soon, and then you'll be on your own again.'

'Rhys, will you try and explain to your mother that I'll have to look after Averyl when we get a place of our own,' Sara pleaded time and again but Rhys only shrugged, or pulled her into his arms and began making love to her.

Much as she loved him, Sara found his sanguine acceptance of the situation maddening. She wanted for them to have a place of their own, not to go on living as they were. Their bedroom was the one Rhys had used when he lived at home and it was so cramped that there wasn't room for Averyl's crib, and so Olwen had it in her bedroom. Rhys's old bed was too small for comfort with the two of them in it, and she was afraid to speak above a whisper in case Olwen could hear what she said. Lloyd's coughing was so loud that they might have been in the same bedroom.

Aided and abetted by his mother, Rhys became adept at evading the issue. Whenever his father was around his mother would suggest that the two of them went down to the Miners Club for a drink.

'Fine by me,' Lloyd would agree, 'but wouldn't

you sooner spend the time with your wife and baba?'

'We're only going for an hour,' Rhys would say. 'I think Mam wants us out of their way while they're fussing around with the baby, see.'

When Rhys announced that he would be off on another trip in a matter of a couple of weeks, Sara looked at him in dismay, her eyes filling with tears of frustration.

'We'd better start looking for our own place right away then? I'd like to be settled in before you leave,' she said anxiously.

'We'll start looking when I get back,' he promised.

Sara shook her head. 'I can't stay here for ever, it's not fair on your Mam. Anyway, I want my own place.'

'Don't worry about it, this time I'm going to America so I'll only be away for about six weeks,' he said placatingly.

'Then we'd better start looking now. That will give me time to get used to living in our new place, and looking after the baby on my own,' Sara said stubbornly.

Rhys had agreed reluctantly but their plans were brought to an abrupt stop at the end of the week when Lloyd arrived home early, his face ashen.

'Hello, and what's wrong with you then, boyo?' Olwen asked with concern. 'You look as though you've had the fright of your life.'

'Worse than that, *cariad*,' he told her between bouts of noisy coughing. 'I've been stood off.'

'You're already on short time so how can you be one of the ones to be stood off?' she asked angrily.

'Pit boss said I wasn't fit enough for the job. This cough of mine, see.'

'You shouldn't have told the buggers about it,' Olwen railed.

'Tell them! I didn't tell them, they can bloody well hear me hacking and hawking.'

'All miners have a cough, so why pick on you?'

'The others don't bring their sodding lungs up each time they bloody cough, that's why,' he told her bitterly.

'So you're back on the dole again, are you?'

'No, not enough stamps on my card since the last time I was off,' he said dispiritedly.

Olwen turned pale. 'What are we going to do when our bit of savings are gone? Then it will be the means test for us.'

'Bugger that! I'd rather starve,' Lloyd said fervently.

They talked of nothing else that night. Rhys could see that it wasn't helping his father's condition. Each time he coughed it was more rasping, more violent, than the time before. Even more worrying was the fact that he was bringing up blood as well as phlegm.

Rhys made a sudden decision. He knew he should have talked it through with Sara first, but he was sure she'd appreciate the predicament he found himself in.

The relief on his father's face when he told him what he intended to do convinced Rhys that he was doing the right thing and that Sara would understand when he explained everything to her.

'All right if we tell your Mam, boyo? Worried out of her mind, she is, see.'

'Well, since it depends on her being willing to have Sara and the baby here for a while longer, hadn't we better ask her, not tell her?' Rhys suggested diplomatically.

'Of course she'll want them to stay! Between you and me, boyo, it's given her a new lease of life. Like a spring chicken, she is, with that baba to look after. In her element, see.'

Sara was anything but pleased when Rhys took her to one side and said, 'Look, *cariad*, I think it would be better if we waited for a place of our own until after I get back from America.'

Her face clouded. 'I don't understand?'

'The thing is, Sara, I haven't been able to save as much as I thought I would, see. Anyway, I'm handing over what I have saved to Mam to help them out now my Da has lost his job.'

'You're doing what?' Her dark eyes widened with shock and disappointment.

Rhys held her close. 'I'd have had to hand over half of the money I've saved to them anyway to cover for the time you've been living here. My Da's been on short time for months so I can't expect them to keep you for nothing, *cariad*!'

'Oh, Rhys. I know they've been very good having me and Averyl here and looking after us so well, but I was so looking forward to having a place of my own. As long as I'm living here I have to do things the way your Mam wants them done. She's practically taken over our Averyl. She won't even let me give her a bath.'

'She's only trying to help. She's probably afraid you might drop her, she's such a little mite!' he grinned. 'Another six weeks, Sara, that's all I'm asking.'

'If you haven't enough money for us to move now, after a six-months' trip, then how will you be able to afford it after one of a mere six weeks?' she asked, looking puzzled.

'Don't worry about it, *cariad*. I'll sort things out.' He pulled her into his arms, kissing her, and holding her so tight she could hardly breathe. 'I'll be a lot happier knowing you are living here, with my Mam and Da keeping an eye on you and the baba, than I would be if you were living heaven knows where in some stranger's house.'

'It's not fair, though, Rhys. I want us to have a life of our own.'

'And so you shall, *cariad*. As soon as I get back from America we'll look for a place.'

'Do you mean here in Tonypandy?'

'If that's what you want.'

Sara shook her head. 'No, I want us to be on our own. If we stay here then your Mam will be visiting us every day and telling me what I should and should not be doing for Averyl. I know what to do, I brought Myfanwy up, didn't I!'

'Mam's only trying to be helpful,' Rhys said lamely.

'I know that. I understand that she wants the best for Averyl but it's interfering and I don't like it.'

'Then we'll go back to Cardiff and find somewhere there, unless you want to go back to Ponty. It doesn't matter much to me where our home is if I am away at sea.'

'Well, it does to me,' Sara argued. 'I want a proper home this time so that once we are settled in I can have Myfanwy to live with us. I did promise her she could,' she defended when she saw the expression on Rhys's face.

'Yes, I know you did but that was a long time ago. She must have friends at school now so she won't want to leave Ponty.'

Sara shook her head. She was only too aware that Myfanwy was growing up and that made it all the more important that she should take her away from Taff Court as soon as possible. She was tempted to explain the reason to Rhys but the moment passed before she could gather up the courage to do so.

'If you don't like living here with my parents then why didn't you stay on at Polly Price's place in Daisy Street?' he asked, puzzled.

'She wanted me out when she knew I was expecting. She doesn't like kids, especially babies. Said they were messy, smelly little things that disrupted the whole house.'

'Well, she got that one right,' Rhys grinned.

Sara looked affronted. 'Don't you like her either?' she said in a hurt voice.

'Like her? I don't just like her, I love her! Almost as much as I love her mother! That's why I want the best for her. I don't want us moving from one dingy room to the next. I want a proper home with a living room, bedroom and somewhere to do the cooking.

I've always wanted that for us, but it's more important than ever now we've got Averyl.'

Reluctantly Sara capitulated. 'Six weeks then, you promise?'

'Six weeks to the day, *cariad*. Get the flags ready to put out!'

Chapter Twenty-two

The next six weeks were some of the longest Sara had ever known. She wrote down the dates on a piece of paper, and crossed each one off, and when it came to the final day Sara could hardly contain her excitement.

All day she watched from the window, or from the front door, waiting to see Rhys turn the corner. She was afraid to go anywhere, even to the corner shop, in case he arrived home and she wasn't there.

She checked and re-checked to make sure she hadn't missed out a day when she'd been crossing out, but every one of the forty-two days were there, every one of them neatly scored through as they'd occurred.

By nine o'clock in the evening, and time for Averyl's last feed, the anxiety was making Sara feel quite ill. After she'd handed the baby back to Olwen to settle for the night, she had an irrational sense of impending disaster.

She stayed downstairs long after Olwen and Lloyd had gone to bed, listening to every footfall, waiting with ears strained for a tap on the door. Finally, so tired she could hardly keep her eyes open, she crept upstairs to bed, and cried herself to sleep.

It was three months before Rhys came home. Sara

was in a perpetual state of tension in case something dreadful had happened to him. Olwen and Lloyd were worried that the money he had given them would run out before he came back. Tempers became strained, and there were harsh words on both sides.

Sara was becoming increasingly annoyed by the way Olwen insisted on being the one to do everything for Averyl.

'Poor little mite, the way things are going she won't know which one of us is her Mam,' Sara told Olwen crossly.

'There's daft you talk,' Olwen said sharply. 'She knows I'm her Nan, and that it's her Nan that looks after her, and does everything for her. Her Mam's just there for her when she needs feeding, and that won't be for much longer, not now we've got the little pet started on proper food.'

It was mid-morning on a sunny day in late September when Rhys finally arrived home. Averyl was in her pram in a shady corner of the small back yard, and Olwen was gently rocking it to try and get her off to sleep. Sara was pegging out washing. Both women stopped what they were doing, and with exclamations of surprise rushed to greet him. He dropped his kitbag on the ground and put an arm round both of them at once, hugging them to him, and kissing them alternately.

'Are neither of you two housewives going to offer a poor sailor a cuppa then?' he joked.

'Go and put the kettle on, Sara,' Olwen ordered.

Disturbed by all the commotion, Averyl began to

grizzle, and Sara went over to the pram to try and pacify her.

'I'll see to the baba, you go and put the kettle on,' Olwen said firmly. 'No point in shushing her off to sleep again now, Rhys will want to see her.' She picked Averyl up and held her in her arms. 'And you want to see your Dada, don't you my little lamb.'

Tears stinging her eyes, Sara went indoors to make the tea. It was three months since she had seen Rhys, and she felt hurt and disappointed that he hadn't asked his mother to make the tea so that they could be alone together for a few minutes.

Hastily she dried her eyes on the edge of her apron as she heard steps behind her. Before she could turn round his arms were about her waist, pulling her body back against the hardness of his own. With his face buried in her hair he murmured how much he'd missed her.

She wriggled round to face him. She wanted to see if he looked any different after their long separation. She wanted to feel the warmth of his lips on hers, not on the back of her neck.

He was still as good-looking as ever, she decided as she ran her fingers though his dark curly hair and traced the outline of his firm jaw and sensitive mouth with her forefinger.

They clung to each other again; their mouths locked in a deep, passionate kiss. Her relief that he was home at last made her feel so weak that she was sure that if he wasn't holding her so tightly she would collapse in a heap on the floor.

'I've some good news for you,' he whispered.

'I've found somewhere for us to live. We can leave here tomorrow, or the next day.'

Sara pulled back and stared at him in disbelief. It was as if all her dreams were coming true at once. Rhys home, and now a place of their own.

'Where is it?'

'Cardiff! Not down at the docks, though,' he went on quickly as he saw her face fall, 'this is in Cathays, a nice part of Cardiff. You can walk from there to Cathays Park, you know, that park you thought was so lovely the day we went to the City Hall.'

She nodded, her dark eyes wide with happiness. 'Can we afford to live there?'

Rhys grinned. 'It's all arranged. A living-room and a bedroom of our own and we share the kitchen.' He held up a hand as she was about to protest. 'It won't be like Daisy Street, I promise you. The chap who is renting us the rooms, Dai Roberts, is a mate from the boat. He says you and his wife, Fran, will be company for each other while we're both away at sea.'

Sara looked disappointed. 'You mean you're going back to sea again and leaving me there on my own?'

'Not for a long while. I haven't signed on for the next run. I've got a temporary job running a bakery in Elm Street. The man who owns it is a friend of Dai's. He's been ill, and wants a bit of a rest, so I'll be at home for a few months. Long enough for you to get settled in.'

'What about Averyl? Will they mind having a young baby in the house?'

'That's the beauty of it all. They have two kiddies

of their own, a girl of five and a boy of four, and she's expecting another. That's why you'll be such good company for each other.'

When later on in the day he broke the news to his parents they were very upset.

'You mean you're taking Averyl away from us just like that!' Olwen exclaimed angrily. 'I'll tell you one thing, boyo, you'll regret it! You'll be bringing her back to me again in a week. That Sara has no idea at all how to look after her.'

'Now, now, *cariad*,' Lloyd tried to calm her. 'Be fair to the girl, you never give her a chance. She's willing enough only you won't let her.'

Rhys laughed. 'She's brought her own sister up. Myfanwy was only three months old when their Mam died. Everything will be fine, don't you worry.'

'Are you two implying that I'm interfering, then?' Olwen demanded.

Lloyd put his arm around her shoulders. 'Of course not, my lovely. Wonderful, you are, with the baba, and so will Sara be, you'll see!'

Rhys would not change his mind. As far as he was concerned the whole thing had worked out far better than he could ever have hoped. He had somewhere decent for Sara and the baby to live, he had a job he knew he would enjoy doing, and he would not be going back to sea for several months.

Patiently he explained all this to Olwen and Lloyd and saw the look of relief on their faces when he added, 'I'll even be able to manage to send you some money each week until you are back on your feet again.'

Dai and Fran Roberts were both ten years older than Sara. Dai was heavily built with a shock of tight brown curly hair and a broad face with a large chin and nose. Fran was tall with straight carrot-red hair and a wide band of freckles around her green eyes that stood out against her pale skin like a brown rash. Five-year-old Hilda was dainty with long fair hair and Robbie, a year younger, was stocky with brown curls and a serious face.

Their terraced house in Coburn Street had a small paved back yard with an outside brick lavatory. The front door opened on to a small hallway that had two living-rooms off it and led through to the kitchen. There was a scullery off this with a gas stove, a sink and a wash boiler.

Rhys and Sara had the middle room downstairs which had a glass-panelled door that opened on to the back yard. By using this they could go across to the scullery without going through the Robertses' kitchen. Their bedroom was above their living-room and Fran had put a drop-side cot for Averyl alongside the double bed.

After the confines of living in one room at Daisy Street, it seemed like heaven to Sara. Even sharing the cooking and washing facilities didn't seem so bad because she could go into the scullery without intruding.

'I'm sure Fran and I will be able to cook and wash without getting in each other's way,' she told Rhys.

It was all so wonderful that for the first few days even Averyl's persistent crying didn't seem to matter.

'Everything is strange to her,' Sara explained to Rhys. 'She'll settle in a day or so.'

'Well, as long as she shuts up at night when I need to get to sleep, I don't suppose it matters too much. Better ask Fran if she's got a pram or something that you can borrow, and then we can take her out. We could walk to Cathays Park. Lovely there!'

The opportunities for Sara and Rhys to take Averyl out for a walk were few and far between. He started work at four each morning in order to have hot bread ready for those who wanted it fresh for breakfast. He rarely got home before six in the evening. By the time he had eaten the meal Sara had waiting he was so tired he often fell asleep in a chair. If Dai was around, though, he'd rouse himself and they'd go to the Cardiff Arms for a beer.

Sara hated the fact that Rhys had started drinking again. 'Don't come near me, you smell disgusting,' she told him, pushing him away when he tried to take her in his arms. 'I'm here on my own all day so when you're not working you should keep me company, not go off boozing,' she added.

'Blame the work, my lovely,' Rhys would say. 'It's so bloody hot in that bakehouse I sweat like a pig. By the end of the day I could drink the Taff dry, and when Dai suggests a trip to the pub I can't resist going.'

For all his misdemeanours Sara still loved him deeply. She knew it was her own fault, for goading him when he'd been drinking, that they had the occasional row.

When he told her that Gareth, the man who

owned the bakery, was now over his illness and thinking of coming back to work, her heart sank because she knew that meant that Rhys would probably go back to sea.

Then there was a slight reprieve. Gareth still didn't think he was well enough to work full-time so he decided not to get rid of Rhys.

'You mean you've got a permanent job there?'

'Seems like it,' he grinned. 'And it will make life a lot easier if someone else is helping with the work.'

'Can he afford to employ you?' She looked worried. 'He won't be docking your money, will he? It's as much as I can do to manage as it is.'

Rhys frowned. 'He hasn't mentioned it. You get all you need for housekeeping, don't you?'

'For housekeeping, yes, but there's very little left over for buying clothes and other things for me and Averyl.'

'You're not as good a manager as my Mam with the old pennies, are you?' he teased.

Sara boiled. 'No, nor as good as your Mam was with Averyl! Go on, say it, you think it anyway.'

'She's certainly the worst squaller I've ever heard. Cry, cry, grizzle, grizzle, a right spoilt little brat.'

'It's only because she's teething,' Sara defended quickly. 'Anyway, your Mam would never let her cry. The slightest whimper out of her and she was there picking her up and cuddling her. That's probably why she needs so much attention and is such a mardy little madam when she doesn't get it!'

When she started talking like that Rhys usually walked out. He'd call out to Dai to see if he was going with him for a beer, and then the two of them would disappear for the rest of the evening.

'Your Rhys is getting my Dai into bad habits with all this boozing,' Fran complained.

'Not my fault your husband can't say no to him,' Sara snapped.

'Well, not much good us two quarrelling over them, now is it,' Fran smiled. 'Come on into my place and we'll have a cuppa.'

Fran was easier going than Sara was. Now, almost seven months' pregnant, and with two older children to look after, she was content to let life flow past her. Running out of things was her worst problem. She never made a shopping list, and more often than not she would return home without the very thing she had gone out to buy.

'Could you nip over to the corner stores and get me a packet of tea, I've run out,' she said as Sara came into the kitchen with Averyl in her arms.

Sara made a face. 'It's raining cats and dogs out there. I've got some tea, let's use that.'

'If you like, *cariad*,' Fran agreed. 'I'll have to nip out later for some bacon for Dai's breakfast so I can get tea then. The corner shop doesn't shut until late.'

'I'll pop over after we've had our cuppa,' Sara promised.

'I'd send young Robbie and Hilda, but it's a bit late for them to be out on their own,' Fran told her. 'Anyway, I'd better pop up and put them to bed.'

'Yes, the nights are really drawing in,' Sara agreed. 'It will be Christmas in next to no time!'

When Fran came down again they sipped their

tea, gossiping about their husbands, the neighbours and the latest goings-on in the newspaper. Fran was full of a story about an airship crashing.

Sara sighed. 'A terrible thing to happen, but it won't affect us much, will it? I can't see either of us ever being able to afford to fly in one of those things.'

'Perhaps not. In fact, I don't know if I even want to do so,' Fran admitted. 'It's still sad though,' she went on, 'that forty-eight people lost their lives.'

Sara stood up. 'I think I'll take Averyl upstairs. She's nodding off and I might even be able to put her down without her waking up.'

'I thought you were going to nip over to the corner shop for some tea and bacon for me, *cariad*?'

'I'll do it after I've put Averyl down. I don't want her waking up and screaming for hours.'

'Oh, don't bother,' Fran said testily. 'It will be too late by then, they'll be closed. I'll go myself.' She picked up a shawl and wrapped it round her swollen figure. 'I'll just go up and make sure my two are in bed, but listen out in case either of them wakes up. I should only be a few minutes.'

It took Sara ages to settle Averyl. Although her lids were heavy she wouldn't let sleep claim her. She held on to Sara's hand, and each time Sara tried to move away she let out a thin wail. Sara would quickly shush her, and stroke her forehead to try and get her to sleep.

When Hilda and Robbie appeared at her bedroom door Sara felt that was the last straw. 'Whatever are you two doing out of bed?' she scolded. 'Your Mam will be very cross with you.'

'Our Mam's not downstairs and your baby was crying,' Hilda told her, 'so we thought you'd both gone out.'

'What silly nonsense! Off you go, back to bed this minute, both of you.'

Averyl seemed to be as far from settling as ever. Sara wondered what was keeping Fran so long. Gossiping, probably, she decided.

It was almost another ten minutes before Averyl finally dropped off to sleep. Her back aching, and her legs stiff, Sara debated whether to go back downstairs or simply undress and get into bed.

As she stood there undecided she was conscious of a smell of burning. It wasn't something cooking, more as if something had been singed. Then she heard the scream. An ear-piercing, shrill scream that went on and on.

For a moment she wondered if Fran was starting with the baby, but it wasn't a woman's cry. It sounded more like that of a child. She remembered that Hilda and Robbie had been out of bed, and rushed to see if it was one of them, and to find out what they'd done.

The moment she opened her bedroom door the hot smell of smoke hit her in the face. She slammed it shut, then opened it more cautiously.

'Robbie, Hilda, where are you?' she called. She started to creep along the landing towards their room, but the billowing smoke was so acrid that she could hardly breathe.

Sara was overcome by panic as memories of the fire at Taff Court when she'd been fourteen came crowding back. She froze, her heart thudding, her pulse racing. Averyl was not much older than her sister Myfanwy had been then. It was history repeating itself. She'd saved Myfanwy that time, now she must save Averyl.

She could hear Robbie and Hilda screaming, but she knew she couldn't reach them. It was terrible to leave them where they were, but she had Averyl to think about.

She edged her way back into her bedroom and shut the door. She hadn't seen any flames so the fire was probably in the lower part of the house, she told herself. If she stayed where she was, with the bedroom door tight shut, then she and Averyl might be safe.

'I must keep calm,' Sara told herself out loud. Fran must be back from the corner shop by now so she would do something about rescuing them.

Averyl was whimpering again so she picked her up and nursed her, finding comfort and reassurance from the feel of the warm soft little body against her own.

It seemed an eternity before she heard the sound of the fire engine arriving, and even longer before two helmeted figures appeared. One fireman took Averyl from her arms, and another helped her down the stairs.

Chapter Twenty-three

It was a long time before the effects of the fire faded from Sara's mind. She felt terribly guilty about not helping Robbie and Hilda.

She kept telling Fran and everyone else that it was because she'd been trapped in her bedroom by smoke and fumes that she'd been unable to do so. In her heart, she knew the real reason was that the smell of burning and the smoke had brought back frightening memories of the night her mother had burnt to death.

Fortunately, Robbie and Hilda had also been rescued unharmed and there was little damage. The fire had not spread much beyond the living-room curtains which the two children had managed to set alight. But Hilda and Robbie were badly shaken by the experience, and there was tension between Fran and Sara. For a couple of weeks there were no shared confidences or cups of tea. For a time they avoided each other as much as possible since when they did meet there were recriminations on both sides.

Rhys managed to steer clear of most of these arguments. Even so, he caused a rift between himself and Fran by saying that if she hadn't stayed gossiping when she went to the corner shop then the fire would never have happened. Whereas she left Rhys in no doubt that she blamed him and Sara for it all.

In spite of this, Rhys and Dai remained firm friends. Their visits to the pub together became a nightly event.

Dai laughed the matter off. 'You don't have to take too much notice of what a woman says when she's in that state, boyo,' he said affably. 'Turns their minds, see. Give it time, she'll get over it in a few weeks once the baba's here.'

Sara also persuaded him to ignore what Fran had said. 'Let bygones be bygones,' she soothed.

Rhys said no more, but it still rankled in the back of his mind, especially when Fran wouldn't let matters rest.

When Fran went into labour almost six weeks earlier than she should have done she was convinced that it was because of the stress and upset she'd been through over the fire.

The new baby, Emlyn, was a crier. No matter what Fran did she couldn't quieten him. Neither feeding, cuddling, nor rocking him, or even singing to him, had any effect. He never seemed to sleep, night or day, and the house echoed with his thin piercing wail.

Sara began taking Averyl out every day simply to get away from the sound. She would walk all the way to Cathays Park, or sometimes take a tram to Roath Park where Averyl enjoyed watching other children sailing their toy boats on the lake.

Frequently Sara lost all sense of time, or journeyed much further than she intended. Often she was so late back that Rhys came home to an unmade bed, dirty clothes and dishes lying around, and no meal ready for him.

Dai found himself in much the same situation. Fran had become more and more slovenly since the new baby arrived. She said she didn't feel well, she was tired all the time, and that Emlyn took up all her day.

In desperation Dai appealed to Sara to help Fran a bit more. 'Can you take the other two off her hands for an hour or two?' he pleaded. 'Let her get some rest, or the time to straighten the place up. It's for your good as well as ours,' he added. 'Look at this scullery, it's absolutely filthy! There are bluebottles and maggots everywhere. Sooner or later one of us is going to be ill.'

'Why don't you clean it up then, instead of going off to the pub every night?' Sara asked sharply.

Dai looked taken aback. 'No need to be like that about it, girl. It's women's work keeping the place clean, not my job. I wouldn't know where to start.'

'Then it's time you found out, and this is your chance to do so,' she told him spitefully and flounced off back to her own room.

Once she'd had her say, Sara felt rather shamefaced. Dai was out all day doing a heavy job at the docks so he probably was too tired to tackle household chores when he got home at night. Usually, he had to put Robbie and little Hilda to bed before he could sit down for his meal, and sometimes, she knew, he even had to cook that for himself.

The next morning Sara set to and cleaned up the scullery. She threw out all the stale food that had accumulated as well as the half-eaten cakes, the bottles with an inch of sour milk at the bottom, lumps of mouldy cheese, and scraps of meat that had obviously been a bluebottle's delight judging by the maggots on them.

Then she washed up all the dirty cups and plates that had been abandoned, and scoured all the surfaces she could reach. As a final touch, she took down the net curtains at the window, and plunged them into a bowl of soapy water along with the dishcloths, teacloths, towels and face flannels.

By the time she'd finished, the rank nauseating smell that had hung over the place for weeks was gone. Everything was gleaming clean, all the things she had washed were out on the line, and the dishes and cups neatly tidied away.

She felt so pleased with herself that when she prepared a casserole for their own evening meal she put in a double quantity, so that there would be enough for Fran and Dai as well.

It sealed a truce. Sara agreed that as long as Fran didn't leave her dirty dishes piled up in the scullery then she would make sure that it was kept clean. She also offered to cook a main meal each night that they could all share. With more time to see to Robbie and Hilda, Fran was able to have them fed and ready for bed when Dai got home.

It seemed a perfect solution, and it would have worked wonderfully well if it had not been for Emlyn.

He seemed to wait until they were all in bed and asleep, and then every night, without fail, he would start crying. His loud sobs and piercing screams would waken Averyl who would then add her voice to the noise, disturbing Rhys and Sara.

Sometimes they could pacify her by taking her into their bed, but she wriggled so much that although she went off to sleep again neither of them could do so.

In the morning, they would feel irritable and tired, and often this led to harsh words before Rhys went off to work.

The night Rhys came home and said he'd signed on to go to sea again, although she felt bitterly resentful, Sara was not altogether surprised.

'Is Dai going too?' she asked.

'Of course he bloody well is! He's fed up with being kept awake every night by that squalling little brat of his.'

'And what about your job?'

'Gareth is there most of the time these days, he'll probably be glad to see me go. More money in his pocket, see, if he's working on his own.'

'And more work on his shoulders. Not good, that, for a man who has been so sick.'

'Don't worry about that bugger. He'll soon sort himself out. Plenty of boyos on the dole willing to work for him to get them some extra cash to buy beer and baccy.'

'And what about me and Averyl?'

'You stay on here with Fran, of course. You'll be company for each other, see.'

'You never bothered to ask me what I felt about it, or if that was what I wanted to do, though, before you decided to go to sea again, did you?' Sara grumbled.

Rhys looked uncomfortable. 'Too late now. I've already signed up so I've got to go. You'll be all right here with Fran, won't you?'

'And screaming little Emlyn?'

He shrugged. 'Those things don't worry women like they do men. They're used to kids bawling. It doesn't go through their heads the same.'

'Oh, no?' She stared at him reproachfully. 'And what are we supposed to live on, I'd like to know?'

Rhys hastily averted his eyes. 'No good making a bloody fuss about it, Sara, I'm going and that's that. 'I'll leave you enough money to cover the few months, so you can stay on here. Or if you run short you can go back to Tonypandy to my home, or to your own folk in Ponty. I don't give a damn.'

Three days later Rhys and Dai left Coburn Street. Fran was even angrier than Sara had been, and there was a terrible scene between her and Dai. Cups, plates and even saucepans were thrown, but it had no effect.

The two men had made their plans. Knowing that they would be away from Cardiff for at least two months they could shrug off almost anything their wives said or did. By the time they sailed back into port again, the two men reasoned, both women would have calmed down, and would even be pleased to see them again.

In that, they were both wrong. Once the men had sailed Fran slipped back into her sluttish ways. Robbie and Hilda played out in the street for most of the day. When they were hungry she gave them jam sandwiches, and they squatted down on the doorstep to eat them.

They wore the same clothes for days at a time, until they were so grubby that it was impossible to tell what colour they were. Hilda's pretty hair became a mass of tangles, and hung dark and greasy for want of washing.

The baby was even more neglected. It would lie for hours, crying miserably, its nappy soaking or even soiled, and the front of its clothes stiff with sick and dribble. Often Fran would simply leave the urine-soaked nappies to dry out, and then use them again rather than go to the trouble of washing them.

Sara tried her best to help at first, but she soon realised she had enough to do just trying to keep her own things clean and looking after Averyl. The pile-up of dirty pots and pans in the scullery became horrific. Sara took to rinsing out her own, and then taking them back into her own room. She knew that if she left them on the shelf that they had agreed would be hers when she had first moved in, Fran would have no compunction about using them, and then putting them back dirty.

Sara grew more and more discontent. Once again she took to going for long walks, sometimes to the Parks or more often into the city centre to walk around and look in all the shop windows.

It was on one of these window-shopping trips that she bumped into Martha Pritchard.

Sara felt overcome with shame and confusion. It was almost a year since she had been in touch with Martha. Never once had she gone back to Pontypridd to visit Myfanwy as she'd promised to do. Martha had been so good to her and helped her so much after her mother had died, yet when Martha had written saying she had problems of her own Sara had not even bothered to reply.

'Oh, *cariad,* there's pleased I am to see you,' Martha exclaimed as she hugged her and kissed her. 'I was beginning to think I'd never set eyes on you again.

'So whose little baba is this, then, Sara?' she asked when she had calmed down a little. 'It's never yours, is it?'

'Yes, this is Averyl. She's seven months old now.'

'*Duw anwyl*! I can't take it in. She's the spit of her Dada!' She gave Sara a questioning look. 'You and that Rhys Edwards are still together?'

'Yes, Rhys and me are still together. He goes to sea, though, so he's not here in Cardiff at the moment,' Sara said evasively.

Martha Pritchard looked concerned. 'There's lonely it must be for you.'

'It is a bit! I'm sharing a house with Fran Roberts whose husband, Dai, goes to sea the same as Rhys does. They're on the same boat.'

'And you live close by, do you?

For a moment Sara was too taken aback to answer. She knew if she said she did then Martha would expect to be asked back, and she knew she couldn't do that because the place was indescribably filthy. She hadn't cleaned her own room for over a week, and when she'd walked out this morning to get away from Emlyn screaming she had even left the tin bath, in which she'd washed Averyl, in the middle of the room.

'It's a tram ride away,' she murmured. 'Next time

you're coming to Cardiff, let me know, and then I can meet you and you can come back and see it.'

'I'd like to do that,' Martha smiled. 'A much better idea though, *cariad*, would be for you to come to Pontypridd, and see if you can sort Myfanwy out,' Martha told her.

'Sort her out?' Sara was immediately alert. 'What do you mean? Is she in some kind of trouble?'

'Not trouble, *cariad*, but the poor little dab is so cowed looking that it breaks my heart to see her. Mind you, I've been that caught up with my own affairs lately that I haven't seen all that much of Myfanwy.'

'Your mother is still with you then?'

'Well, she is and she isn't. She's in hospital just now. That's how I've managed to get to Cardiff today. Tied down, I am, most of the time.'

Sara nodded sympathetically, but it was what Martha had said about Myfanwy that was uppermost in her mind.

'Who do you think is to blame for Myfanwy looking like that, Gwladys or my Dada?'

'I think they're as bad as one another. Myfanwy's at school now, but Gwladys takes her right to the school gate, and she's there waiting for her when she comes out. Then it's straight back home, and no playing out afterwards. Like a little prisoner she is, see. On Sunday it's chapel in the morning, Sunday school in the afternoon and in the evening all three of them go to chapel again.'

Sara felt uneasy. She must do something and do it soon before anything happened to Myfanwy and it was too late, she thought guiltily.

'Apart from being so protective does Gwladys treat her quite well?' Sara asked anxiously.

Martha shrugged her ample shoulders. 'Depends on what you mean by well,' she prevaricated.

'Is she looking after her, feeding her properly, that sort of thing.'

'She's thin as a rake, but then your Dada hasn't worked for a while so perhaps things are hard for them.'

'But they're good to her otherwise?' Sara pressed.

'I can't really say. They never have anything to do with me, *cariad*. It's not like it was in the old days when your Mam was alive and we used to have a chat and a cuppa together, and I'd lend her my love-story books.'

'Does Myfanwy seem happy, though, Martha?' Sara persisted.

'She does an awful a lot of crying at night. I can hear it through the wall, see.' Her plump face looked unhappy. 'Pitiful, it is! I don't know whether they smack her a lot, or what it is that is wrong with her,' she said cautiously.

Sara's stomach turned over as she recalled her own experiences. Surely her father wouldn't do anything like that to Myfanwy? Not at her age; she was a mere baby!

She gave Martha a tremulous smile. 'Look, I have to get back because it's time for Averyl's next feed, but I really will try and come to Pontypridd, and see if I can find out what's going on.'

'Good! Don't leave it too long, *cariad*. And when you come to see Myfanwy, make sure you find the time to pop into my house for a cuppa.'

Chapter Twenty-four

Sara found Martha Pritchard's news about Myfanwy so disturbing that she could think of nothing else. Even so, she couldn't bring herself to make the trip to Pontypridd and find out for herself exactly how things stood.

She was less worried now that there would be gossip about her and Rhys; instead she knew it was mainly because of her own feeling of guilt. When she'd left Pontypridd she'd promised Myfanwy that as soon as they had a place of their own she could come and live with them. She'd promised to come back for her, and yet she had never once been near Taff Court, not even to visit her.

It had been such a long time since she'd seen any of them that she was afraid that if she did go there now, her Dada would be hostile even if Gwladys wasn't.

Gwladys would probably be frosty, and if she was at home alone then she might refuse to let Sara in. If that happened her journey would have been for nothing, she told herself. She could always go next door to see Martha, but it would still be a wasted trip since Martha had already told her all she knew.

There was Betti to visit as well, of course, but since she and Rhys had hardly been in touch with

Betti since the letter they'd received from her when they were first in Cardiff, Sara wasn't sure how welcome she would be, especially if she was visiting on her own.

Sara thought over and over again about all the things Martha had told her. What worried Sara the most was Martha saying that she sometimes heard Myfanwy crying at night.

She remembered how she'd cried when she'd been that age. Usually it had been because her Dada had taken off his leather belt and thrashed her across her bare bum with it.

She didn't know which had been worse, the pain or the indignity of having to take off her knickers and bend over a chair. As she grew older, and he still insisted on thrashing her in that way, she'd found it shameful. That was why she could never tell anyone, not even Martha, either about that or the other terrible things he did to her later after her mother died.

A dozen times during early December she made up her mind to go to Pontypridd, then at the last minute abandoned her plan. She was too scared to revive the past and too uncertain about what her reception would be.

She knew she was being a coward, but she tried to appease her conscience by telling herself that her visit might only make things worse for Myfanwy. Not at the time, of course, not while she was there and could protest, but afterwards. Sara envisaged her Dada creeping into Myfanwy's bedroom after she was asleep, like he used to do when she was a child. She remembered his visits so well, his belt in hand, stripping back the bedclothes, pulling up her nightdress and forcing her on to her face.

Each time she reached that point Sara tried to stop. She didn't want to let herself think about the stinging lashes, her screams, and her tears. Brooding over the past did no good at all. It was the present that mattered. Somehow she must do something. She couldn't bear to think of Myfanwy suffering the way she'd done.

If only she could talk to Rhys she was sure that between them they could come up with some sort of plan.

The days became weeks and they were halfway through December before Sara had a brilliant idea. It was so simple that she wondered why she'd never thought of it before. She'd go to Pontypridd and ask if Myfanwy could come and stay with her for the Christmas holiday.

Sara resolved to use the small bit of money she'd scraped together for Christmas on the train fare to Ponty instead; even if it meant she couldn't afford to buy any presents for Myfanwy or Averyl, it would be a joy in itself for them all to be together. They'd have a lovely time. She'd be able to take Myfanwy into the city centre to see all the lights in the shop windows, and it would be a wonderful treat for her.

Of course, she told herself, she mustn't tell her Dada that was what she wanted to do or he'd regard it as the temptation of the Devil, and refuse to let Myfanwy come back with her. She'd tell him that she was on her own and with Rhys away at sea she needed someone to help her with the baby. Myfanwy was old enough to do that.

Once she'd got Myfanwy in her care she was sure she'd manage to hold on to her. Gwladys might even be glad to be free of the child. She'd probably seen enough young children in her life as a schoolteacher. The more Sara thought about it the better the idea seemed to be.

It was a crisp cold morning in late December when she finally plucked up the courage to put her idea into action. As she set out with Averyl, both of them bundled up in coats and scarves and a big warm carrying shawl which she wrapped around Averyl and her own body, there were butterflies fluttering in her stomach.

She hadn't mentioned anything about the trip to Fran because she might have said it was a bad idea, and anyway the whole thing was so personal that Sara felt shy about discussing it.

As she stood on Cardiff station waiting for the train, she felt so scared that she thought she was going to be physically sick.

'So you've decided to pay us a visit at long last,' Ifor Jenkins sniffed when he answered the door to Sara's tentative knock. 'I suppose you want something, otherwise you wouldn't be here.'

'Hello, Dada!' She was taken aback by the change in him. He had aged visibly. His hair was now almost white and looked thin and lank. His face was lined, and there was a sour twist to his thin mouth.

He looked at Averyl speculatively, 'This yours, then?'

'Yes, Dada. Your first grandchild. Her name's Averyl. She's eight months old.'

'A child born to a godless household, so may the

Good Lord protect her,' he muttered as he turned away and started to walk back inside the house. 'You'd better come in, I suppose.'

As Sara followed him into the living-room, so many childhood memories came flooding back that she felt apprehensive. Her father might look older but he hadn't really changed. As he sat down at the table, his bible open in front of him, and ignored her, all her old fear of him returned.

'I didn't expect to find you at home, Dada,' she said awkwardly, to break the uneasy silence.

'I've been stood off again for the last three months,' he snapped. 'Pit caved in, see, broken right arm, so I doubt if they'll take me back this time. No point when I can't swing a pick, see.'

'I'm sorry to hear that,' Sara murmured. 'I didn't know.'

'Well, you wouldn't when you never come near us. Mind you, the cave-in was reported in all the newspapers,' he added sharply. 'Don't you get newspapers down in Cardiff?'

'I don't buy one very often,' Sara admitted.'

'Why's that then? You and that man you ran off with can both read?' he said tersely.

'We've better things to do with our money,' Sara laughed, kissing Averyl who sat quietly on her lap. 'A young baby is expensive. It takes every penny we've got for food and clothes.'

'And you think we don't know that? That young sister of yours costs us a pretty penny, I can tell you.'

Sara's heart leapt. She had been right. She was

sure they would like to get rid of Myfanwy. All she had to do was handle it carefully.

'Where is Myfanwy? Still at school?'

'She comes home at midday; Gwladys has gone to fetch her so they'll be here any minute.'

'Lovely, I'm dying to see her. She must have grown?'

'So eager to see her that you've never once come back in almost a year?' he said snidely.

'Well, there have been reasons. It's been difficult for me, see.'

'But not now? So what's changed?'

'Rhys is away at sea so I have a bit more time to myself. Lonely it is, though, sometimes.'

'You've got the baba!' he said, glancing at his granddaughter.

'Yes, and she takes up most of my day, but she's not got much to say for herself, not yet.'

Ifor sniffed. 'Give her another year and if she's like your sister you'll be wishing you could shut her up.'

'Our Myfanwy is a little chatterbox, is she?'

'Spoilt little madam if you ask me. And I know who's to blame for that. Ruined that child, you did, and you'll probably do the same with your own. The only thing she understands is the strap,' he said grimly.

Sara's heart pounded. She could feel hate and anger rising inside her like an unstoppable tide as she looked at the hard, thin-featured man in front of her. She took a deep breath to try and calm herself, biting back the words that sprang to her lips, knowing she would ruin all her plans for Myfanwy if she antagonised him.

The door opening saved her.

Sara was shocked by the change in Gwladys too. She not only looked older than Sara remembered, but she was also not nearly so smart although she was just as formidable.

'So you've finally decided to visit us, have you,' she snapped.

Sara smiled, but her eyes were on her little sister. Myfanwy was so thin and wan that she felt dismayed. Everything Martha Pritchard had told her seemed to be true.

'Myfanwy!' Sara balanced Averyl on one knee, and held out her free arm to welcome her little sister.

For a moment Myfanwy stood stock still, her dark eyes saucer wide, and for one brief second Sara was afraid she didn't recognise her.

'Sara?' Myfanwy gave an uncertain little smile that quickly became a frown. 'You never came back for me, like you promised,' she scowled.

'I know, *cariad*. I'm sorry about that but it wasn't possible. I'm here now, though.'

Sara waited patiently, still with her arm extended, inviting her little sister to come to her.

Almost reluctantly, Myfanwy edged closer until she was near enough to be encompassed by Sara's arm.

'Are you going to stay?' she asked suspiciously.

'For a little while, *cariad*.' Sara kissed the top of Myfanwy's head, and hugged her even tighter. 'Look who I've brought to see you!' She released her hold on Myfanwy, and moved Averyl on to the centre of her lap. 'Isn't she lovely?'

Myfanwy stared at the baby in silence.

Sara took Myfanwy's hand and with one of the fingers gently stroked Averyl's face, making the baby chuckle.

'She's trying to eat me!' Myfanwy giggled as the baby reached out, grabbing at her finger and pulling it towards her mouth. 'What's her name?'

'Averyl. Do you want to hold her?'

Myfanwy held out her arms and gathered the baby to her chest in a bear-hug.

'Careful!' Sara warned. 'She's quite heavy, see.'

'Stop all this nonsense! Myfanwy, sit up at the table and eat your food,' Ifor Jenkins snapped. 'You have to be back in school in twenty minutes.'

Disappointment showing on her face, Myfanwy obeyed.

'You eat your dinner, *cariad*, and then I'll walk back to school with you,' Sara said quickly as she took the baby from her.

Obediently, but with her gaze still fastened on Sara and Averyl, Myfanwy sat at the table and began eating the wedge of bread and dripping that Gwladys slapped on to a plate and put down in front of her.

'Stop!' Ifor Jenkins roared. 'Put that bread down this instant. You know better than to ever touch a morsel of food until you have put your hands together and thanked the Good Lord for the bounty that He has provided for you.'

'Sorry, Dada, I forgot.' Myfanwy was shaking like

a leaf, her face ashen as she dropped the slice of bread and dripping back on to the plate.

'Forgot, did you?' He stood up, and for a moment Sara thought he was going to take off his belt to the child. Instead he bent over the table and took away the plate of food. 'Well, now you can forget this as well,' he snarled. 'And there will be no supper for you when you come home tonight either.'

'Please, Dada . . .'

'Don't you dare answer your Dada back,' Gwladys snapped, slapping Myfanwy across the face. 'I'm warning you, see! Don't think that your sister suddenly turning up out of the blue means that you can get away with anything, my girl. Come on, off back to school with you, and when you get hunger pains in your belly this afternoon remember to ask the Good Lord to forgive you.'

Sara felt inflamed as she watched Myfanwy climbing down from the chair. She felt as if she was living her own childhood all over again, though at Myfanwy's age Sara at least had had her mother to cushion her a little from Ifor's brutality. Hesitantly she looked at Myfanwy, whose pleading eyes seemed to be trying to remind her of her promise to walk back to school with her.

Sara thought quickly. 'I'll have to pop out to get some milk and Farley's rusks for Averyl, so I'll walk Myfanwy back to school, Gwladys, and save you the trouble.'

With Averyl in her arms, warmly wrapped up in the big shawl, she pushed Myfanwy out of the door in front of her before either Gwladys or her father could say or do anything to stop them.

She turned a deaf ear to Gwladys's expression of annoyance and to her father's stentorian order to stop.

As soon as they had rounded the corner, Sara hunkered down and wiped her sister's tear-stained little face with her handkerchief. Gently she touched the bright red patch on Myfanwy's cheek where Gwladys had slapped her.

'Come on!' She stood up, Averyl in one arm, holding Myfanwy's hand with the other, and hurried her along. She knew they passed a corner shop on the way to school, and she intended to make sure that even though Myfanwy hadn't had anything to eat at home she certainly wouldn't go hungry all afternoon as her Dada and Gwladys intended she should.

'What do you like eating most of all?' she asked Myfanwy as she pushed open the shop door, and the jangling bell brought the owner out of the back room to serve them.

'Chocolate! I had it once; it was ever so lovely!'

Sara smiled. She should have expected that answer, she thought wryly, but it wasn't really very filling for a hungry little girl. 'And what else? What about biscuits?'

Myfanwy's eyes widened with excitement and she nodded enthusiastically.

'So what kind do you like best?'

Myfanwy didn't answer, merely looked bemused.

'Biscuits then, is it?' the woman behind the counter asked impatiently. 'Broken ones?' She took the lid off a big square tin and poked around in the contents. 'She can have an assortment then, even the odd cream one in here, see.'

Sara shook her head. 'No, thanks all the same, but we won't have the broken ones. Do you have a packet of mixed biscuits?'

'A whole packet, is it?' The woman shrugged and reached down a packet of Betta biscuits, the outside wrapper a galaxy of colour. 'There you are then! That will be threepence.'

'Thank you!' Sara brought out her purse and rummaged inside it. 'And a penny bar of chocolate as well,' she said as she placed fourpence down on the counter.

As they continued on their way to school, Myfanwy happily munched away at her biscuits. Sara wanted to tell her that she was going to take her back to Cardiff, but knew she daren't do so in case she failed to persuade her Dada and Gwladys to let Myfanwy return with her.

The afternoon bell was ringing as they reached the school gates.

'I mustn't take these into school,' Myfanwy said reluctantly, 'it's not allowed.' She handed the remainder of her packet of biscuits and the bar of chocolate to Sara. 'Will you come and meet me?'

'Of course,' Sara promised. She quickly broke off a piece of the chocolate and popped it into Myfanwy's mouth. 'Go on, you can manage to eat that up before you go into the classroom,' she smiled.

Sara walked slowly back to Taff Court, stopping to buy rusks and milk for Averyl on the way. She was tempted to call in to the cake shop but decided it would be better if next time Rhys came home from sea they went to see Betti together.

Gwladys looked on in distaste as Sara sat at one end of the table and spooned a dish of rusks and milk into Averyl's hungry little mouth and then gave her half a dry rusk to chew on.

'Not going to make a mess with that, is she?' Gwladys asked sharply.

'I'll clear it up if she does,' Sara promised.

'I've got enough to do without having more work foisted on me,' Gwladys grumbled. She lowered her voice to a whisper. 'Your father being at home all day doesn't help matters, I can tell you. Under my feet, see.'

'Perhaps things would be a bit easier for you if Myfanwy came and stayed with me. Keep me company while Rhys is away.'

'And be led into the world of sin! Cardiff is a den of iniquity and incurs the wrath of the Lord,' her father intoned solemnly.

'She won't come to any harm, I'll see to that,' Sara promised. 'Please, Dada, it would do her good.'

'And what about her education? Take her out of school, would you, as well as plunge her into a world of sin?'

Sara thought quickly. 'No, no! I wouldn't dream of doing that, Dada. She will be off school for a while over Christmas so why not let her come to stay with me then? It would be a break for both of you, see,' she added, looking at Gwladys in the hope that she would offer her support.

'Christmas is the time for celebrating the birth of Our Lord, not for gadding about and indulging in the pleasures of the flesh,' Ifor intoned. 'The child stays here where I can see she prays to the Good Lord and studies His word in the Bible,' he added ominously.

Chapter Twenty-five

Sara's journey back to Cardiff was a nightmare. Being disrupted from her usual routine made Averyl irritable. Sensing that her mother's attention was not fully on her, she became all the more fractious, and kept up a whining cry for most of the way.

Sara tried half-heartedly to console Averyl, but her mind was still back in Pontypridd. The hatred that was building up inside her for her father and Gwladys alarmed her. And the concern she was feeling over the way they both treated Myfanwy disturbed her even more. She kept wondering just how far her father's bestial torture had gone, or whether there was still time to rescue Myfanwy before her innocence was taken from her.

How was she ever to do that, she asked herself? She hadn't even managed to persuade them to let Myfanwy come and stay with her over Christmas. The memory of her little sister's woebegone face when she was leaving would stay etched on her mind for ever.

She hadn't even seen Martha Pritchard. Alun Pritchard had been there, but he said his wife had gone to visit her mother who'd been taken into hospital after having a stroke.

'Getting on, the old dear is,' Alun sighed. 'Never been the same since her husband died. Martha told you the pit owners turned her out of her home, didn't she?'

'Yes, she told me all about it when we met in Cardiff.'

Alun sighed again. 'It hasn't really worked out having her living here with us. She was used to having her own place. And you know what they say about two women in one kitchen.'

'I know all about that,' Sara grinned. 'I've been sharing kitchens ever since I left Ponty.'

'Not like the old days,' he confided, filling up his pipe with tobacco. 'When your Mam was alive she and my Martha enjoyed a cuppa, and a good old gossip. Your father has never been one to have anything to do with his neighbours. Chapel as many times a week as you like, Bible bashing and hymn singing, but try to have a chat about anything else and he doesn't want to know.'

'I think Gwladys is the same,' Sara smiled.

Alun lit his pipe, puffing on it until it was going. 'There's a cruel streak in both the buggers, you know, *cariad*!' He shook his head sadly. 'I wouldn't treat a dog the way they treat little Myfanwy.'

Since Alun was a man of few words, and usually much too kind-hearted to criticise his neighbours, Sara found this confirmation of what Martha had said to her in Cardiff particularly upsetting.

By the time she'd reached Coburn Street, washed and fed Averyl, and made herself a cup of tea and a sardine sandwich, Sara was so tired that she felt the best place for both of them was in bed.

Her living-room was in chaos, but she felt too exhausted by her journey, and by all the things

Alun Pritchard had told her, to sort it out. It could stay that way until morning.

After a good night's sleep she'd have more energy to see to it. She'd even leave the dishes she'd been using where they were on the table, she decided. If she went through into the scullery to wash them up she would probably bump into Fran, and have to stand there for half an hour listening to her moans about being left on her own all day with three kids.

Averyl would be awake by six thirty ready for her early-morning bottle. Instead of bringing it back upstairs, and taking Averyl into her bed to feed her as she usually did, Sara promised herself she'd get dressed the moment she woke up and sort the place out.

For once Averyl failed to act as an alarm clock. When Sara eventually surfaced from a deep sleep it was to hear Fran yelling up the stairs that there was someone down there waiting to see her.

Grabbing her coat, and putting it on over the old grey flannel shirt of Rhys's that she used as a nightdress, Sara padded along the landing and peered down the stairs to see who it was.

Her heart galloped. Standing in the hallway, smartly dressed in her brown winter coat with its thick fur collar and matching brown fur hat, was Olwen Edwards.

Sara's first thought was the state of her living-room, and the realisation that there was absolutely nothing at all she could do about it.

For one frantic moment, Sara wondered if she could retreat into her bedroom and pretend to be asleep. Even as the thought crossed her mind, Olwen looked up. Their eyes locked, and Sara knew it was too late.

Pushing her uncombed hair back from her face, Sara went down to greet Rhys's mother. As she led the way into the room and heard Olwen Edwards's gasp at the chaos that met their eyes, Sara mentally cringed.

Olwen thinks I always live like this, she thought guiltily. If only I'd stopped to tidy up before going to Ponty instead of dashing off and leaving such a muddle, with unwashed dishes on the table. In one corner there was also a pile of dirty clothes that she was intending to wash as soon as she had given Averyl her breakfast.

'This is a surprise,' Sara said, moving Averyl's coat and bonnet off a chair so that Olwen could sit down.

Olwen smirked. 'Caught you on the hop by the look of things, or do you always live like this?'

Sara smiled apologetically. 'I overslept this morning, see. Usually Averyl is awake by half six and I'm up making her a feed.'

'Really? Well, it's half past nine now, girl! I was up before six making sure my Lloyd had some breakfast inside him before he went off to the pit,' Olwen commented snidely.

Sara looked defeated. 'I had no idea it was that late. Can I make you a cuppa?' she asked, trying to ignore Averyl's distressed wailing cries that were now coming from the room above.

'Better see to that baba first, hadn't you? Or are

you so used to her crying that it doesn't bother you?'

Sara took a deep breath and squared her shoulders. She mustn't let Olwen put her down or upset her. This was her home; she should be the one in charge, the one making decisions. Even if the room was a tip, that was her affair. Once she was washed and properly dressed she would be able to handle things better, she told herself.

'Yes, I'd better bring Averyl down before I do anything else. Why don't you take your coat off, and then when I've fed her we can have a nice cuppa.'

'Take my coat off? It's freezing in here, girl! Enough to give you pneumonia!'

Once she was upstairs, and she saw the state of her bedroom, Sara wished she could wake up and find that this wasn't happening, that it was all a bad dream.

Averyl was standing up in her cot, screaming; her face was blotched, her eyes were red from crying and her nose was running. Her sobs were thick and mucus laden as if she had a heavy cold and it had gone on to her chest.

Sara didn't know which to do first: get dressed herself or take Averyl downstairs. She caught a glimpse of her reflection in the piece of cracked mirror that was part of the wardrobe door and shuddered. She had never looked worse.

Quickly she put on the clothes she had been wearing the day before. They were crumpled because she'd been so tired when she got home from Pontypridd that she'd thrown them down in a heap, but they looked better than Rhys's old grey shirt and her coat.

Averyl was soaking wet, and her nappy smelly, so Sara took it off, wiped her clean with her nightie, fastened on a dry nappy, and popped the dress she'd been wearing the day before over her head.

'Here she is,' Sara announced, carrying her into the living-room. 'Look who's come to see you, Averyl. Do you remember Nana Edwards?'

Olwen almost snatched the baby from Sara's arms. 'Of course she remembers her Nana. Cared for her right from the minute she was born, didn't I? Are you a hungry little baba, then?' she crooned. She turned to Sara. 'Hurry up and get her food ready then, girl, and I'll feed her.'

Sara looked round helplessly. There was nothing in the room to give her except the couple of rusks left in the packet she'd bought in Pontypridd. She crumbled them into a dish, wondering if there was any milk or whether she would have to dash across to the corner shop for some.

To her relief there was a half-bottle of milk on her shelf out in the scullery.

'That doesn't look very fresh,' Olwen commented when she came back with it. She took the bottle out of Sara's hand and sniffed it before Sara could pour it on to the rusk.

'This milk is off, girl! It's as sour as can be; rancid, in fact. What are you trying to do, poison the poor little mite? No wonder she looks such a pitiful little scrap if that's the way you're looking after her.'

'If you'll hold her for just a minute I'll nip out to the corner shop and get some fresh milk,' Sara told her. She held out a piece of dry rusk to Averyl. 'Here, my love, chew on that and you can have a proper breakfast in a minute.'

'Put a comb through your hair before you go out into the street or you'll frighten someone,' Olwen advised. 'Here,' she opened her capacious handbag and handed her own comb to Sara. 'You'd better use this, I don't suppose you have one or even if you have you'll never find it in all this jumble.'

Sara bit down on her lower lip to stop herself from answering back. She ran the comb through her hair and then handed it back to Olwen.

'Here, take this,' Olwen told her, handing her a half-crown, 'and buy something nice for little Averyl. See if they've got some honey, she used to like that on a crust. Go on, girl, take it,' Olwen persisted. 'I'm not short of a bob or two now that Lloyd's working again.'

Ten minutes later Sara was back with fresh milk, a loaf, some butter and a jar of honey. The cold December air had whipped some colour into her cheeks and restored a little of her confidence, and now she felt ready to face Rhys's mother.

The living-room was empty. There was no sign of either Olwen or Averyl. Sara plonked her shopping down on the table and looked round her, bemused. They couldn't have followed her to the shop or she would have seen them. She looked out into the small back yard in case they were in the scullery, but they weren't there either. Then she heard the footsteps overhead and her face flamed. Olwen was up in her bedroom! Sara dashed upstairs, trying not to think about the state the room was in. She found

Olwen up there, busily collecting Averyl's few clean clothes together in a pile.

'What are you doing?' Sara demanded.

'Oh, you're back at last.' Olwen pushed Averyl into Sara's arms. 'You'd better feed her then, the poor little mite is absolutely starving. Go on, take her downstairs and give her some breakfast. You did get something for her to eat, didn't you?'

'Of course I did. And I got her some honey like you suggested.'

'Good! Go on then, see to her. I'll be down in a minute.'

Sara hesitated. She wanted to demand that Olwen stopped gathering Averyl's clothes up into a pile, and came out of her bedroom, but her tongue seemed to have stuck to the roof of her mouth, preventing her from speaking.

Tearfully she turned and took Averyl downstairs.

Without stopping to warm the milk because that would have meant going outside to the scullery, Sara tipped some over the rusk, mashed it up and fed it to the child.

Averyl was ravenous. She gulped it down so fast that she started choking. As Olwen came downstairs and into the room, Averyl was sick, bringing up not only the breakfast that she'd eaten too fast, but also the mucus that had been clogging her chest.

'My God, girl, that child is in a right state,' Olwen exclaimed. 'Not fit to look after her, you're not. I'm taking her back to Tonypandy with me! She needs proper care or she's going to be really ill.'

'Hold on, you can't do that!' Sara protested furiously.

'Can't I? Wait until I see my Rhys when he gets home from work, and I tell him what I think of you both.'

'You'll have a long wait,' Sara snapped. 'He's away at sea.'

Olwen looked so taken aback that Sara wanted to laugh. 'Well, I can't say I blame him if he has to live in a sty like this. Not used to it, see. My Rhys was always brought up decent, like. He always had clean clothes waiting for him, good food on the table, and lived in a nicely kept home. He'll understand. He'll only have to look at this place, and the state of you, to know why I have taken little Averyl back with me.'

There was so much truth in what Olwen was saying that Sara could think of no reply. She held out her hands to Averyl, seeking comfort from the feel of the tiny arms around her neck, but Averyl turned away and clung on to Olwen.

Sara felt it was the last straw. She was losing everything. Even her own child didn't want her. She looked around at the shambles that was their home and felt sick inside. If only Rhys was here he would know how to handle his mother. As it was, she had no idea when he would be home again.

Sara felt her entire world was in turmoil. She was no longer able to think clearly. She looked at Averyl snuggled up in Olwen's arms, and felt her heart would break. Then she thought of her own little sister Myfanwy and the spartan clean home she lived in, and wondered if cleanliness and tidiness were as important as love and care.

'I'd better make that cuppa I promised you,' she said in an effort to pull herself back to normality.

'Oh, don't bother. If there's no chance of seeing Rhys then we'll be on our way, see. Find the baba's coat, will you? And a big shawl if you have one, it's bitter outside. You can let me have the rest of her things when you've washed them.'

'But you can't take my baby from me like that, I don't want her to go,' Sara argued, her face white with anger.

Olwen stiffened. 'Don't try to stop me. You've obviously been neglecting the child. Look at the state I found her in. Her little chest is wheezing with every breath she takes. She'll have pneumonia if she stays here any longer.'

Struggling to keep calm, Sara took a deep breath. She knew Olwen had her at a disadvantage. There was no excuse for the state her home was in, but no one, not even Olwen, could accuse her of neglecting Averyl.

'Oh no, she won't! She's got the snuffles but that's only because she had a long day yesterday. I went to Pontypridd for the day so she's a bit tired, see.'

'Rubbish, girl, it has nothing to do with that!' Olwen said contemptuously.

'Averyl is teething. She always gets a bit of a cold when she's teething, and it usually goes on to her chest,' Sara explained.

'Excuses, excuses! Stop trying to blame the child for the state she's in,' Olwen scolded. 'I know a bad chest when I hear one, girl! This poor little mite is underfed, neglected and living in a pigsty, and that's all there is to it. I'm taking her back home to Tonypandy with me, so don't you dare try to stop me.'

Chapter Twenty-six

The day after Olwen took Averyl away, Sara stayed in bed all day. She felt ill, her head was muzzy, every bone in her body ached, and even her eyes hurt when she lifted a corner of the curtains to see what sort of day it was.

She would have stayed there the next day as well if Fran hadn't come hammering on her bedroom door.

'I'm all right, leave me alone,' she called out, hoping Fran would go away.

'Come on then, get dressed. I'll put the kettle on and we can have a cuppa before I leave.'

Sara forced herself awake. 'What are you talking about?' she called back groggily.

'I'm leaving Cardiff, and going back to my Mam's place.'

'You mean for Christmas?' Sara yawned.

'No, I don't bloody well mean for Christmas, I mean for good!' Fran said defiantly. 'So hurry up and come downstairs.'

Sara sat up in bed, feeling bemused. She was sure she must have got it wrong. Fran couldn't be leaving; Coburn Street was her home. And if Fran went, then what would happen to her? Fran was the one renting the house; she was only Fran's tenant.

'Hang on, *cariad*, wait while I pull on some clothes

and then you can tell me all about it,' she called out. Hurriedly she dressed yet again in the clothes that she had worn to Pontypridd, and which were still lying in a heap on the bedroom floor.

'Christ, you look rough!' Fran grinned when Sara shambled into her room, rubbing the sleep from her eyes. 'Have you been having a bad night with the baba?'

Sara ran her hands through her hair, trying to tidy it. 'No, nothing like that. I think I must have a cold. I feel a bit better today than I did yesterday, though, so I'll probably be all right in another day or two.'

'Why didn't you sing out and I'd have brought you something up? I could have looked after Averyl for you. Where is she, by the way? I haven't heard her crying for the past couple of days.'

'Averyl's not here,' Sara said bleakly. 'When Rhys's Mam came the day before yesterday she took her back to Tonypandy with her.'

Fran nodded approvingly. 'There's handy. Wanted to give you a bit of a rest, like, until you were over your cold and feeling better, did she?'

Sara shook her head. 'No, nothing like that. Turning up out of the blue, she caught me on the hop, see. I'd been to Pontypridd the day before to find out how my little sister was getting on, and my rooms were in a terrible mess. Pigsty she called it. Said it wasn't healthy for a baby to live here, and that I wasn't fit to look after her.'

Fran puffed out her cheeks in disbelief. 'There's a nerve! And she took your Averyl back to Tonypandy?'

Sara nodded, fat tears streaking down her cheeks.

'And you let her, you silly cow!'

'What else could I do? She was right, see. It was a tip, and I had no food in the place. Right old mess, I was in.'

Fran ran her hand through her own straggly hair. 'Right pair, aren't we!'

Sara gave her a watery smile. 'What's all this about you going back to your Mam's, then?'

Fran shrugged helplessly. 'Seems the only thing I can do. I've not had any word from Dai since the day he sailed.'

'So? I haven't heard from Rhys. You don't really expect to hear from them, do you?' she asked with a grimace.

'I don't bloody know. The trouble is I've got no money left. It's Christmas next week, and I can't even buy a sodding cake or an orange and an apple to go in Robbie's and Hilda's stockings.'

'Well, that's not the end of the world now, is it!' Sara protested. 'At least you've still got your own place. If we pool what we've got then we won't have such a bad time over Christmas.'

Fran shook her head. 'No, I've had enough pinching and scraping. My Mam and Dad have a small farm a few miles outside Caerphilly, see. Plenty of milk and eggs for the kids, and fields for them to play in. Lovely, see! Mam's been on at me for ages to go back home, so that's what I'm doing.'

Sara's face fell. 'What about this place? If you move out, Fran, then I'll be out on the street, won't I?' she asked accusingly.

'God, you must think I'm a right cow if you think

I'd do that to you,' Fran snapped, her voice tight with indignation. 'Of course I've thought of that. Glenda Williams is taking over the tenancy. She's not married, and can afford the rent each week. In fact, she's paid off the back rent that I owed. The landlord and Glenda have both agreed that you can stay on, so that's all settled.'

'Been busy, haven't you!'

Fran laughed. 'About time I got myself organised, and once I get an idea I like to put it into action straight away. I hope it isn't too much of a shock to you, *cariad*, but I've been that busy with arrangements, and so excited. I feel happier than I have for years. Mam's pleased, too. Loves the kids, see, and she's been fretting because she never sees Hilda and Robbie. She's only seen Emlyn once since he was born.'

'That's because she's only been here to see you once, and then she only stayed about an hour,' Sara said indignantly.

Fran sighed. 'I know, but she is getting on, see, and the journey down to Cardiff is a bit too much for her. Poor Mam, she's not too good on her legs. Anyway, this way I'll be there to give her a hand around the place, and she'll be able to see all she wants of her grandchildren.'

'Have you told Dai?'

Fran shook her head. She poured out two cups of tea and pushed one across the table to Sara. 'Not much point in writing to tell him, now is there? He'll probably be home before the letter reaches him, you know how it is.'

'So how will he know where you've gone?'

Fran shrugged. 'You can tell him I've gone back to my Mam's place when he gets here. He knows where it is.'

Sara bit her lip. 'I can't say I relish the idea of doing that. He's bound to be flaming angry.'

'Don't worry about it, Sara. If Glenda Williams is around she'll tell him.'

'So when is this Glenda Williams moving in?'

'Right away. As soon as I move out. A van's coming to pick up my bits and pieces of furniture, and the kids' things, in about an hour's time.'

Sara raised her eyebrows. 'You certainly don't waste time, do you?' she said.

'The kids and me are riding back to Caerphilly in the van as well.' Fran laughed. 'That's why they're so quiet. Robbie and Hilda are both up in the front bedroom watching out for the van and Emlyn is still asleep.'

Sara drained her cup. 'Do you think I'll get on with this Glenda Williams?' she asked anxiously.

'Oh yes! She's lovely. Bit older than us mind, but lively, if you know what I mean. Gets out and about a lot. Likes going to the pictures and all that. Plenty of friends, so she tells me, and she won't be sitting around in your place all day making a nuisance of herself.'

'A neat and tidy old maid!'

'No. You've got the wrong idea about her. She's not like that at all. She's on her own now, but she was married for years until her husband died.' Fran laughed. 'Tidier than us, mind you, but then it would be hard not to be.'

Sara pulled a face. 'I'd better clean my rooms up before she gets here or we'll get off to a bad start.'

Fran shrugged. 'I've done the scullery out, looks as neat as a new pin.'

Sara stood up. 'It shouldn't take me long. Help fill in my day. It seems awfully empty without Averyl.'

'Then go and get her back!'

Sara nodded. 'I'll give it a day or two, until I'm feeling better,' she prevaricated. Although she didn't want to complain to Fran, Sara was feeling weaker and dizzier than she had since Averyl was born.

'If you do that Rhys's mother will insist on keeping her over Christmas, it's only a week away, you know.'

'I'll have her home for the New Year and make a fresh start then,' Sara promised.

Fran laughed drily. 'Same as me! I thought the start of 1931 would be a good time to get my life in order. Foolish I've been, sticking around here and Dai away at sea more than he is at home.'

'But you love him, *cariad*?'

Fran shrugged. 'When he's here. When he's not, my mind goes blank. Sometimes I can't even remember what he looks like.'

Sara laughed. 'You've only got to look at young Robbie! He's the spit of his Dada except that he's got your freckles.'

Fran shook her head. 'It's not the sort of life I want, though, see. I want my man at home every night. I don't want to have to struggle to bring up the kids on my own, with them never seeing him, and him being like a stranger when he does turn up every three or four months.'

'Going home to your Mam is not going to change that.'

'No, I know that, but Robbie needs a man in his life and my Dada will be there for him. Robbie's getting cheeky, see. Answers me back a lot, and Hilda has started copying him.'

Sara sighed. 'You're probably doing the right thing. Take no notice of me, I'm being selfish because I don't fancy being left here with a stranger. Got used to you, *cariad*.'

'You'll get used to Glenda. You'll like her. Lovely, she is. Like I said, older than us, but not all that much. Seen life, has Glenda.'

Sara's eyebrows shot up. 'What sort of work does she do?'

'She doesn't need to work! Her husband died about six months ago and left her well provided for. He was years older than her. She used to be a nurse at Cardiff Infirmary, and that's where they met. After they married they lived in Caerphilly and she became friendly with my Mam. One day Mam told her I was fed up on my own in Cardiff and was thinking about going back home and she said if I did that then she would like to have my place here in Cardiff. That's how it all happened really.

'I explained that you'd want to go on living here and that she may have to wait for your rent until Rhys comes home next month and she's quite happy about that, so stop worrying, *cariad*. Use what money you've got to feed yourself and Averyl.

And for God's sake, go and get Averyl back. Do you hear?'

'Yes, I will. Give me a few days to sort myself out, and then I'll go to Tonypandy.'

'Did you say you'd been to Pontypridd the day before Mrs Edwards came here?'

Sara nodded. 'I went to see how my little sister was. I couldn't bring myself to tell you about it beforehand because I was so nervous, and it was something I had to do on my own.' She shook her head dolefully. 'The way they treat her, I felt as if I was a kid again and living it all over again.'

'Christ! That bad!'

'Gwladys works her like a little slave and smacks her for the most trivial things. And my Dada is so taken up with the Lord, and living according to the Bible, that even the slightest slip makes him go wild. Myfanwy forgot to say Grace before sitting down to a piece of bread and dripping when she came in from school at midday so he took it off her, and made her go back to school without anything. Threatening her he was, telling her that she'd get nothing at tea time either.'

Fran's eyes blazed. 'Wicked old bastard! What did you do?'

'Told them I was nipping out to get some rusks for Averyl so I'd walk Myfanwy back to school. I bought her a bar of chocolate and a packet of biscuits on the way.'

'Poor little dab!'

Sara sighed. 'I feel guilty about her, Fran. Before I left home I promised Myfanwy she could come and live with Rhys and me once we got our own place.

She thought that was why I'd come back. I begged them to let her come and stay with me over Christmas, but they refused. Broke my heart having to leave her there, knowing she'd probably get a thrashing from Dada for even wanting to be with me.'

The sound of little feet running overhead, and the excited voices of Robbie and Hilda screaming, 'The van's coming, the van's here,' brought Fran to her feet.

'This is it then, *cariad*.' She gave Sara a quick hug. 'Glenda will be here later today or some time tomorrow, and I know you'll like her, so good luck to you both.'

'Can I do anything to help?'

'No, *cariad*. Everything is packed, even the baby has been fed ready, see. The driver will carry all the boxes and cases out for me. All we have to do is pile in. You don't look at all well, I'd suggest you go back to bed. Make sure you come and see us when Rhys gets home.'

Sara stood on the front step, shivering in the December cold, her dark eyes misted with tears, as Fran, her children and all their belongings were packed into the van. She wouldn't even have their company over Christmas, she thought glumly.

Chapter Twenty-seven

Sara felt desolate as she watched the van carrying Fran, her family and belongings, turn out of Coburn Street into Crwys Road. Her head drooped dejectedly as it disappeared into the distance. It was the end of an era for both of them!

Fran was right, though, she must pull herself together and go back to Tonypandy, bring Averyl home and build a new life before Rhys came home in the New Year.

There were still four days to go to Christmas, and another week after that before she needed to make that fresh start, she consoled herself as she went upstairs, and crawled back under the blankets.

Eleven days to dream about the sort of new life she wanted with Averyl. I mustn't forget about Myfanwy, she reminded herself. I am probably the only one who really knows what that poor child is suffering.

Gwladys and her Dada had such an air of respectability about them that no one would believe how evil they could be. Only Martha Pritchard had ever guessed that something not quite right was going on when she had lived at home.

She wished Rhys was at home so that she could confide in him, and he could tell her what to do for the best. She should have told him everything that had happened years ago, before they had come to Cardiff, in fact.

He deserved to know the truth, but she had always felt so ashamed. Even Fran thought her concern about her little sister was because Gwladys and her Dada were so strict with Myfanwy, and punished her so harshly.

Rhys had only been away a couple of months, but it seemed like eternity. His brief spell ashore, working for Gareth, the baker in Elm Street, had given her a taste of what their life together could be like, and now she felt the same way as Fran did. She didn't want to go on living on her own for months at a stretch, trying to make ends meet, and never knowing when there would be any more money.

If Rhys had been in the navy then he would have had to make her a regular allowance, and she would be able to go to the shipping offices down at the Pier Head and collect it every month. As it was, she had to eke out what money he left behind without even knowing whether it had to last her for two months or five.

As the daylight faded she drifted off to sleep. When she woke several hours later she had no idea of the time, or even what day of the week it was. She felt terrible. Her body was one gigantic ache, and a hammer was pounding inside her head as if it was going to break her skull wide open at any minute.

She forced herself to get out of bed, wrapping herself in her coat, intending to go downstairs and make a hot drink. She managed to get as far as the landing before a wave of darkness seemed to envelop her, and she felt the ground rising up and crashing into her.

When she next opened her eyes she was back in bed again and a stranger, a woman she had never seen in her life before, was holding a glass of something hot and aromatic to her lips. Sara gulped at it thirstily; coughing and choking as it hit the back of her throat with a burning stab that took her breath away.

'Come on, *cariad*, finish it all up and then go back to sleep again,' a voice gently ordered.

Obediently she did as she was told, too exhausted to argue, or even ask the woman her name. She'd do that next time, she told herself, when she started her new life, whenever that was.

Afterwards, Sara couldn't remember whether this had happened once, twice or a dozen times. All she did recall was that it was the same woman, the same kind of drink, and each time she felt a little less exhausted. Nevertheless, she was quite happy to sink back on the pillow and drift off to sleep again as soon as she'd swallowed the mixture.

When she eventually came back to reality she lay for a long time staring up at the ceiling, trying to remember what it was that was so important. Unable to focus her mind, and wondering why everything was so incredibly quiet, she got out of bed and padded across to the window.

Drawing one of the curtains aside, she stared out in amazement. The entire street was blanketed in snow. Dazzling, white, unmarked, pristine snow. It covered the road, the pavement, and the doorsteps, and had even lodged itself into the window-sills and crevices like thick white cotton wool.

Shivering, she crept back under the blankets, but she could no longer curl up and sleep. Her whole body was as tense as a geared-up engine. She felt restive, needing to get up and do something physical, something positive.

When she looked for her clothes on the chair where she usually left them they weren't there. For a moment she was panic-stricken. What had happened? Who had taken them?

'Calm down!' she told herself out loud. 'Try and think where they will be?'

Gradually her mind stopped spinning, and she began to reason more lucidly. Her blue dress and her grey skirt and two cream blouses, she discovered, were all hanging up in the wardrobe where they should be. Her stockings and underclothes were in the chest of drawers all clean and neatly folded, ready for her to wear.

Her fingers were clumsy as she tried to get dressed. All the time she was conscious that something was missing. Something, or someone. She wasn't sure which. Then she remembered, and panic flooded through her like a gush of scalding water. Averyl! Where was her baby? What had happened to her?

Without stopping to comb her hair she ran from the room and down the stairs. Her living-room was so tidy that it looked as if no one ever used it. There was a faintly musty smell as if it had been shut up for a long time.

Looking apprehensively round the deserted

room, she could see that there wasn't even a trace of Averyl or any of her belongings. So what on earth had happened to her? Had someone taken her away? Worse still, had something happened to her? On the brink of panic, Sara shied away from that line of reasoning, too afraid to let her mind dwell on the worst possibility of all.

The sound of the front door opening made her hold her breath. She heard a woman's steps on the linoleum in the hallway and relaxed.

'Fran? Is that you?'

As her door opened Sara stared open-mouthed. It wasn't Fran who stood there, but a tall handsome woman in her forties, or perhaps older, with rich chestnut hair and startling green eyes. She had on a grey fur coat, and as she undid the fastenings Sara saw she was wearing a bright red wool dress under it.

'So you're up at last!' The woman smiled. 'I was beginning to think you were never going to come back to the land of the living!' She removed her leather gloves. 'I'm Glenda Williams, by the way,' she said, stretching out a hand.

Sara hesitated, then slowly reached out and took the woman's hand. She was a stranger and yet not a stranger. She couldn't remember having seen her face before, but she was sure she'd heard that deep rich voice.

'I've taken over Fran's tenancy on the house. She's gone back to live with her Mam in Caerphilly,' Glenda explained.

Vaguely, Sara started to recall Fran telling her that someone called Glenda Williams was moving in, and she remembered standing on the front doorstep watching the van that came to collect Fran, the children and their belongings, disappear down the street. After that, though, everything was hazy, almost a blank.

'You were out for the count for almost a week,' Glenda said conversationally. 'You had a touch of pneumonia to go with it, or so the doctor said.'

'And you looked after me?'

The woman smiled broadly, showing perfect white teeth. 'Well, yes, you came with the tenancy, see, so I felt it was my duty to get you back on your feet. And I used to be a nurse, I expect Fran told you?'

'Yes. That was very good of you. I'm grateful. Thank you very much.'

'That's all right. It's satisfying to see I've been so successful. Instead of standing here freezing, why don't we go to my room and have a cuppa, and get to know each other better? Fran told me a bit about you,' she smiled, 'but it's not the same as hearing it from the horse's mouth, so to speak, now is it?'

Sara nodded, following her as if being led on a piece of string. She was so weak that she couldn't think straight, and her knees felt as if they would buckle under her at any minute. All she wanted to do was sit down.

The tea revived her spirits and cleared her head. She looked round, noticing the many changes Glenda had made to Fran's living-room, and thought how different it looked.

Slowly she remembered the things Fran had told her about Glenda. That she seemed to have money, that she liked everything nice and neat, that she was a widow.

So she probably didn't have any children, Sara reasoned. Was that why Averyl wasn't here? Had Glenda Williams sent her away because she didn't like the noise and mess that children made?

Sara swallowed another mouthful of tea and studied Glenda. She was very striking to look at with her gleaming chestnut hair and brilliant green eyes. She had a good figure, too, and her red wool dress, cinched at the waist by a navy leather belt, showed it off to advantage.

She seemed to be kindly, intelligent and capable, with a quick probing mind. Sara guessed she must be in her mid to late forties, but she was so well made up with powder and lipstick, even at this time in the morning, that it was difficult to be sure.

No, Sara decided, she didn't look the sort of person who would do something like that. But she had to know. She cleared her throat. 'Where's my Averyl, then?' she asked bluntly.

'Averyl?' Glenda Williams looked puzzled. 'Is that your baby's name?'

Sara nodded. 'That's right, so where is she then?'

'I'm not sure, *cariad*. Fran said something about you having a baby, but there was no baby in the house when I arrived. Only you here on the floor unconscious.'

Then everything jolted into place. The visit to Pontypridd to see her little sister, Myfanwy, and then the very next morning, before she was even up, Rhys's mother arriving, and insisting that Averyl wasn't being cared for properly. They'd exchanged strong words, and then Olwen had insisted on wrapping Averyl up in a shawl and taking her away.

'What day is it?'

'Tuesday! Why? What's wrong, Sara?' Glenda asked, her green eyes watchful. 'You look as if you've seen a ghost.'

'No, what date is it, I mean?'

'It's the thirtieth of December.'

Sara's voice rose. 'You mean Christmas is over?' she asked shrilly.

'I'm afraid so, *cariad*. It's New Year's Eve tomorrow.'

Shuddering, Sara put both hands over her face. 'I was going to sort everything out by the first of January. The New Year was to be the start of a whole new life.'

'You've still got time,' Glenda told her quietly. 'What sort of new life are you planning on having?'

'I want to get my baby back. Her Nana, Olwen Edwards, came and took her away before Christmas. Now it's too late to do that. I'd never even manage to get up to Tonypandy in this snow.'

'You're probably right,' Glenda agreed, 'but you can still make your plans before the New Year starts. Then the moment the weather improves you can go to Tonypandy.'

Sara sighed. 'It sounds easy, but you don't know Rhys's mother! She is so strong-willed that now she's had Averyl all this time, without a word of protest from me, she'll never give her up.'

'Nonsense! Averyl's your child.'

'I know that, but Olwen will say that I'm not fit to

look after her. The day she came here she said the place was looking like a pigsty and not fit for the baby to live in.'

'That was then, this is now. She couldn't say that if she saw your room looking as it does today!'

'True enough, but that's thanks to you, not me,' Sara sighed despondently.

'Let's get the facts straight,' Glenda persisted. 'You say Olwen Edwards arrived unexpectedly? You hadn't invited her?'

'No! Indeed I hadn't,' Sara agreed. 'I had no idea she was coming.'

'So why was your room in such a mess?'

'I'd been to Pontypridd the day before, visiting my own family. I was tired out when I got back, and not feeling too good, so I decided to leave everything until the morning, and then I overslept.'

'So you weren't up when she arrived?'

'I wasn't even awake!'

'No wonder your place was a bit of a tip!'

'It was petty grim, I must admit that,' Sara said ruefully. 'The bag with all Averyl's dirty nappies, all her clothes, and the cups and things we used when I got home, were all lying around.'

'Hardly the crime of the century.'

'There's more! I'd no milk to make a cup of tea for Olwen or to give Averyl. I'd even run out of bread and had to pop over the road to the corner shop to get some.'

Glenda shrugged. 'It happens. Even if you'd had milk in, it would probably have gone off by the next day.'

Sara smiled. 'You make it sound so normal.'

'Well, *cariad*, let's face it, we all run short of things from time to time. It was sheer bad luck happening to you when someone that mattered chanced to drop by. If she'd let you know she was coming you'd have had the place looking like a new pin, now wouldn't you? And you would have been up and dressed, and had the baby all ready and waiting for her.'

'That's true.'

'So really there's no problem at all. Not for you, at any rate. All we have to do is wait until the weather improves, and then pop up to Tonypandy and collect Averyl, and thank Olwen for looking after her while you've been ill.'

'We?' Sara looked astonished. 'You mean you'll help me?'

Glenda smiled broadly. 'I'll do my best.'

'And you'll come with me to Tonypandy?'

'Of course I will, and believe me, it won't be my fault, *cariad*, if we don't bring your little Averyl back home with us.'

Chapter Twenty-eight

The pristine white snow had turned to a miserable grey mush, and the sky was as leaden as Sara's mood when she and Glenda Williams set out for Tonypandy. Although her heart ached to hold Averyl in her arms again she was quaking inwardly at the thought of facing Olwen.

'If we don't go today then we may get another fall of snow and the roads could become impossible again,' Glenda insisted when Sara suggested postponing their trip.

'Another few days and before we know it we'll be into the middle of January. New Year resolutions are supposed to be started on the first day of the New Year, not halfway through it.'

'Yes, I suppose you're right.' Sara picked up the thick grey shawl she was taking with her to wrap Averyl in, and buried her face in its softness. She'd hardly slept for worrying whether or not she was doing the right thing in bringing Averyl back to Cardiff. She desperately wanted her, hungered for her, but she couldn't forget Olwen's accusation that she wasn't fit to be a mother.

'Here, *cariad*, hold this for a moment,' Glenda said, handing Sara a shopping bag. 'This Olwen Edwards mightn't even ask us in when she knows why we've come, let alone offer us a cup of tea or anything to eat, so I thought we'd go prepared. I've made some sandwiches to take with us.

'Now, if we've got everything I'll lock up. I've banked down the fire in my place so it should be lovely and warm in there when we get back.'

Shivering, Sara tightened the scarf around her neck. 'It's awfully good of you, Glenda, to go to all this trouble, taking up your time like this.'

Glenda smiled and patted her arm. 'Don't you worry your head about it. It's time I took a little bit of a holiday, see.'

Sara sighed. 'Olwen and Lloyd aren't going to be very pleased about what we're doing. I don't think I'd have the nerve to go through with it on my own.'

The moment they knocked on the door of the Edwardses' house it became obvious that Sara was right. When she saw the pair of them standing on the doorstep, Olwen scowled, and tried to slam the door shut again, but Glenda was too quick for her.

'Hello, Mrs Edwards,' she said cheerfully, putting her foot over the threshold. 'You don't know me, but I'm a friend of Sara's. She rents rooms in my house, see.'

Olwen's lip curled. 'That tip!' she sneered. 'Be better off back there cleaning up the mess, wouldn't you. Never saw such a pigsty in my life. Downright filthy it was. No place for a baby!'

'I want Averyl back, we've come to fetch her,' Sara said, her voice quavering.

'What you want and what you get are two different things. One thing you're not going to get is that baby. It would be criminal letting her go back to live in that filthy hole.'

'The day you called I was ill . . .'

'Ill? Ill!' Olwen shrieked. 'Been out gadding about, more likely. I know your sort,' she went on derisively. 'The moment their husbands' backs are turned they let their homes go to pieces, neglect themselves and their children!'

Lloyd appeared from the back of the house, puffing on his pipe, a worried look on his face. 'What on earth is going on, Olwen? Who is it you're talking to? I can hear you out in the back yard.' He paused, and there was a welcoming smile on his face the minute he saw Sara, 'Hello, my lovely, come to take little Averyl home, have you?'

Sara took a deep breath of relief. The shouting had frightened her, and she'd been sure that Olwen would never let Averyl go, but Lloyd's calm manner restored some of her optimism.

'Hello, Lloyd. This is Glenda Williams, my landlady.'

'Pleased to meet you!' His blue eyes studied Glenda appraisingly as he shook hands with her.

'How is Averyl?' Sara asked anxiously.

'Oh, she's doing fine. Crawling everywhere and pulling herself up on to her feet now. She'll be toddling round on her own in next to no time. Going to have your hands full when that happens, *cariad*.'

'I can't wait to see her.'

'Well, come on in then, don't stand there on the doorstep,' he insisted. A coughing spasm hit him.

'Come on in and warm yourselves, you both look frozen,' he gasped.

'They're not coming into my house, Lloyd Edwards,' Olwen declared, defiantly folding her arms across her chest.

'Don't talk so bloody daft, woman,' he puffed. 'What's the bloody sense of us all standing here letting all the heat out of the house and all the cold in?'

He firmly elbowed Olwen to one side. 'Come on in now, my lovelies, and get yourselves warm, while Olwen makes us all a nice cup of tea.'

'Where is Averyl then?' Sara asked anxiously as they went into the cosy living-room.

'Having her morning nap. Pleased to see you, she'll be, keeps asking for her Mammy!'

'There's lovely,' Sara beamed. 'I was afraid she might forget me, see.'

Lloyd nodded understandingly. 'Heard from our Rhys lately?' he asked, coughing noisily.

Sara shook her head. 'Not since he went to sea. He should be back soon, though. He doesn't usually bother to write while he's away because he's usually back in port before I get the letter.'

Lloyd tamped on his pipe, lighted it with a spill and drew on it deeply. 'Funny business, this going to sea. Not much of a life for a married man, or for his wife and family.'

Sara sighed. 'I know, but like I told you it was all he could get.'

'Oh, I do understand. This damn Depression has messed up all our lives, especially here in the Valleys. Miners always seem to be on strike, or on short time. One's much the same as the other since it means there's no money coming in. Is your Dada still working?'

'No.' Sara shook her head. 'There was an explosion, and he was caught in the fall and his arm was broken. Can't swing a pick now so he's no use to them.'

Lloyd shook his head, drawing heavily on his pipe. 'Where's Olwen with that tea?' he muttered, going out into the kitchen to look for her.

Glenda and Sara exchanged glances, and Glenda raised her eyebrows and grinned, but neither of them spoke for fear of being overheard.

It was Lloyd who brought the tray of tea in. Olwen stayed out in the kitchen, clattering dishes, but refusing to come and talk to them. Sara wondered what to do next. They couldn't sit there all day drinking one cup of tea.

Her dilemma was saved by a thin wailing cry from upstairs. Olwen shot through from the kitchen, into the hall and up the stairs without a word to anyone. The minutes ticked by with agonising slowness. Sara's eyes were riveted on the door, waiting for her to appear with Averyl.

'Dammo! Where's the woman got to with that baba?' Lloyd said irritably. He walked across to the hall door and shouted up the stairs, 'Do you want me to come up and carry her down?'

There was no reply. Lloyd sighed. 'I'm glad you've come to collect Averyl, too much for Olwen, she is, see. Not that Olwen will admit it, mind you, but she can hardly lift her. It's not that Averyl's all that heavy, but she wriggles like a little eel.'

'Shall I go and bring her down?' Sara suggested.

Lloyd shook his head. 'Better not, *cariad,* it will only put Olwen's nose out of joint. She's probably changing Averyl's nappy before she brings her down, so give it another minute and then I'll go up.'

When Lloyd eventually went upstairs and brought Averyl down, Olwen looked so red faced and angry as she stumped down the stairs after them that Sara was afraid she was going to have a seizure.

Once in the living-room, Olwen tried to snatch Averyl from him before he could hand her to Sara.

'Where's her food then?' Lloyd demanded, holding on to the baby and refusing to let go of her.

'Who is this, then?' he murmured, turning Averyl round so that she was facing Sara. 'Is this your Mam come to see you, my lovely?'

Tears in her eyes, Sara held out her arms to her baby and Averyl gurgled happily as Lloyd passed her over. Too choked to speak, Sara smothered her with kisses, cuddling her so tight that Averyl squirmed and began to whimper.

'Stranger, you are to her, see,' Olwen said spitefully, coming through from the kitchen with a bowl of sops. 'Frightening her to death, you are. Come on,' she held out her arms to the baby, 'come to Nana and have something to eat.'

'Let Sara feed her,' Lloyd said quietly.

Olwen angrily pushed the bowl of bread and milk across the table, spilling some of it on the cloth. 'Now look what you've done,' she ranted at no one in particular.

Sara began spooning the food into Averyl, feasting her eyes on the appealing little face, the big blue eyes and the dimpled little hand that kept grabbing at the spoon.

When Averyl had finished, she stood her up on her lap. 'Ready to go home, precious?' she asked, bouncing her up and down.

'You'll have the child sick all over the place, doing that when she's only just finished eating,' Olwen snapped.

Sara stopped what she was doing and handed Averyl to Glenda. 'Will you hold her for a minute?' Turning to Olwen she said, 'Can I have her clothes and things, please, and then we'll be off.'

'You're doing the right thing taking her back home with you,' Lloyd murmured.

Sara nodded. 'I know, and thank you both for taking such good care of her.'

'That baba's not leaving this house,' Olwen declared. 'Not fit to look after her, you're not. Filthy, she was when I came to your place, and your home a pigsty.'

Sara sighed wearily. 'You've said all that time and time again, Olwen. Can't you understand I was ill? I'm more than grateful to you for looking after Averyl, but I'm better now and her place is with me.'

'Her place is here where she'll be properly looked after,' Olwen argued sourly.

'Come on, *cariad*, be reasonable,' Lloyd intervened. 'Sara's right. She's the child's mother, and she's the one who should be looking after her.'

'Fat lot you know about it!' Olwen exclaimed

scornfully, her face dark with anger. 'You didn't see the place. Dirty clothes and unwashed dishes everywhere.'

'Sara's explained why it was like that; she was ill. That's all in the past, *cariad*! Look at her, she's better now, the picture of health!'

'Plastered with paint. Probably daubed that on to save washing her face,' Olwen said cattily.

'We really ought to be going,' Glenda intervened. 'I'd like to get home before it's dark; the days are so short, and the roads are treacherous now the snow's melting.'

'Hang on a minute, then, while I wrap the shawl round her,' Sara said, 'and we'll be off.' She turned to Olwen. 'You can parcel up the rest of her things and post them on to me.'

'Oh no, you don't!' Olwen positioned herself between them and the door into the hallway. 'You're not taking that baba from here. She's staying here with me until our Rhys gets home, you understand?'

'That may not be for weeks, a couple of months even!' Sara reminded her.

'I don't give a damn whether it's weeks, months or even years. She's staying here with me. You're not fit to care for her.'

'And what makes you think you are?' Sara demanded. 'Far too old, you are, Olwen, to look after a young baba. You can hardly lift her! One of these days you'll drop her, and then what will Rhys say? I'll be the one he blames for leaving her with you!' She looked appealingly at Lloyd. 'Can't you say something to make her see sense?'

He nodded, putting his arm around his wife's shoulders. 'Let the little one go, *cariad*. Sara will bring her back up to see us again soon, won't you, my lovely?'

'We'll come to visit you as soon as Rhys gets home,' Sara promised.

'If you take that baba away from here,' snapped Olwen, her eyes gleaming with anger, 'then I never want to set eyes on you again.'

Chapter Twenty-nine

Dai Roberts and Rhys Edwards returned to Coburn Street in the middle of the night in late April. The loud banging on the front door roused Sara from a deep sleep and it took her a while to realise what was happening.

Glenda Williams had already opened her bedroom window, and when she saw two men standing there she'd called down to know what all the racket was about.

Grabbing her coat from the back of her bedroom door, and putting it on over her nightdress, Sara shouted to Glenda that it must be Rhys home from sea, and then she raced downstairs to let them in.

The moment they were inside the door, Sara flung her arms around Rhys, hugging him tightly, her tears of relief that he was home at last flowing freely.

'*Darw*! What's all this, a bloody flood the moment I step over the doorstep?' Rhys joked as he hugged and kissed her in return.

She shook her head, too choked to speak. It had been so long that he even seemed different from when he had left. He still had the same dark curly hair and vivid blue eyes, but his shoulders seemed to be broader and either he was more muscular or he had put on weight. Fresh air and sunshine had tanned his skin and he was so handsome that just looking at him made her heart beat faster.

As Dai dropped his kitbag in the hall, and made to bound up the stairs, Sara let go of Rhys and grabbed at Dai, trying to stop him.

'Fran's not up there,' she warned.

'Then who was it bloody well shouting out of the bedroom window?'

'Glenda Williams.'

'Who the hell is she?'

'She's taken over the house. Fran's in Caerphilly.'

'She's bloody what?'

'Fran and the kids are living at her Mam's place. They moved back there before Christmas,' Sara told him.

'Christ! I don't believe it!' Dai sat down on the stairs, his head in his hands. 'What the hell has she done that for?'

Sara shrugged. 'Fran was lonely with you away and she couldn't manage the kids on her own, not with the new baby as well. Right handful, they were, I can tell you.'

'You could have helped her, couldn't you?' he said accusingly. 'That was why we let you have the rooms here, so that you and Fran would be company for each other when I was away at sea.'

'I did what I could, but I've got my own baba to look after,' she pointed out.

'Bloody hell, I know that, woman, but it was a case of you two looking out for each other,' Dai exploded angrily.

'So who is this woman who's living here now

then, the one shouting out of the window?' Rhys asked.

'Glenda Williams. She's someone Fran knew. She helped Fran pay the back rent that was owing, and then the landlord agreed she could take over the rent book. Fran asked Glenda if I could stay on.'

'Christ! So that means I've got no bloody home!' Dai ranted.

'Yes, you have! Your home is with Fran at her Mam's place. Fran said you knew where that was. You do know where the farm is, don't you, Dai?'

'Of course I damn well do! That doesn't mean to say I want to go there. Bloody hates me, does Fran's Mam,' he said defensively. 'She thinks I'm not good enough for her precious daughter. I may as well bugger off back to sea right now.'

'You will go and see Fran first, though?' Sara persisted anxiously. 'She'll be heartbroken if you don't.'

'*Duw anwyl*, do you take me for a fool?' Dai snarled. 'If she had any thoughts at all about me then she'd have waited here for me. This was our home, wasn't it?'

'You mean it was where you left her when you cleared off to sea,' Sara said heatedly.

'I left her with a roof over her head and money in her purse,' Dai argued doggedly. 'What more could I do for her? As my wife it was her duty to wait here for me.'

'And so she did until her money ran out,' Sara retorted. 'Pinching and scraping, feeding the kids and going without herself. Waiting and worrying about your safety and wondering when, if ever, you were going to return!'

'I've been worried about her and the kids, too,' he defended sulkily.

'If you were so worried about her then why have you never written? Not one word has either of us had from you two since you left,' she added angrily, though she knew she was being unreasonable.

'There wasn't much point in writing, *cariad*,' Rhys intervened. 'We can't post the letters until we reach a port and then there's every chance that we will be home again before the letter reaches you. You know that.'

'It would still be nice to know that you are thinking about us,' Sara grumbled.

'We talked of nothing else but our families back home and our kids, isn't that right, boyo?' Dai said morosely.

'Well, I don't suppose there's much point in arguing about it,' Sara said exasperatedly. 'You'd better remember that line to tell Fran when you see her. Hard time, she's had, with a young baba as well as the other two to look after.'

'That's a wife's job,' Dai muttered in a disgruntled tone. 'And it's her job to look after her man's home while he's away earning a living, not bugger off to her Mam's the minute things get a bit difficult.'

'You are going to Caerphilly, to the farm, to see her?'

'Suppose I'll bloody well have to if I want to see my little ones.' He bent down and picked up his kitbag, and hoisted it on to his shoulder.

'Hold on, mun,' Rhys intervened. 'You can't

bugger off like that, not without some food and a hot drink. Bloody freezing outside and there won't be any trams, or trains, for a couple of hours yet, not until daybreak.'

When Dai eventually prepared to leave early next morning, Sara made him promise to let Fran know that she was managing all right. 'Tell her that everything is working out well with Glenda, but that I miss her.'

'I still haven't met this bloody Glenda woman,' Dai muttered. 'I thought you said the pair of you got on well.'

'We do!'

'Gone out already, has she? Where does she go?'

Sara shrugged. 'I don't know. She's never said and I've never asked her. It's none of my business. I like her, she's always willing to keep an eye on Averyl for me when I nip to the corner shop . . .' she stopped, her face scarlet with embarrassment. She'd forgotten about the incident with Robbie and Hilda, on the day Fran had left them with her while she went across to the corner shop, and they'd set fire to the curtains.

Dai didn't seem to remember either, or if he did he had no intention of making an issue of it.

'I'm off then, boyo,' Dai said, picking up his kitbag and slapping Rhys on the shoulder. 'See you when we sign on for the next trip.'

Sara was more than pleased to see him leave. She wanted Rhys to herself; she didn't feel comfortable with Dai there. All the time they'd been drinking tea and eating she was studying Rhys and marvelling at the change she saw in him. He was still devastatingly handsome but now he seemed more mature, more considerate and quieter than she remembered.

'Does that mean you're going back to sea again, then?' Sara murmured unhappily as the door slammed behind Dai.

'I don't know if I'll be going back to sea or not,' Rhys told her, pulling her into his arms. 'It depends on whether I can find any work ashore.'

His lips sought hers. 'Anyway, we don't have to worry about that at the moment,' he whispered. 'There are far more important things to do,' he added, taking her hand and leading her towards the stairs.

'Quiet,' Sara warned as they reached the landing, 'I can't put on a light or we'll waken Averyl.'

Rhys nodded and followed her into the bedroom. He paused to peep into the cot squeezed in at one side of the double bed and Sara heard his quick intake of breath as he stared down at the sleeping child.

Then he took her in his arms and everything, even Averyl, was forgotten as she melted into the strength of his embrace.

They made love gently, with such tenderness that Sara was transported back to the days when they had first left Pontypridd. His mouth was warm and eager, his hands gentle and caring as they stroked and explored her willing body.

Sara had never felt more happy, so much a part of Rhys. It was as if their minds and bodies fused into one as they satisfied each other's needs.

She could have lain there in his arms for eternity

but she was brought back to reality by a movement from the cot alongside their bed and a plaintive little voice calling out to her.

Reluctantly she pulled herself free from Rhys's arms. Shivering, she pulled on her nightdress before going over to lift Averyl from her cot and bring her back to the warmth of the double bed.

As she snuggled back down, Averyl cushioned between them, she'd never felt happier or more content. After the months of anxiously waiting for news, worried in case her money ran out completely before Rhys returned, having him beside her was sheer bliss no matter what the future might hold.

She watched with delight as he and Averyl took stock of each other. There was an anxious moment when Averyl puckered up her face and was on the verge of tears as she pulled away from Rhys. To Sara's relief it passed in seconds.

She'd already taught her to say Dada and Rhys was delighted when, gurgling happily, Averyl prodded him in the chest, repeating the word over and over again.

When they finally went downstairs Averyl clung to Rhys, wanting him to help feed her. At first he seemed clumsy with her, but it made no difference, Averyl demanded his attention rather than Sara's. She even protested when Sara tried to dress her, wriggling from her grasp and clutching at Rhys.

Seeing how delighted he was with his little daughter, Sara seized the opportunity to try and find out if he really intended to go back to sea again.

Rhys looked uncertain. 'It's been a long trip; I've saved most of my wages so we have no money worries at the moment. As to the future, well, it depends on whether or not I can find work ashore. For the moment, though, all I want to do is spend some time with you and get to know this gorgeous little girl,' he said, swinging Averyl up into the air until she choked with laughter.

'I suppose the first thing you must do is go to Tonypandy and see your parents,' Sara reminded him.

Rhys shook his head. 'Not yet. There's something far more important that we have to do.'

Sara looked puzzled. 'What's that?' she frowned.

He placed Averyl down on the floor and took Sara in his arms. Tilting her head back so that she was forced to look straight into his vivid blue eyes he said softly, 'Get married, of course! That's if you still want to?'

Sara's dark eyes filled with tears. Sinking her fingers deep into his dark curly hair, she pulled his face closer until their lips were only a fraction apart. 'Of course I do,' she breathed, kissing him passionately, 'more than anything in the world.'

'Right. Let's clear up here and head for the registry office, then,' Rhys told her. 'There won't be any problem this time about paying,' he grinned, jingling the loose change in his pocket.

It was a crisp bright spring morning as they set out for the City Hall. They caught a tram from Crwys Road that took them to within walking distance of the magnificent Portland stone building that glistened like an Eastern palace in the morning sun. Even the enormous dragon on the pinnacle of the roof seemed to exude happiness.

This time, as Rhys had promised, there were no problems. When the date and time for their actual marriage was fixed he turned and hugged Sara.

'Now we'd better go and see your parents,' Sara told him as they emerged and walked down the wide steps. 'Your father's cough is so bad that he's not at all well.'

'Are you sure that's what you want to do?' Rhys asked. 'You look so radiant at the moment I don't want to do anything to spoil that.'

Their visit to Tonypandy went better than Sara had expected. On the way she told him that his mother had taken care of Averyl over Christmas while she'd been ill, but she said nothing about the row there had been afterwards when she went to get her back. They agreed to say nothing to his parents about their forthcoming marriage.

'Since they think we are already married there doesn't seem to be any point in stirring the dust up now, does there,' Rhys pointed out.

'Not unless you want them to be our witnesses,' Sara grinned.

Rhys pulled a face. 'I can see my Mam's face if we asked them to do that. Have a fit, she would, if she knew we weren't already married.'

Olwen was surprised to see them and caustic about the fact that they hadn't let her know they were coming. She was immediately critical about the way Averyl was dressed, scolding Sara for not wrapping her up more warmly.

Taking her from Rhys's arms she plied her with biscuits and milk and berated Sara for not having been to see her since Averyl had stayed with them over Christmas.

Sara was about to point out that she'd told her never to darken her door again, but thought better of it. Why spoil the day and mar her own feeling of happiness, she decided. Rhys was home and at long last they were to be married; her dearest wish was coming true.

'I'd have had some food ready for you and been able to make you a bit more welcome, if you'd let me know you were coming, see,' Olwen told them as they sat down for a meal of cawl followed by bread and cheese and some of Olwen's home-made chutney.

'Rubbish, Mam. This is a feast in itself after the hard tack we get at sea,' Rhys told her, giving Sara a wink.

'Well, maybe,' she conceded, but if I'd known to expect you then I would have cooked a shoulder of spring lamb. Lovely, it is, done in cider and honey. It used to be your favourite.'

Lloyd said very little. He seemed to be increasingly short of breath and his bouts of coughing appeared to leave him completely exhausted. He still puffed away at his pipe even though the smoke made him cough all the more.

When the meal was over Lloyd looked expectantly at Olwen. 'Well, *cariad*, are you going to tell them or shall I?'

Sara saw Olwen's mouth tighten and feared that an outburst of some kind was to follow.

'I'll tell them!' She smoothed down the front of her

dress. 'I didn't want to upset our Rhys the minute he walked through the door, now did I?' she railed.

'So what have you got to tell me that might upset me?' Rhys looked from his mother to his father enquiringly.

Olwen squared her shoulders, pursed her lips and patted her carefully waved hair. 'I don't know how you are going to take this,' she said. 'It's Lloyd's idea, really, but of course I've had to go along with it.'

'It's as much the bloody pit owner's idea as mine,' Lloyd spluttered, 'and after we'd talked it over you were just as keen on doing it as I was.'

'Yes, well, I could see it was what you wanted,' Olwen prevaricated.

'Come on, Mam, let's hear what it's all about, then,' Rhys said quietly.

'Well, it's like this, see. We're moving.'

'Away from Tonypandy?'

'Oh, yes. Right away. Going back to work after the last time he was laid off with the cough only made his chest worse, and now the doctors all say that your Da has silicosis, see. So the pit owners have told him he's not fit to work any more. After all these years, mind you, they turn round and say that!'

'They've offered me a pension,' Lloyd cut in. 'But of course they want this house back. It's a tied tenancy, see.'

'I thought I was telling this tale,' Olwen interrupted sharply. 'As I was saying, we're leaving Tonypandy. We're moving right away and going to Somerset. We've found a cottage there. Lovely little place it is, right out in the country and it has a nice garden, so Lloyd will have plenty to keep him occupied. We did wonder about keeping a few chickens so that we would have fresh eggs, but we'll have to see how things go. It's not too far from the village so we won't be completely cut off, see.'

'There's a general shop and a post office as well as a pub in the village itself so we'll be all right, see,' Lloyd added.

'Well, this is a surprise,' Rhys told them. 'When are you going?'

'Very soon. At the beginning of June, we thought. That's not all, though,' Olwen added.

'If we manage to get settled before you go back to sea, Rhys, then perhaps the three of you could come and stay for a week,' Lloyd suggested.

Chapter Thirty

At the end of May, three weeks after Rhys arrived home from sea, he and Sara were married at the registry office in Cardiff City Hall.

The week before, Rhys had insisted on taking Sara into the city centre on a shopping spree to buy her a new dress for their special day as well as something for Averyl to wear.

Catching sight of their combined reflection as they walked through David Morgan Arcade, Sara felt as if her heart would burst with joy. Rhys looked so broad and handsome that she felt fiercely proud to be at his side.

She'd often been window shopping in the Arcade, dreaming about how wonderful it would be to walk into Howell's or one of the other big department stores and ask to try on one of the beautiful dresses displayed in the window. Now, when it was about to happen, she felt that it was like a dream come true.

Sara felt uncomfortable and nervous as the liveried doorman opened the glass-plated door and ushered them into the carpeted showroom. When an assistant, wearing a neat black dress with white piqué collar, hurried forward to help them she was completely tongue-tied.

After Rhys had told the assistant what they were

looking for they were taken into another room where there were racks of dresses, blouses and skirts. Several of these were displayed on stands around the room and Sara moved from one to the other mesmerised by what she was seeing.

Rhys was offered a comfortable chair where he could sit and nurse Averyl while the assistant helped Sara to look through the dresses hanging on the racks and to select those she would like to try on.

They were all so enchanting, the fabrics wonderful to the touch and the styles so smart that Sara felt spoilt for choice. She wanted to try them all on, but she knew that Averyl would soon become restless, and Rhys, too, would probably become impatient if she spent too long in the changing room.

The assistant was so helpful that in the end Sara confided in her that she needed an outfit for a very special occasion.

'Is it for a wedding?' the assistant asked.

Her face suffused in embarrassment, Sara nodded.

Tactfully the assistant didn't question her further. Selecting three dresses that she suggested might be suitable, she invited Sara to try them on.

Five minutes later she'd chosen the one she liked best. It was pale blue in artificial silk and sprigged with tiny white flowers. As she caught sight of herself in one of the many cheval-glasses dotted around the showroom, Sara gasped in surprise at her reflection.

It was hard to believe it was the same person. The fitted waistline of the dress made her look slimmer and taller than she'd thought she was. The pretty puff sleeves that came to just above the elbow showed off her slender arms to advantage. Suddenly she was no longer a drab housewife with a young baby, but an attractive twenty-year-old with shoulder-length dark hair and shining dark eyes.

She had never felt happier than at that moment. She knew that dressed as she was now she would feel as glamorous as any film star when they went to the City Hall for their wedding in a few days' time.

The assistant viewed her critically, tweaking at the hem, straightening a fold, making sure the dress was smooth across the shoulders with the puff sleeves at their fullest before she would let her walk across the room to let Rhys voice his opinion.

He nodded his approval as she slowly turned round in front of him, his vivid blue eyes conveying his delight in her appearance.

'For such a special occasion you will need the right hat, Madame,' the assistant told her.

Sara was about to protest, but Rhys agreed immediately.

'Of course she needs a hat. Will you fetch something that you think would be suitable?'

Sara waited until the woman was out of earshot. 'Can we really afford it?' she whispered, knowing they would already be making a dent in their savings if she bought the dress.

'You know what sailors always say,' Rhys grinned, ' "Why spoil a ship for a ha'porth of tar." You look wonderful in that dress and with the right hat you'll be sensational. I might even be persuaded to marry you?'

Sara looked round nervously, then relaxed when she saw there was no one who could overhear what they were saying.

The pale blue hat of finely woven straw with its large drooping brim was the very latest style and a perfect complement to the dress.

'It would look even smarter if Madame had her hair a little shorter and curled at the bottom,' the assistant told her.

While Sara's purchases were being carefully wrapped they went to the children's department to find something suitable for Averyl. The selection was tremendous but they both agreed it had to be something that looked right with Sara's new dress. In the end, they chose a plain white muslin with the yoke smocked in blue and edged with a garland of tiny blue rosebuds, and Averyl looked like an exquisite little doll in it.

On the way home, though, Sara and Rhys debated whether or not they were doing the right thing in taking Averyl with them on the big day.

'Perhaps we should ask Glenda Williams to look after her for a couple of hours,' Rhys suggested.

'Eleven o'clock in the morning might be difficult for Glenda,' Sara pointed out. 'It might mess up her plans for the day.'

'It's hardly fair to ask her to do that,' Rhys agreed, 'but what else can we do? We can hardly stand there in front of the registrar nursing Averyl, now can we!'

Sara looked crestfallen. 'No, I suppose not,' she admitted.

'So what do we do?'

'I feel she ought to be there, though,' Sara mused.

Rhys grinned. 'I think so too. In fact, I'd like her to be with us but I don't think it would be acceptable.'

'We could take her in her pram and park it in a corner of the room,' Sara suggested.

Rhys ran a hand through his thick dark hair. 'They might let us do that, I suppose. Perhaps after all we should have told my Mam and Dad what we were planning to do and then they could have looked after Averyl for us.'

'If we'd told Olwen we weren't already married she'd have been scandalised,' Sara reminded him.

Rhys laughed. 'What about asking Martha Pritchard, then?'

'It's a long way to take her back to Ponty for the day, and if my Da or Gwladys found out that we'd left Averyl with Martha they'd start poking their noses in and wanting to know why.'

'No need to tell them, *cariad*! I'm sure Martha wouldn't say a word if you asked her not to.'

'I know, but Myfanwy might see Averyl with Martha and mention it at home.'

There seemed to be no answer to their problem, but then Sara had a brilliant idea.

'Instead of asking Glenda to look after Averyl, why don't we invite her to come with us as a guest,' she suggested. 'If we did that Glenda could sit and hold Averyl while we were being married. Afterwards, we could all go and have a meal together to celebrate.'

'That sounds like a perfect solution,' Rhys agreed. 'It would be a nice way of saying thank you to Glenda Williams for being such an understanding landlady and helping you out when Fran decided to go home to her mother's place.'

Sara's face clouded. 'You don't think Glenda might turn against us when she hears we've been living in sin all this time?' she mused.

'I don't know her, but she doesn't look that sort. Anyway, that's a chance we'll have to take,' Rhys said philosophically.

Glenda was delighted by their invitation and when Sara showed her the new clothes Rhys had bought for her and Averyl she promised she would dress up for the occasion as well.

On the day, Glenda insisted that they should have a taxi to collect them from Coburn Street and take them to the City Hall in case it rained.

'My treat!' she told them. 'I don't want my new outfit to be spoilt, see. Brand new, it is! First time I've worn it. Like it, do you?'

Rhys told her she looked extremely smart in the beige linen dress with its matching three-quarter-length jacket.

'If I was as young and as pretty as your Sara then I'd have gone for one of these new-fangled big-brimmed hats like she's wearing. I thought at my age, though, I'd better stick to the style that I'm used to.'

They arrived at the City Hall with ten minutes to spare. Rhys led the way into the special office that was set aside for weddings and they were told to wait in an adjoining room until it was their turn.

Sara felt alternately sick with apprehension and ecstatically happy because at long last her union with Rhys was to be legalised.

So many thoughts rushed round and round in her head as she sat tensed on the edge of her chair. She wished her mother was still alive and could be there to witness what was happening. She felt uneasy because they hadn't told either her father or Rhys's parents about what they were doing. And she felt guilty because she knew what their reactions would be if they ever found out that they had been living together all this time without being married.

She kept looking anxiously at Rhys to try and work out if he was having similar qualms. He was sitting back in his chair, jogging Averyl up and down on his knee to amuse her, and seemed to be completely relaxed.

At least he's not having second thoughts, Sara told herself. And in less than an hour's time we will be legally man and wife and Averyl will be legitimate.

The waiting seemed interminable and there was further delay because they needed two witnesses. Finally, Glenda was accepted as one of them and a clerk from the City Hall staff as another. The ceremony, once it actually started, was so brief that it was all over and they were signing their names before Sara realised what was happening.

It seemed to her that Rhys had barely handed Averyl over to Glenda before he was taking her from Glenda again and they were outside the gleaming white building and standing in the sunshine wondering what to do next.

'It's a little too early to have a meal,' Glenda said, looking up at the clock face on the tower of the City Hall. 'Since the sun has decided to shine after all and it's a wonderful occasion, what about us all taking a stroll in Cathays Park. The spring flowers are at their best and I'm sure Averyl will love the chance to show off her walking.'

'That sounds a great idea,' Rhys agreed, 'and then we can stroll back into the city centre and find a really nice restaurant.'

Worn out by their busy morning and all the fresh air, Averyl fell asleep in Sara's arms almost as soon as they were seated in the restaurant.

'Let's leave her be,' Sara advised. 'It means we can eat our meal in peace. If we wake her up she will only be grizzly and spoil things for the rest of us.'

Glenda insisted on buying a bottle of wine to have with their meal so that she could toast the newly married pair. There were tears in her eyes as she wished them every happiness. She expressed the hope that they would stay on with her in Coburn Street for a long time to come.

'Lonely, I am, see,' she said with a smile. 'In my fifties now, even if I don't look it. Not likely to ever get married again and even if I did I'd be too old for children, so it's lovely to be able to watch your little moppet growing up.'

'I bet you don't think that when she wakes up full of beans at six in the morning,' Sara said ruefully.

'Even then I think she's lovely,' Glenda assured them.

They sat for a long time over their meal. Rhys

regaled them with stories about some of the fascinating places he'd visited and about the many hazards of living and working on board ship. It was as if they didn't want to break the spell and return to the everyday world.

'Now look, you two,' Glenda said to them when Averyl finally woke and they decided they must go home, 'this is the most memorable day of your lives, one you should look back on with pleasure. You sort Averyl out and when you've fed her and you're ready to put her down to sleep, take yourselves out for the evening. Enjoy what's left of your special day, I'll keep an eye on her so you can be as late home as you like.'

Sara smiled at her gratefully. It had been a perfect day, one she would always treasure. Only one thing could have made it even more wonderful and that would have been to have Myfanwy there.

Chapter Thirty-one

Over the next few months it became obvious to Sara that Rhys and Averyl had bonded so well and that the two of them were so inseparable that it would be upsetting for Averyl if he went away for any length of time.

Averyl was now eighteen months old and with her dark curls and vivid blue eyes she looked like a tiny replica of Rhys.

He doted on her and every minute she was awake she wanted to be with him. He couldn't move from his chair without her clutching at his trouser leg and trying to walk alongside him.

All through the summer, the pair of them had enjoyed daily outings, usually to Roath Park to feed the ducks. Rhys refused to push her there in a pram so Sara dressed her in one of the dainty little dresses Rhys had bought for her and a pretty cotton bonnet to protect her head from the sun, and Rhys would carry her in his arms.

Sometimes Sara went with them, but more often than not she let Rhys take Averyl on his own. She was eager for them to form as close an attachment as possible so that he would be reluctant to leave her and go back to sea.

She didn't mind staying at home because it left her time to herself and she would go over in her mind how much her life had changed and how lucky she was.

Having a man around had not only meant more cooking, but extra cleaning as well, but she didn't mind. She wanted Rhys to enjoy his home and feel comfortable, and since they only had two rooms that meant keeping everything neat and tidy all the time.

Rhys said it didn't bother him that they only had two rooms because he was used to living in a confined space on board ship. He agreed with her that they were fortunate in having such an understanding landlady as Glenda Williams. They rarely saw her and she never interfered in any way. In fact, living in Coburn Street was perfect apart from having to share a bedroom with Averyl.

Whenever they made love they were both on tenterhooks in case they disturbed Averyl. Sara worried about this a great deal because she was afraid it might create a barrier between her and Rhys.

Several times Sara thought of asking Glenda Williams if they could put Averyl's cot into the small back bedroom. It would be worth paying out another shilling a week for the privacy that it would give them. If Rhys didn't go back to sea, she decided she would go ahead and do so because they couldn't go on sharing a room with Averyl indefinitely.

The only cloud in the sky was that Rhys wasn't having much success in finding a job ashore. He had already asked Gareth, the baker he'd worked for before in Elm Street, if he needed any help, but

Gareth had taken on a young lad and was managing quite well. He had promised to ask around, though, but so far there had been no word from him.

Rhys had also visited most of the local shops and companies looking for work, but no one wanted to employ a baker no matter how skilled he might be. As the months passed, and autumn approached, Sara became more and more worried because it looked as if Rhys would have to go back to sea whether he wanted to or not.

Dai Roberts had already decided to. He'd called in to see them on his way to the shipping offices and had tried his hardest to persuade Rhys to go along with him and sign on.

'Come on, mun,' he coaxed, when Rhys declined. 'It won't bloody well hurt to sign on, now will it! It could be weeks before we manage to get a ship.'

Sara had been eager for news of Fran and the children, but he'd dismissed them with a few words.

'All cosy back on the farm with her Mam, aren't they?' he snarled.

'I know that, but have they settled in? It must be very different for the children to be living in the country after spending all their life here in a big city like Cardiff.'

Dai shrugged. 'Kids soon adapt, don't they,' he said dismissively.

'Do Robbie and Hilda both like being at the village school?'

'I suppose they do. Too young to worry about such things, aren't they. Simply do as they're told.'

'And they like it on the farm with all the animals and so on?'

'Yes, and all the muck and mess. They enjoy it more than I bloody well do.' He pulled a face. 'Stinking place. I can't get away from there fast enough.'

He turned to Rhys. 'Come on, mun, let's get down the Pier Head and sign on, you know it's the best thing to do.'

Rhys picked Averyl up in his arms. 'I'm not sure you're right about that, Dai. I'd miss this little one growing up if I went away again now.'

'Your three will miss you, Dai,' Sara butted in, 'and Fran will. She gets desperately lonely when you're away at sea, you know.'

'She doesn't need me now, she's got her Mam,' Dai snapped. 'No good me staying on there, we fight the whole bloody time! Got no time for me, see, any of them.'

'Fran will still miss you,' Sara repeated stubbornly. 'I know I'd miss Rhys if he went back to sea again. Wonderful, it is, having him at home.'

'It won't be so bloody wonderful when the money runs out,' Dai scowled. 'That's all Fran thinks I'm good for, providing her with money. Nag, nag, nag, night and day. The kids always seem to be needing something new. If it isn't shoes then it's clothes and no sooner have they got them than they've grown out of the bloody things. Sick to death, I am, of hearing about it. Can't wait to get away to sea again.'

Sara waited with bated breath for Rhys's reaction. When he shook his head and said he wasn't ready to sign on for another trip she felt so choked she couldn't speak.

After Dai left she flung her arms around Rhys and hugged him, tears streaming down her face.

'Come on, *cariad*, don't take on so. I won't go back to sea at all if you feel like this about it,' he told her, gently wiping the tears from her face.

'You promise?' Her dark eyes were shining with hope as her gaze held his.

He puffed out his cheeks and then released his breath slowly. 'I promise I won't even think about going back to sea if I can find some sort of work in the next few weeks, but I've been at home over four months now and the money I earned is running out, *cariad*.'

Some of the elation faded from Sara's face. 'There doesn't seem to be much chance of that happening, does there. No one in Cardiff seems to want a baker,' she murmured sadly.

'Something will turn up, I feel sure of it,' he said confidently. He stood up. 'No point in sitting here worrying our heads about it. Let's make the most of things while I have some free time. Now, what is it to be, Cathays Park, or Roath Park where we can feed the ducks?'

September came and went. In her heart Sara knew that the longer Rhys was at home the harder the separation was going to be if he did have to go back to sea.

She tried not to think about it but sometimes as she lay in his arms after they had made love she was so at peace with the world that she felt she couldn't bear the thought of being parted from him ever again.

She had never known such happiness as she'd experienced since he returned home in April. They might not have much money but they had each other, and they had Averyl. Rhys was so loving, so attentive and so wonderful with Averyl that she felt it was almost too good to be true.

She thought back to all the misery she'd had to endure when she'd been growing up in Pontypridd and the struggles she and Rhys had faced when they'd first moved to Cardiff, and had been living in Daisy Street. Now she could have dismissed them like half-remembered nightmares were it not for the fact that Myfanwy was still living in Taff Court.

There were days when something inside her warned her that this tremendous bubble of happiness couldn't last for ever. Some day it was bound to burst, and she was fearful about what would happen then.

The first grey clouds appeared towards the end of September. Rhys had still not found any work and their money was almost all gone.

Sara did everything in her power to economise. The days were still warm so they didn't need a fire every day, only once a week when she had to heat up enough water to fill the big tin bath that hung on the wall outside the scullery so that she and Rhys could have a bath. She had hers first, then Rhys had his and afterwards she washed their clothes in the same water.

A kettleful of hot water heated up on the gas cooker Glenda had had installed in the scullery which they shared was enough for Averyl's daily bath in a tin bowl, and then Sara rinsed out the baby's clothes in the same water afterwards so that they were clean for the next day.

Rhys played his part. When they went to the park, or out shopping, he would carry Averyl in his arms, rather than spend money on tram fares.

When he stopped going on his occasional trips to the Hope and Anchor, the pub run by Barbie Buckley in Tiger Bay, Sara thought he was economising too far.

'Barbie said she'd keep her ear to the ground for any jobs going that might be right for you,' she reminded him.

'I know, *cariad*, but the sort of jobs she tells me about are not the sort I want, are they. They're navvying or labouring on the dockside.'

He held her tightly, kissing her on the brow. 'Don't worry your head about it, keep hoping, you never know what is around the corner. I've put out so many enquiries that I'm bound to be lucky soon. Something will turn up out of the blue when we least expect it.'

Two days later Rhys's prophecy came true, but not in the way either of them had anticipated.

Chapter Thirty-two

The arrival of Gwladys on their doorstep brought any further speculations between Rhys and Sara about their future plans to an abrupt halt.

'Gwladys?' Sara couldn't believe her eyes. Gwladys hadn't been in touch with her since she'd left Pontypridd and she hadn't a good word to say about her either, according to Martha.

Gwladys looked distraught. Although she was wearing her neat grey dress and coat she looked unkempt. Her hair, instead of being brushed and combed into its usual neat chignon, was scraped back into a knot at the back of her neck and long strands had escaped from under her hat and hung round her face.

Immediately Sara was filled with foreboding that something must be wrong with either her father or Myfanwy.

'Can I come in?' Gwladys said abruptly.

'Yes. Of course you can!' Sara stood aside for her to enter. 'It's the middle room. Go on in, you'll find Rhys in there with Averyl.'

'I'll leave this here in the hallway,' Gwladys stated as she put down her heavy suitcase.

Sara looked at it in alarm, hoping that Gwladys wasn't expecting to stay with them. 'Leave it there and I'll get Rhys to bring it on through to our room,' she offered.

'Oh, don't fuss, Sara,' Gwladys snapped. 'Leave it where it is, I'm not going to be here that long.'

As Sara followed her into the living-room she saw the look of surprised anger on Rhys's face. It was the first time he and Gwladys had met face to face since the day he and Sara had announced they were getting married, and Sara was on tenterhooks about how he would react.

'Well, this is a surprise, Gwladys,' Sara said in an attempt to break the uneasy silence. 'Have you come to Cardiff to do a bit of shopping then?'

'Shopping! There's daft you talk, Sara. Where would I have the money for shopping?' She hesitated, glaring at Rhys as if wishing he wasn't in the room.

Rhys quickly took the hint. 'I'll go and put the kettle on, shall I?' he asked, catching Sara's eye. 'Leave you two to discuss whatever it is that Gwladys has come all this way to tell you.'

The moment he left the room, taking Averyl with him, Gwladys turned to Sara. 'You'd better sit down. Spot of bad news, see.'

Sara looked alarmed. 'My Da? He's ill or something?'

'Ill! No, he's not ill, not unless it's in the head,' Gwladys snorted.

'Myfanwy then? There's something wrong with Myfanwy,' she repeated as Gwladys avoided her eyes. 'Come on, tell me! What's wrong? She's ill? There's been an accident?'

'Calm down, Sara! Why do you always have to be

so dramatic,' Gwladys snapped. 'It's nothing like that. I came here to tell you that I'm leaving your father and moving right away from Pontypridd. I'm not staying in the same house as him, wicked old sinner that he is.' She shuddered and buried her face in her hands.

The colour drained from Sara's face as Gwladys spoke. She didn't need any further explanation. She caught sight of the revulsion in Gwladys's eyes when she mentioned Ifor's name, and she had a premonition about what Gwladys was going to tell her and she couldn't bear to hear it.

At that moment she felt as if her insides were all churned up; she felt sick with horror as all the terrible memories came crowding back. Shivering, she closed her eyes to try and shut out the spectre of her father's long hard face and scrawny neck, the glint of his dark eyes, the cruel twist to his lips as his face loomed over her while she lay pinioned beneath him.

She tried to obliterate the sounds in her head, his harsh breathing and guttural panting as his frenzy mounted, but they were as clear in her ears as if he was right there in the room.

Her nostrils were filled by the acrid smell of coal dust. She could feel his grime-ingrained fingers digging like steel talons into her tender flesh, probing, invading, and inflicting excruciating pain that spiralled from the most intimate parts of her body directly into her brain.

She couldn't speak or move. She felt paralysed with fear and foreboding. Her face was so ashen and so tense that when Rhys came back into the room with the tray of tea things he was alarmed. 'Sara, are you all right?' he asked, putting the tray down on the table and placing his arm around her shoulders.

His voice, warm and concerned, brought her back from the dark abyss of her past. Opening her eyes, she stared past him and glared at Gwladys with loathing.

'What's going on?' Rhys, perplexed, looked from one to the other of them. Angrily he turned to Gwladys. 'What have you been saying this time to upset Sara?' he demanded.

'Nothing at all, not yet,' Gwladys said dully.

'Then why is Sara sitting here looking like a corpse?' His arm tightened around Sara. 'Tell me what she's said,' he demanded, tenderly stroking her hair back from her ashen face.

'I haven't told her anything yet,' Gwladys protested.

'Then whatever it was you were going to say, she seems to think she knows what it is in advance,' Rhys snapped. 'So what have you come here to tell her? Is it something to do with her father? He's not died, has he?'

'No, more's the pity. The Good Lord should smite him down. Wicked, he is! Led me to believe he was a pillar of respectability but all the while he'd been one of Satan's henchmen. Lecherous! Evil in the eyes of man as well as the Lord!'

'What the hell are you on about?'

'No, Rhys, don't ask,' Sara moaned. 'I don't want to hear her say anything more.'

'Well, I do,' he told her firmly. 'I'm not having her coming here and upsetting you like this without knowing what is going on or what she's on about.' He turned back to Gwladys. 'Go on then, out with it!'

She bit down on her lip, struggling to find the words, her face mottled red as if she were too embarrassed to continue. 'Ifor and Myfanwy,' she gulped. Gwladys looked across at Sara. 'She knows! She'll tell you.'

Sara pulled Averyl towards her, then picked her up and cuddled her, burying her face in the child's hair.

Rhys looked from one to the other. 'Are either of you going to tell me what it's all about and what is going on?' he asked irritably.

'You'd better drink your tea and then say whatever it is you have to say,' Sara muttered, staring across at Gwladys.

In her heart she knew what it was going to be and she felt more frightened than she ever had in her life. Once Gwladys voiced her accusations aloud there would be no going back. Everything would be out in the open. Rhys would know the vile secret that she had guarded all these years.

She felt awash with shame. Her hand was shaking as she picked up the cup of tea Rhys had poured for her. She found she had difficulty swallowing, her throat felt so tight and constricted.

'Right, well, can we get on with it,' Rhys said impatiently. 'You haven't come all this way from Pontypridd just to sit and drink tea with us, so what is this all about?'

'It's to do with Myfanwy and her father,' Gwladys said hesitantly. 'It's not easy to explain. I only found out a few nights ago and I've no idea how long it's been going on, but I refuse to stay under the same roof as him so I'm getting out. I won't spend another night breathing the same air as that vile creature.'

'What the hell are you getting at?' Rhys looked nonplussed. What's Ifor done that . . . ?

Gwladys sat up very straight in her chair and squared her shoulders. 'I found him in Myfanwy's bedroom staring at her while she was asleep in bed . . .'

Rhys looked puzzled. 'You did what?'

'He had pulled back the bedclothes and lifted her nightdress up above her waist and he was standing there, staring at her with a gloating look on his face.'

Rhys looked stunned. His arms tightened around Sara. 'Take no notice of what she's saying,' he told her. 'She's lied before. Don't forget what she said about us having to leave Pontypridd in a hurry because I'd got you into trouble.'

'All right, Rhys, I admit that I jumped to the wrong conclusion when you left in such a rush and that what I said was all a pack of lies,' Gwladys mumbled contritely, 'but this isn't. As the Good Lord is my witness I am telling you the truth.' She looked from one to the other. 'You must believe that.'

Rhys looked scornful. 'Must we? After what you said about us?'

'I've already said I'm sorry about that. This is quite different. It . . . it's not just a mortal sin, it's perverted!'

'What the hell are you blabbing on about,' Rhys

muttered. He stopped and his mouth dropped open. 'Are you saying what I think you're insinuating?' he asked incredulously.

Gwladys nodded, her thin mouth a tight line, her face registering disgust.

For a moment Rhys couldn't speak. He stood clenching and unclenching his hands. 'If you were a man I'd thrash you for implying a slur like that about Sara's family. Now get out!'

'No, wait, Rhys,' Sara intervened.

'You sit there and listen to her outrageous lies and let her slag your old man off like that!' he said contemptuously. 'I know he's a sanctimonious old sod and I can't stand the old bastard, but I don't think you understand what she is accusing him of doing.'

'Oh yes, I do, Rhys. I know only too well,' Sara said quietly.

'You do?' Rhys stared at her in disbelief.

'You needn't bother to explain any further,' Sara said sardonically to Gwladys, 'except to tell me why Myfanwy isn't here with you.'

'Christ, you haven't left her back there on her own, have you?' Rhys demanded.

'She's at school. I packed her up some food and told her to eat her midday meal there,' Gwladys said wearily.

'And what about tonight when she comes home from school?' Sara asked in alarm.

'Ifor's on nights. I told Myfanwy she was to go to Martha Pritchard's when she came home from school.'

'You've explained to Martha why she's doing that?'

Gwladys's mouth tightened. 'Of course I haven't told Martha the reason why.'

'Not even told her that you are leaving for good?'

'No, of course not. It would be all round Ponty in five minutes if I did that.'

'So if Martha takes her back home and puts her to bed, then she's going to be there on her own when my Da gets home from work,' Sara said in a horrified voice.

'You're a selfish bitch!' Rhys shouted. 'You're every bit as immoral as he is. Probably if you'd been a proper wife to him this would never have happened.'

Gwladys went ashen. 'May the Good Lord forgive you, Rhys Edwards,' she gasped piously. 'I've cooked and cleaned for that man and his daughter ever since the day we married.'

'You mean you made me cook and clean when I was in Ponty,' Sara said bitterly, 'and since I've left home it's been poor little Myfanwy who has had to do it.'

'I've simply been teaching her to be useful, that's all I've done,' Gwladys blustered. 'Spoilt the child, you had. Proper little madam, she was, when I first moved in.'

'And a proper little skivvy after you'd been there for a few months,' Sara retorted. 'Don't bother to deny it,' she added, as Gwladys was about to speak. 'Martha Pritchard has told me about her having to whiten the step, take out the ashes, get the coal in and clean the grate before she goes to school in the morning. She's told me everything. Even about the way you make the poor little mite sew samplers and kneel for hours at a time praying until her poor knees are red raw. Wicked, you are, Gwladys.'

Gwladys made a tremendous effort to regain control of the situation. 'That's not what I came here to discuss though, is it, Sara,' she said haughtily.

'So why have you come?'

'I wanted you to know that I'm leaving your father and Pontypridd for good.'

'And leaving Myfanwy to the mercy of Ifor Jenkins!' Rhys exclaimed. 'Christ, you're as wicked as he is! She's barely eight and you're walking out on her! Have you no conscience, woman?' he demanded heatedly.

'Of course I have a conscience. I'm a devout Christian and a follower of the Lord,' Gwladys bristled. 'I wouldn't have taken the trouble to come all this way to warn you about the situation and to tell you that I am leaving him if I didn't have a conscience. She's not my child, remember,' she said stiffly, 'so I'm not responsible for her. What has happened is probably as much her own fault as not. She's the most disobedient child I've ever had to deal with, and what's more to the point, she's always showing off and trying to be the centre of attention.'

'Lies, all lies!' Sara yelled. 'You know better than that. You know that's not the truth. Myfanwy's not to blame!'

Gwladys's lip curled. 'You know more about him than me, Sara. Very much more!'

The colour drained from Sara's face and her body

shook uncontrollably. She tried to speak but choked on the words, tears streaming down her cheeks.

Gwladys stood and picked up her suitcase. 'I'll be off now. I don't expect we'll ever meet again. It's up to you now, Sara, whether you go and look after your sister, or whether you leave her there with her father,' she added pointedly.

Chapter Thirty-three

Sara started to make preparations to leave for Pontypridd right away.

Rhys felt there was obviously a lot he didn't know about what had happened in the past, but decided that this wasn't the right moment to ask questions.

'I'm coming with you, Sara, no argument,' he said firmly.

'We'll catch the bus from the stop near the City Hall,' she said. 'It's easier than going all the way to Central Station for the train. Are you ready?'

Sara hardly spoke throughout the journey. Rhys nursed Averyl and in a very short time, lulled by the motion of the bus, she fell asleep. He didn't mind, it gave him time to think and to try and puzzle out exactly how serious the situation was that it was worrying Sara so much.

His mind went back to the days when he and Sara had worked together in Ponty. The shy, gauche young girl who had responded to his wisecracks and smiles so readily that she'd made him feel ten foot tall.

Things had been going so well for them. His job with his Aunt Betti had offered reasonable prospects, he'd fallen in love with Sara and he'd wanted to marry her and would have done so then if Sara had agreed.

Looking back, rushing off to Cardiff with very little money and nowhere to live had been childish and had let his Aunt Betti down.

Then going off to sea and leaving Sara on her own had been a callous thing to do. It had worried him all the time he'd been away, especially when he discovered that their sailing pattern had been changed and they would be away months longer than he'd expected to be.

He hadn't known Sara was pregnant, of course, but he wasn't sure if it would have made any difference if he had known, not then. He'd been irresponsible and so angry at the world and everyone in it that he couldn't think of anyone but himself.

Bleak months at sea had changed all that. It had mellowed him and made him realise that the world didn't revolve around him.

He'd missed Sara. Not just the sex but for her warmth, her personality and her way of looking at life. Hardly a night had passed when he hadn't wished he'd treated her better.

He'd intended to write to her, had tried once or twice, but he was no hand at writing. When he put the words down on paper they were completely different from what had been in his head. They were so impersonal that the message seemed all wrong.

He'd tried holding imaginary conversations with Sara in his head and the words he used then were warm and beautiful. Yet the moment he tried to commit them to paper they came out so stilted and cold that they sounded ridiculous.

Over and over again he'd wished he could obliterate the last few weeks they'd spent together in Daisy Street. He knew he'd been foul-mouthed and evil tempered. At times he'd practically raped her yet she'd never complained.

He'd left her there all on her own in one of the meanest streets in Tiger Bay. He knew she would have to tolerate the whims of Polly Price, their landlady, who had seemed to resent them being in her house from the moment they moved in. Not only that, but he had left her practically penniless.

He looked down tenderly at the child asleep in his arms and with his free hand reached out and found Sara's.

'Do you know,' he said softly, 'when I first set eyes on Averyl I felt trapped. I had no idea when I sailed that you were pregnant. I felt so guilty because I'd left you to cope all on your own, Sara. I even felt jealous because she demanded so much of your attention.'

He squeezed her hand more tightly. 'I should never have listened to my mother or let her take over like she did. She's always been over-possessive. I knew she was trying to shut you out, wrong-footing you whenever she could, and I should have done more to stop her. Do you forgive me?'

Sara stared at him in surprise, then nodded and gave him a tremulous smile. 'Moving into Coburn Street with Fran and Dai would have been all right if you'd been able to go on working for Gareth or found some other job ashore.'

He looked uncomfortable. 'Yes, but with both Averyl and Dai's new baby disturbing us all at nights I began to think that perhaps I wasn't cut out for family life. That's why, when Dai decided to go back to sea, it didn't take much persuading on his part to get me to go along with him, did it?'

'No, not really,' she agreed.

'I told myself that I would only sign on for a short run and be back home again in a couple of months,' he explained. 'I intended to leave you enough money to keep you and Averyl for that long and I really did believe that you'd be happy enough with Fran for company.'

Sara sighed. 'I suppose it wasn't your fault that once again the ship you were on didn't keep to its schedule. You couldn't have known that Fran would change her mind about living in Coburn Street and go back to Caerphilly to live with her Mam.'

Rhys leant sideways and kissed Sara's cheek. If he'd been a praying man he would have sought forgiveness. Since he wasn't, he'd resolved to spend the rest of his life trying to make up to Sara for what he'd done and the pain and grief he'd caused her.

Time and again since he'd come ashore he'd tried to explain all this to Sara, but the words wouldn't come. They were all there in his head, but in the same way as when he'd tried to write his thoughts down in a letter and couldn't, so he found that when he tried to say them out loud they didn't sound right.

Even asking her to marry him had been an ordeal. He'd let her down once and he was afraid she might remember that and turn him down, and then his entire life would be in ruins.

He loved her so deeply that he wanted to be with her every minute of the day and he was in mortal dread of losing her. When she'd said yes and had gone along to the registry office to file their details he had felt the happiest man alive.

Getting married was such an important milestone. He'd wanted to tell the whole world what they were doing. He'd wanted to shout it from the rooftops, but instead, because he had behaved so stupidly in the past, they had to do it as secretively as possible.

Most women would have been angry about that, but Sara had been as anxious as he was to keep it all a secret. He suspected it was because she felt uneasy for having claimed his name without having the legal right to do so, but he knew she had done this because of Averyl.

Even his own mother would have been quick to condemn them if she'd ever found out that they hadn't been properly married when Averyl was born. And as for Ifor and Gwladys, they would have brought the wrath of the Lord down around his ears if they'd heard so much as a whisper, he thought wryly.

Now, when all that was behind them and their marriage was not only legal, but also all their early differences were forgotten, it angered him that Gwladys had brought this fresh cloud to hover over them.

Rhys wished he knew the whole story of what had gone on. The look of horror on Sara's face,

Gwladys being so outraged and refusing to talk about it, meant there must be far more to it than Gwladys finding Ifor standing in Myfanwy's bedroom in the middle of the night, simply looking at her.

As he looked sideways at Sara he knew there was something terribly wrong, something even worse than the accusations that Gwladys had made about Ifor. He wasn't even sure he believed them himself, surely no man could be so evil, but somehow Sara had been convinced. She was staring unseeingly out of the window, her hands clenched tightly together in her lap. The colour had drained out of her face and she was chewing nervously on her lower lip.

All sorts of unspeakable thoughts circulated inside Rhys's head; things he didn't want to dwell on. He kept telling himself that he was reading far more into the situation than it merited, but he feared that wasn't so.

They approached Pontypridd and turned off Pentrebach Road and went over the bridge into the Broadway; Averyl wakened and let out a cry of protest as he moved her into a more comfortable position to carry her off the bus.

He tapped Sara gently on the arm. 'We're here,' he warned, as the bus shuddered to a stop.

She looked at him blankly, as though she had no idea where they were, but followed him blindly off the bus and on to the pavement.

In silence they walked the short distance to Taff Court. It was the first time he had been back there since they'd left for Cardiff and he was aware of the waves of anger against the unknown rising up inside him.

'Had we better go and tell Martha Pritchard we are here first?' he asked as Sara walked towards her old home.

She hesitated, then nodded in agreement.

Martha was wearing a small frilly apron over her smart red dress. She opened the door immediately, almost as if she'd been watching out for them.

'There's glad I am that you've come,' she greeted them, hugging Sara to her ample bosom. 'Come on inside, we've time to have a cup of tea and sort out what we're going to do before Myfanwy gets back from school.'

'You know Gwladys has gone for good, do you?' Sara asked sharply.

'Well, *cariad*, she as good as said she was thinking of doing so and when I saw her leaving this morning with that heavy old case then I said to Alun I didn't think she'd be coming back. Things haven't been going too good with them for quite a while now, so I can't say that I'm all that surprised. Came to see you in Cardiff, did she?'

'Yes, she came to tell us that she was leaving Ifor and Pontypridd,' Rhys said.

'Well, good riddance and all, I say. Never could stand the woman and the way she's treated that poor little Myfanwy has been shocking. Like I told you, she's made a little slave out of her.'

Martha bustled around, putting the kettle on and finding a biscuit for Averyl, Alun joined them the minute he heard their voices and his face beamed as he hugged Sara and kissed her on the cheek.

As they sat drinking their tea he endorsed every word that Martha had been saying about Gwladys and Ifor.

'It's what they do when they are not praying that worries me,' Alun said gloomily, passing a hand over his greying hair. 'I expect Martha has told you that since they've not been getting on so well Gwladys has been circulating all sorts of terrible gossip.'

Martha nodded. 'Some of what she says makes my blood boil and my skin crawl.' She looked directly at Sara. 'They do say, though, that there's no smoke without fire.'

Sara didn't answer but Rhys saw the fear in her dark eyes and his own unease increased.

Chapter Thirty-four

For the next hour, until Myfanwy arrived home from school, the four of them sat talking things over in the Pritchards' comfortable living-room.

Rhys felt more and more astounded by what he was hearing. He had always known that Sara's childhood had been hard, but she'd never really spoken about the years right after her mother died.

At first Sara said very little, but sat brooding and looking so morose that Rhys knew there was a great deal more involved than the mere vagaries of the Jenkins household.

He listened as Martha and Alun repeated their concern about Ifor's obsession with attending the Tabernacle Chapel and his fervent involvement with religion.

'All of us hereabouts were brought up to go to chapel and to Sunday school, and most of us brought our own children up to do the same,' Martha proclaimed.

'Indeed, but none of us became so besotted by religion that we let it rule our lives,' Alun stated heatedly.

'Ifor Jenkins didn't either when he and Gwen first moved into Taff Court,' Martha pointed out.

'No, that's true! Hard-working, hard-drinking man, he was, in those days,' Alun agreed. 'Down to the pub with the rest of us on a Saturday night and cursing and swearing with the rest of us as he rolled back home. Strong union man, Ifor was, then. He could talk for hours! Eloquent, too, not ranting religious babble like he does now.'

Martha sighed. 'Losing so many babas was what changed him, there's no doubt about that. After Sara was born, poor Gwen had so many miscarriages that he was convinced the Lord was punishing him for his wicked ways, so he turned to religion to try and atone for his sins.'

'Yes,' Alun took up the story. 'Ifor stopped drinking and swearing and began telling the rest of us that we were all doomed to the stinking pit of damnation and would rot there in Hell unless we did the same. We laughed at him, of course. Some of the boyos thought he was joking!'

'Oh, yes,' Martha said disdainfully. 'Ifor Jenkins took his religion very, very seriously, and he took it underground with him, preaching and ranting at the coalface whenever there was a cave-in or a blowout or some other kind of accident. He'd insist that it was the Lord's retribution for their dastardly ways.'

Martha sighed. 'Poor Gwen used to worry herself sick over it all. After Myfanwy was born she hoped he might stop his ranting and raving, but he didn't.'

'A sickly little baba she was, see!' Alun said, shaking his head sadly as he looked at Rhys. 'Puny little thing, like a skinned rabbit, clinging on to life for all she was worth.'

'Feeding her drained every ounce of strength from poor Gwen.' Martha sniffed and wiped a tear from her eye with the corner of her apron. 'Never the same woman after Myfanwy was born.'

'You know all about that, don't you, Sara? You were the one who had to nurse her, poor soul,' Alun murmured sadly. 'And then, of course, there was the fire. I'll never forget the night that happened. A terrible tragedy, that was.'

'Things were never the same in your house from that day onwards, were they, Sara?'

Something in Martha Pritchard's voice alerted Rhys and he looked quickly at Sara. Her face had flamed a brilliant red and then the colour had drained away, leaving her grey and shaking.

'I don't think we should talk about it,' she muttered.

'You mean the fire?' Alun asked. 'That wasn't your fault, Sara. It was your Mam that left a candle burning, the fire chief told me so after he'd carried out the investigations. You did all you could that night. You rescued Myfanwy, she owes her life to you.'

'It's not the fire we're talking about, Alun,' Martha told him sharply. 'Sara knows what I mean. I've never mentioned it before, *cariad*, but I had my suspicions about what was going on. Wicked old bastard, and so mealy-mouthed and pretending to be so religious.'

Rhys frowned, looking from Martha to Sara in bewilderment. 'I'm afraid I don't understand what we are talking about.'

'You've lost me as well,' Alun admitted.

Martha chewed on her lower lip, looking sideways at Sara as if trying to determine whether she ought to say any more or not. 'You'd better ask Sara if you want to know any more. As I said, I was pretty certain that I knew what was going on, but you can't face a man on suspicions alone, now can you?'

Sara reached out and took Rhys's hand, holding it so tightly that he winced. Her voice was barely a whisper as she said, 'Martha's right. I should have said something but I was too frightened to do so. I thought people would blame me, even you, Martha.'

'Oh, my poor love.' Martha left her chair and went over to put her arms around Sara. 'Don't say another word if it upsets you so much.'

'No,' Sara said dully, 'it's time I spoke out, time Rhys knew the truth.' She shuddered. 'It went on for so long that in the end I even managed to stop thinking about what was happening to me.'

'I could hear you crying, *cariad,* and to my shame I never asked what was wrong. I didn't want you to think I was interfering, see.'

'So what was happening? Was your father ill-treating you? Beating you?' Rhys questioned, trying to conceal his increasing anxiety. It was as though he didn't want to accept the truth.

'Oh, he used to beat me, all right. Even before I started school, given the slightest reason he'd take off his leather belt and thrash me. Always where it wouldn't show.'

'The wicked old bastard! Wait until I get my hands on him!' Rhys exploded.

'That wasn't the worst thing, though,' she said

dully. 'I was so used to being thrashed that I almost expected it. Afterwards I would curl up into a ball and sob myself to sleep. It wasn't so easy to do that later on when the things he did to me were so much worse.'

Rhys tensed, clenching and unclenching his fists. 'Tell me.'

Sara took a deep breath, then plunged into new revelations. 'It started soon after the fire. The night you painted my bedroom, Alun. You and Martha said I wasn't to sleep in there that night because of the paint fumes. You told me to use my Da's bed because he was on nights. Do you remember?'

She paused, waiting for them to nod their heads.

'I was still in his bed asleep when he came home next morning. Perhaps if I had been more obedient and I'd been up and had his breakfast and his bath waiting for him like he expected, then it would never have happened.'

She sighed. 'I overslept and that was when it all started. After that it became a regular thing. If he was on nights he expected me to be in his bed waiting for him when he got home. When he was on days then he ordered me into his bed before he went to sleep ...' Her voice broke and shudders shook her.

'I hated it, I hated him, but nothing I said made any difference. If I complained he took his belt to me first, and when that happened he took even less care about the way he used me. He could be so brutal that I could hardly move afterwards.'

She pulled her hand away from Rhys. 'I don't

suppose you want me now, you're probably wishing you'd never married me,' she whispered, holding her bottom lip between her teeth to stop it quivering.

Rhys swallowed hard. Even after what Gwladys had told them he found it difficult to give credence to what Sara was saying. He had met some rough types when he had been at sea, but he still found it hard to believe that any man could treat his own young daughter in such an evil, brutish manner.

Quickly he took her into his arms, holding her tenderly, reassuring her of his love for her. His heart ached, and more than ever he wanted to protect her, to cherish her. He vowed to himself that he would make sure that she never had to face an ordeal of that kind ever again.

Sara's dark eyes were full of pleading as they searched Rhys's face. 'So now do you understand why Myfanwy mustn't stay here in Taff Court?'

'Of course I do,' he told her gently. 'We'll take her back with us, we'll look after her. She must never be allowed to suffer like you did, *cariad*.'

'It may be too late, boyo,' Alun said quietly. He looked across at Martha, waiting for her to continue with the story.

'We've heard her crying at night, just like we used to hear you, Sara. We know he thrashes her for the slightest wrongdoing, but whether anything else goes on or not . . .'

'I don't think so,' Sara told them quickly. 'I don't think Gwladys would have stood for that. I think she walked out on him because she saw him in Myfanwy's bedroom. He was only looking at her,' she added quickly. She looked at Rhys for support. 'Isn't that right?'

He shook his head. 'I hope you're right, but I think that Gwladys is as evil as he is. She certainly led us to believe that she objected to whatever was going on, but whether she has only just found out, and that is why she was so incensed, I wouldn't know for sure.'

'Myfanwy is the only one who knows the truth,' Sara said. 'She probably won't tell us and I'm not sure that we should ask her. I always felt so ashamed about what he did to me and I think she will probably feel the same.'

'The important thing is to get her right away before her Da comes home and then no one, except the four of us, need know anything about it,' Rhys stated.

'You won't say anything?' Sara begged, looking first at Martha and then at Alun.

'Not a word, you can rest assured on that score,' they both told her.

'We'll go and pack up her belongings then,' Sara told them. 'Can you keep an eye on Averyl while we're doing that?'

'Of course we will,' Martha agreed. 'Take your time. I'll get some tea ready while you're gone. Myfanwy will be hungry when she gets home from school.'

'It's kind of you, Martha, but perhaps we should leave right away,' Sara protested.

'Nonsense! Ifor's shift doesn't finish until five o'clock so you'll have plenty of time. Rush things and you might upset the child. As it is you can let her think she's going on a little holiday.'

Sara shook her head. 'I'm not sure what to tell her,' she admitted. 'She's bound to wonder what is going on.'

'Look, *cariad*, you can leave her here with us if you like,' Alun suggested. 'We've got a spare bedroom and we'd love to have her, wouldn't we?' He looked across at Martha for support.

Martha looked doubtful. 'I'm not sure it would be for the best, not while her Da is living right next door. It might cause all sorts of trouble, you know what he's like when his temper is up.'

'Martha's right,' Sara said quickly. 'Myfanwy wouldn't be safe here. He'll be inflamed as it is when he finds Gwladys has left him and he'd take it out on Myfanwy at every chance he got. Apart from anything else, he's very handy with the old belt,' she reminded them.

Chapter Thirty-five

Myfanwy was ecstatic when she arrived home from school and found that Sara and Averyl were waiting for her in Martha Pritchard's house.

'I wondered why I was told to come here, instead of going straight home,' she exclaimed, her elfin face beaming. 'I thought perhaps there was going to be a surprise, but nothing as exciting as this.'

She hugged Sara enthusiastically, then struggled to try and pick Averyl up off the floor and cuddle her.

Myfanwy was so thin and puny that she couldn't even lift Averyl a few inches off the ground, but she looked so happy when the baby laughed at her efforts that it brought tears to Sara's eyes.

'Come and sit here in this big chair, *cariad*, and then Sara will put Averyl in your lap so that you can cuddle her,' Alun told her.

Eagerly she did as he suggested and waited for Sara to lift Averyl up and settle her comfortably beside her.

'Now hold on to her so that she can't fall,' Rhys warned.

'I'll make the tea and then you can have something to eat and be on your way before Ifor gets home,' Martha whispered to Sara.

'Right. I'll come and help you,' Sara offered.

In the kitchen, with the door to the living-room closed, the two women freely exchanged their opinions of the situation.

'I'm so relieved that you are taking her back with you,' Martha exclaimed. 'Night after night I've been lying in bed worrying my heart out about her and not knowing what to do. I did hint to you when we met up in Cardiff that time that all was not well.'

'I know you did, and I feel guilty about not doing something sooner,' Sara told her. 'When you said that Gwladys was strict and that she was making a little skivvy out of Myfanwy, it worried me, but I didn't know what I could do about it, not right then. With Rhys at sea it was all I could do to manage on the money he'd left me. It was impossible to have her living with me because I knew I wouldn't be able to afford to feed her.'

'I know, I know, *cariad*,' Martha murmured understandingly.

'Sometimes I worried in case my Da was beating her but I kept telling myself that Gwladys wouldn't let him do that. I had no idea if he was hurting her in any other way,' she explained unhappily.

'Wicked they are, the pair of them,' Martha agreed heatedly. 'Take her back with you, *cariad*, before he breaks her spirit. She's not as strong as you were, remember.'

Myfanwy's face fell when Rhys took the baby from her and told her to sit up at the table, but she obeyed instantly.

'I don't want anything to eat,' she whispered. 'I'd sooner play with Averyl.'

'So you can later, but Averyl wants her tea now,'

Sara explained. 'Perhaps if you sit next to me, and I have Averyl on my lap, then you can help me to feed her.'

Martha was on edge throughout the meal. She kept plying them with more tea and her home-made *bara brith* and bakestones, but all the time she was hurrying them and Sara knew she was anxious for them to be on their way.

When she wiped Averyl's hands and mouth clean and asked Rhys to pass her little cardigan so that she could get the baby ready for the journey home, Myfanwy once more looked unhappy.

'When are you bringing Averyl to Ponty again, Sara, so that I can play with her?' Myfanwy asked.

'Not for a long time,' Sara told her. 'You can come and stay with us, though, if you like.'

Myfanwy stared at her in disbelief. 'Do you mean in Cardiff?'

'That's right, *cariad*. Would you like to do that?'

Myfanwy nodded eagerly, her elfin face radiant, her big brown eyes shining with excitement.

'Get your coat on, then.'

'You mean I can come now? Right away?' she gasped.

'Yes, this minute. Hurry up, then.'

Myfanwy's face clouded. 'I'll have to go home first and ask for permission,' she said anxiously.

'No, you won't need to do that. It's all arranged. Isn't it, Martha?'

'Yes, everything has been arranged, *cariad*. We've even got your clothes here all packed up ready for you to take to Cardiff with you,' Martha smiled.

Myfanwy was very quiet on the journey. Rhys

nursed Averyl, and Myfanwy sat cuddled into Sara, her hand clutching Sara's arm as if she were afraid that at any moment her sister might disappear.

It was the first time Myfanwy had been to Coburn Street and she stood stock still in the middle of the room, staring around her in a bemused way.

'You sit in the big chair and nurse Averyl while I get her something to drink,' Sara told her.

Myfanwy nodded obediently and did as she was asked.

Sara steered Rhys out into the hallway and closed the door so that Myfanwy couldn't hear what was being said. 'Where is she going to sleep? We haven't made any arrangements!' she said anxiously.

Rhys ran a hand through his thick dark hair. 'Do you think Glenda would let her sleep in the back bedroom?'

'It might be worth asking her, but what if she says no?'

'Then she'll have to sleep in our bed with you and I'll sleep in the chair downstairs.'

Sara shook her head doubtfully. 'It's not fair to expect you to do that.'

'Well, we can't let her sleep down here on her own, now can we, *cariad*?'

'No, I suppose not, not after what she's been through. She looks frightened to death as it is.'

'You carry on with getting Averyl to bed and I'll go and talk to Glenda about it.'

Glenda was out, but in any case by the time Myfanwy was ready for bed it was obvious to both Rhys and Sara that she would be too scared to sleep in a room on her own in a strange house.

'As a special treat, just for tonight,' Sara told her, 'you can sleep with me in my big bed.'

She thought Myfanwy would be delighted but instead a look of abject fear came into her huge dark eyes and her lower lip trembled as if she was about to burst into tears.

'Don't you like that idea?' Sara asked, pulling the scrawny little figure into her arms and hugging her.

'I . . . I'm not sure,' Myfanwy whispered.

'Why's that then?' Sarah asked gently.

Myfanwy looked away, avoiding Sara's eyes. She fiddled with the buttons on the front of her dress, then asked in a tremulous little voice, 'Is Rhys going to sleep with us as well?'

'No, of course he's not,' Sara assured her. 'There's not room for three of us in one bed, now is there?'

The child's face brightened. 'So where will he sleep?'

'In another bedroom. It's the one where you should be sleeping, but I thought you mightn't like being on your own, not on your first night here. That's why I thought you would like to sleep in my bed,' Sara explained.

Myfanwy relaxed. 'Thank you, Sara,' she said, flinging her arms round her sister's neck and kissing her on the cheek.

'Good. Now if that's settled, what about you going on up to bed and warming it for me,' Sara smiled.

She took Myfanwy upstairs and helped her to find her nightdress from the bag of things they'd brought from Pontypridd.

As Myfanwy took off her clothes, Sara held her

breath in dismay to see the criss-cross of weals on the little girl's back and buttocks.

Memories of when she'd been treated like that came rushing back. She felt suffused with anger against her father as well as against Gwladys for allowing him to beat Myfanwy. Several of the weals were so new that the lacerated skin had not healed properly and she ached to put some soothing cream on them. Only her concern that this might draw Myfanwy's attention to them and revive unhappy memories stopped her. Time enough to sort those things out tomorrow, she told herself.

'In you get then,' she said, turning back the bedclothes.

'I haven't said my prayers yet.'

'Can't you say those in bed?'

'No!' Myfanwy shook her head emphatically. 'Dada says the Good Lord doesn't hear them if you do that.'

'Go on then, kneel down and say them. Do you want me to wait until you've finished, so that I can tuck you in?'

Myfanwy nodded, then looked round as if she'd lost something. 'Did you bring my prayer mat with us, Sara?'

'Your prayer mat? No, is it something special?'

Myfanwy nodded. 'Yes, it's very special. It's a piece of coconut matting and Dada says I have to kneel on it or else the Good Lord won't listen to my prayers.'

As Myfanwy was speaking, Sara glanced down at her little sister's knees and felt sickened by their pitted surface and raw scabbiness. They were the sort of knees a harum-scarum boy who climbed trees or fell down a lot might have, not the knees of a fragile little girl of eight.

'I'm sure the Lord understands that things are different when you're away from home,' Sara told Myfanwy gravely. 'You pop into bed and close your eyes and say your prayers before you fall asleep. He will hear them all right, I promise you.'

Myfanwy looked doubtful. 'I think I'd better kneel down to say them,' she said tremulously.

Sara nodded her agreement and listened while Myfanwy recited a litany of prayer that Ifor had taught her. At the end, she screwed up her face in concentration as she added some extra ones. 'Please, dear Lord, look after Sara and Rhys and baby Averyl and make them very, very happy.'

With Averyl sound asleep in her cot and Myfanwy snuggled down in the big bed, her eyelids already drooping as she was being tucked in, Sara went downstairs again to eat the supper Rhys had prepared for them both.

They had barely taken their first mouthful when they heard Glenda come in.

'Shall I go and ask her?' Rhys said, pushing back his chair and standing up.

'Leave it for a moment, it sounds as though she has a friend with her,' Sara murmured, holding up a hand. They could hear the sounds of a man's voice. The next minute Glenda was tapping on their door and calling out that there was someone to see them.

'My Dada's come to take Myfanwy back! We can't let him do that,' Sara exclaimed in alarm. 'She's covered in cuts and bruises from where he's been punishing her. If we let her go back to Ponty her life will be hell.'

'We won't let him take her away, don't worry,' Rhys assured her as he walked towards the door of their living-room.

It wasn't Ifor Jenkins who stood there, however, but Rhys's own father, Lloyd Edwards.

'What the devil are you doing here?' Rhys exclaimed in surprise. 'I thought you and Mam were in Somerset. Something gone wrong with your plans then? Nothing's happened to Mam, has it?' he asked in alarm. 'Hell of an upheaval for her, you know, moving house at her age.'

'Hold on, boyo, there's nothing wrong with your Mam. It's your Aunt Betti Morgan I've come about. She's had a heart attack, see. They've brought her here to Cardiff Infirmary. She's in a pretty bad way and she's asking for you. You'll have to come with me, boyo. Right now!'

Rhys looked hesitantly at Sara. They'd had a traumatic day and he didn't like the idea of leaving her on her own. He knew she was worried in case Ifor came looking for Myfanwy.

'Hurry up, boyo, or we'll be too late,' Lloyd urged. 'They're not holding out much hope. She's still conscious but they doubt if she'll last the night. Come on! I've got a taxi waiting outside the door, mun, so what's keeping you?'

'You must go, Rhys,' Sara urged. 'After all she did for us in the past, it's only right.'

'It means leaving you here alone . . .'

'Nonsense! Don't worry about that. I'll be all right,' she assured him. 'I'll be tucked up in bed with Myfanwy within five minutes! Go on, now,' she urged, 'your Dada's waiting.'

Rhys didn't return home until dawn was breaking. His father had stayed behind at the hospital to deal with all the arrangements and then he said he had to go back to Somerset. But he promised that both he and Olwen would return for the funeral.

For a long time he sat downstairs, thinking over all that had happened in the last few hours. Then he made a pot of tea and crept upstairs to rouse Sara so that they could drink it together and he could tell her about the night's events.

When she joined him downstairs, Sara was still dazed by sleep and all that had happened the previous day. She listened in uneasy silence as Rhys told her that Betti Morgan had died at four o'clock that morning.

'And we never made our peace with her, never told her how sorry we were that we cleared off to Cardiff and left her like we did,' she said sadly. 'I meant for us to go and see her when we were in Ponty today, but so many other things were happening that I clean forgot.'

'Not to worry, *cariad*, I was able to tell her. She was conscious right to the end. She understood. She'd heard so many awful rumours about the way Ifor and Gwladys were treating Myfanwy, that she realised why you had been so desperate to get away.'

'And did you tell her that we were having Myfanwy to live with us?'

'Yes, and that seemed to ease her mind a great deal.'

'I'm glad she died peacefully and that you were able to tell her how sorry we were about the way things happened,' Sara murmured. She wiped away her tears with the back of her hand. 'She did forgive us?'

'Oh, yes. She'd done that a long time ago.'

Sara shook her head. 'How can you be so sure?'

'Well, she'd made a will, see, quite a long time before she died, leaving the business to us. She wouldn't have done that if she'd held any sort of grudge, now would she?'

Sara stared at him in disbelief. 'Are you telling me that her cake shop and the bakery are ours now?'

'That's right! I'll be doing the sort of work I enjoy and, what's more, we'll have somewhere to live.'

Sara stared at Rhys wide-eyed, unable to take in the enormity of what he was telling her. 'I can't believe it! You're saying she's left us her house and home as well as her business in Ponty?'

'That's right, *cariad*! Wonderful, isn't it! There's only one problem,' he paused and looked searchingly at Sara, 'and that's whether you can bring yourself to go back to Pontypridd to live?'

'Sara shrugged. 'The past is the past, isn't it. Hardly likely to turn down an opportunity like this just because of a few bad memories, now am I?'

'There's a bit more to it than that,' Rhys warned cautiously. 'That's the one thing Betti was a bit worried about, that leaving us everything would force you back there whether you liked it or not.'

'You mean because of my Dada and how he

might react to us being in Ponty, especially if we have Myfanwy living with us?'

Rhys nodded.

Sara chewed her lower lip for a moment as she turned the matter over in her mind. 'It could be a problem, I suppose. I wonder how Myfanwy will feel about it? I don't think I will be too worried,' she said thoughtfully. 'It's not as though you will be going away to sea again. You'll be there all the time to look after us if he ever turns nasty, won't you!'

Rhys hugged her. 'That was exactly what Betti hoped you'd say,' he told her.

Sara's face brightened. 'Oh, Rhys, it's like a dream coming true. Yesterday we didn't even have a bed for Myfanwy to sleep in, and you were convinced you would have to go back to sea any day now, so that we could make ends meet. Now we're going to move into a place of our own and even have our own business.'

'Yes,' he agreed, 'all of a sudden our future is assured.'

'Averyl will be able to grow up in the same town as I did,' Sara murmured thoughtfully. 'Far safer for her there than in a sprawling great city like Cardiff. Mind you,' she added with a sad smile, 'I'll have to make sure she has a happier childhood than I did!'

'That shouldn't be too difficult. Remember, we'll have our very own business and a thriving one at that,' Rhys exclaimed triumphantly.

'Betti certainly did a good trade when I was working there,' Sara agreed.

'I can build it up so that there is an even better turnover,' Rhys said confidently.

'I'll be able to work in the shop, like I used to do,' Sara said eagerly.

Rhys shook his head. 'No need for that, *cariad*, we'll employ someone. Looking after Myfanwy and Averyl will fill your day.'

'I can do that as well,' Sara laughed. 'Remember, I used to look after Myfanwy as a tiny baby while I was keeping house for Dada and running all his errands, and I'm more experienced now. And Myfanwy will be at school most of the time.'

'We'll be able to afford to employ whatever help we need in both the shop and the bakehouse, so perhaps the answer is for you to supervise things in the shop and that will leave me free to concentrate on the baking.'

'Leaving us the business was very generous of Betti,' Sara said reflectively, 'but to leave us her home as well was kindness itself.'

'Nice place she had, as well. I was very comfortable when I was lodging there with her,' Rhys agreed.

'It will be all ours, no landlady telling us what we can and can't do and dictating when we can use the kitchen,' Sara added dreamily.

'The other thing is that it's big enough for all of us, including Myfanwy,' Rhys pointed out.

'Your Aunt Betti had a big heart,' Sara enthused. 'I know when I worked in the shop she was always kindness itself to me.'

'She treated me like a son when I was there,' Rhys agreed. 'I never really appreciated how comfortable I was until after we'd run away to Cardiff.'

Sara laughed wryly. 'That room in Daisy Street was pretty grim!'

Rhys took her into his arms. 'I promised you so much when we moved from there to Coburn Street, but really that wasn't much better. I know you've had a lot to put up with in the past, Sara, but this really is the turning point,' he murmured as he kissed her.

Sara smiled broadly. 'I'm sure you're right about that! In fact, it looks as if the prayers Myfanwy said last night are coming true already.'